THE ASSASSIN'S LEGACY

A MINTE AND MAGIC ADVENTURE

D. LIEBER

Ink & Magick, LLC
Kenosha, Wisconsin
contact@inkandmagick.com

Hardcover ISBN: 978-1-951239-20-6
Paperback ISBN: 978-1-951239-19-0
Ebook ISBN: 978-1-951239-21-3

Cover by Maria Spada

Edited by Samantha Talarico

SPECIAL THANKS

Thank you to my beta readers: John, Megan, Aunt Debbie, and Amy.

A special thank you to my sensitivity reader, Oleg, and Bonny for recommending him to me.

THE ASSASSIN'S LEGACY

BOOKS BY D. LIEBER

Minte and Magic

The Exiled Otherkin

The Assassin's Legacy

Intended Fates

Intended Bondmates

Intended Strangers

Intended Enemies

Council of Covens

Dancing with Shades

In Search of a Witch's Soul

Also by D. Lieber

Conjuring Zephyr

Once in a Black Moon

A Very Witchy Yuletide

The Treason of Robyn Hood

The Curse of Moonseed Manor

The Goblin King's Mischief

The Winter Sorcerer and the Summer Witch

1

The inn tavern was dim and crowded for a sleepy country village. It seemed all the residents spent their evenings listening to the aging musician imbue the rest of his life into his guitar. Men and women alike raised their glasses and off-key voices, singing the songs they had learned long ago.

In the darkest corner, with my back to the wall, I sat as far from their rowdy merrymaking as I could. The shapely waitress, with curls that shined in the soft light, smiled as she delivered my drink. The dimples in her cheeks were becoming, and I knew I only had to give her a wink to feel her warmth that night.

"Thank you," I told her, staring into the amber liquid in the glass she'd given me.

Her plump lower lip pouted when I didn't respond to her silent offer. *She is beautiful, and I know I could help her. But not now. My mind is too full to give her the appreciation she deserves.*

"Oi, Rose!" The bartender beckoned the waitress from across the room.

She clicked her tongue before leaving to answer his call.

I blew out all my breath, then downed the drink. Running my fingertip along the smooth rim of the glass, I considered ordering another. *I should not waste what I have left. I do not know how long it will be before I get another job.* Though my position on the merchant airship had been ideal for staying on the move, I wasn't keen to fly anytime soon after what had happened with the pirates.

Closing my eyes, I could still feel the warmth of their blood as it streamed down my blade to my hand. Mac's astonishment echoed in my mind. "Sasha, where did you learn to do that?" he'd asked as I stared blankly at their lifeless forms sprawled on the deck.

Squeezing my eyes tighter, I sighed to myself. *For all my vows never to spill blood again, I did not hesitate to kill my fellow humans.* My guilt held firm even as I knew the pirates had been the worst kind of men; the world was better from them no longer in it.

And in the end, I handed Charlie over to that agent. I clenched my fist until it shook. *I followed her wishes; she said she was helping Ember.* I sighed again, relaxing my hand, and snorted to myself.

I do not know what I am so upset about. I knew Ember would never love me. I knew she would eventually find her home with Reilley. I was only involved to show them how they felt about each other. I smiled inwardly. *That is right. She could not have loved me, but I helped her still. I showed her she deserved happiness. And now she has it with Reilley, or at least I hope she does... Let it go.*

Placing money on the table, I rose from my seat and started toward the stairs and the room I'd requested for the night. *I should be able to find another job in that nearby city Mac told me of yesterday.* I took some comfort in the knowledge that he was likely back in the loving embrace of his wife and children.

I didn't bother to light the lamp as I entered the small room. I just stretched out on the bed, grateful the whiskey had relaxed me enough for sleep. Letting out a long sigh, I closed my eyes and waited for dreams to take me.

After a few even breaths, my ears pricked as a floorboard creaked ever so softly to my left. I forced myself to continue breathing slowly though my instinct was to freeze.

The strike came from above, and I was barely able to avoid it by rolling to the side. Fabric tore as a knife sank deep into the blankets beneath me.

My hand wrapped around a slender wrist in the dark while my attacker tried to reclaim the weapon.

In a fluid motion, the wrist in my grasp twisted and thin fingers clenched my wrist. I jerked my assailant's arm and pulled her off-balance onto the free spot I'd just occupied before she got a chance to yank the blade out with her other hand. Twisting my hips, I wrapped my legs around her neck, putting her in a choke hold.

Her arms flailed at my hips to no avail as I squeezed my thighs.

"Who sent you?" I asked the assassin in my mother tongue.

She growled in frustration but did not answer.

"Was it the Ubyzniki? My father? Who?"

"Go to Hell," she spat in Russian.

I clenched my teeth and tightened my hold until she went limp with unconsciousness. Sighing heavily, I allowed my tense muscles to relax.

After a few more deep breaths, I slipped off the bed and fumbled for a match on the side table. The warm, flickering light of the lamp illuminated the room and the crumbled assassin in my bed.

Her long, dark hair had begun to loosen from her braid and fell partially over her face. I reached out and gently brushed the soft tresses aside. Her skin had a warm undertone, and a smattering of freckles dusted her cheeks. I held my finger above her full lips and was relieved to feel the telltale signs of life.

Tilting my head, I regarded her. *I have never seen her before. I thought I knew everyone in the Ubyzniki.* I pursed my lips. *Then again, I have not seen them for many years. She could have joined since then. On the other hand, she looks only a few years younger than I. The Ubyzniki train their members young, and they do not let just anyone in. Perhaps it is not them after all.*

I shook my head and pulled my surprisingly light attacker until she lay her on her stomach. After rummaging through the pack I'd salvaged from the pirate shipwreck, I found the rope and used it to tie her hands and feet.

Her knife, which I retrieved from the bed, was a

nicely balanced stiletto. I admired the craftsmanship, running my thumb gently along the sharp edge.

"Very nice," I told her.

But she was still unconscious.

I crossed the room to the washbasin I'd used earlier that evening.

After a satisfying splash, the assassin gasped awake.

"Let us talk," I said when she was done sputtering.

2

The assassin's grey eyes blinked at me in confusion, and then she glared, struggling against her bonds.

"Are you ready to tell me why you tried to kill me?"

Air whistled through her nose as she sucked in a breath.

I sat beside the bed so she wouldn't have to crane her neck to look at me.

"You spoke to me in Russian earlier. And as far as I know, no one else wants me dead quite as much as the Ubyzniki."

She continued to glare at me but didn't speak.

"On the other hand, you could hardly be counted among their ranks. You failed to kill your target. Are you even an assassin at all? You have probably never spilled blood in your life," I taunted.

Her face reddened.

I smirked at her. "I bet you are some backwater whelp who has never had a day of formal training.

So what? You heard of me—Aleksandr Sergeyevich Volonov, assassin of legend, only son of Sergei Nikolayevich Volonov—and decided to try your hand?"

"You call yourself an assassin of legend?" She laughed humorlessly. "Yes, I have heard of you. Many tales. Aleksandr Sergeyevich Volonov, the ruthless killer, master of his trade. But look at you, you are not half the man I was told you would be. The Aleksandr of legend would never have left me breathing. Mistress Yuliya need never have trained me so hard."

My smile broadened. "You are the one who is tied up, Kisa."

She growled at my playful tone, and I stood.

"So it was Yulya who sent you then?" I snorted. "I would have thought she had gotten over her childhood rivalry by now, but it seems she has moved on from competition and gone straight to assassination. She never did do anything halfway. I suppose this means Father has not given her the recognition she so desires?"

I quirked one eyebrow, looking down at the seething woman once more.

Her lips curled as she said, "Master Volonov is dead."

The shock of hearing that my father had joined my mother stopped my heart. "I see," I murmured, then cleared my throat. "When did he go?"

"The day before yesterday."

"Yulya lost no time in sending you after me. While I am impressed you found me so quickly, you need not have bothered. My sister does not need to worry about whether I will come back and lay claim to the family title."

"It does not matter. Your father named you the next head of the family despite your long absence."

I sighed heavily, pinching the bridge of my nose. "Stubborn old man," I muttered.

Using the assassin's stiletto, I cut the ropes that bound her. As soon as she was free, she rolled to the floor then shot to her feet, putting the bed between us.

"Relax." I grinned. "I am not going to fight you."

"My orders were to—"

"I am certain your orders were to dispatch me quickly, but that will not be necessary," I said, waving my hand at her. I snatched my pack and shouldered it, heading for the door. "The day before yesterday, you say? That does not give me much time."

She launched herself at me, spinning me around and pinning my back to the door. "I cannot let you leave alive."

"I will return home to pay respects to my father. And after the funeral, I will renounce any claim I have to lead the family."

She squinted up at me, uncertain. "You truly do not want to hold the title?"

"Of course not. Why would I have left if I had? I will name Yulya heir and be done with it."

Nibbling her lower lip, she considered her options.

It is highly unlikely this woman has ever killed anyone, or if she has, her victim was not human.

"If you are lying, I have no problem taking you down in Saint Petersburg same as here."

I smirked down at her as her weight pressed against me. "You talk so big, Kisa, but I think you cannot best me."

"You think so? Who has whom trapped at the moment?"

I easily switched our positions, pinning her back to the door.

Her eyes widened, then squinted at me.

"You were saying?"

Pursing her lips, she squirmed against me.

"It is a few hours' walk, and I need to get there before morning if I have any hope of making my own father's funeral. Are you finished trying to kill me, Kisa?"

"For the moment," she mumbled. "But stop calling me kitten. My name is Elizaveta."

"As you wish, Liza."

"You do not know me well enough to call me Liza." She glared disdainfully up at me.

"Do I not?" I murmured. "I always felt trying to kill someone was a rather intimate act." I ran my fingertips down her arm.

She shivered and flushed, at a loss for words.

I smiled gently at the attractive blush that bloomed behind her freckles. Then I turned the doorknob near her hand, and she tumbled backward into the hall. Chuckling as she scowled, I strode toward the stairs. At the landing, I looked over my shoulder while she scrambled to her feet.

"Are you coming, Kisa?" I grinned.

She sighed and grumbled as she followed me

down the stairs, but I could feel her cold glare on my back when I didn't stifle my laughter.

"When are you going to stop calling me that?" she asked as we stepped into the cool autumn night.

"When you let me call you Liza. Or would you prefer Lizochka?"

She sputtered. "I will never— Do not even think about it."

I couldn't hold back my chortle, the noise causing the trees near the road out of town to shake as it woke the sleeping creatures.

"Tell me, Kisa," I started, ignoring her look of irritation. "How did you find me so soon after my father's death? This is not exactly a common place to be."

She paused for a while, the only sound the crunching of the dirt road beneath our feet. "Master Volonov never gave up the idea you would return one day to take over the family. He had the mage dowse for you regularly though he could not always find you."

Because I was on the airship. He only would have been able to find me while I was on the ground. "So Yulya asked the mage to dowse for me?"

"No, Master Volonov was planning to bring you home for some reason. He had a big announcement, but Mistress Yuliya did not tell me what it was. When he died, we already knew where you had been and the direction you were going."

Father was trying to bring me home? I never thought he would want me to return after I failed that mission, not that I wanted to come back either. "How long have you served my sister?" I asked Liza after a while.

"Ten years. I am told I arrived shortly after you left."

I nodded, glancing over at the woman as she walked by my side in the dim light of the waxing moon.

"And where were you before then? Serving another Ubyzniki family?"

She tucked the hair that had escaped her braid behind her ears as if just noticing it had come loose. She didn't answer my question.

"If you did serve another Ubyzniki family, they could not have trained you to be an assassin. Your skills are rough and underdeveloped. I would guess you have not trained for even half of those ten years."

She sniffed hard as I damaged her pride.

"Not everyone is a legendary prodigy, oh great Aleksandr Sergeyevich Volonov," she sneered in sarcasm.

"You can call me Sasha."

3

The crunch of our footsteps as we hiked toward the city disturbed the hushed night. Now that the heat of our battle had cooled and we had walked for a while, Liza's anger-fueled aggression seemed to settle into a formal distance. I frowned at her change in demeanor.

"Tell me about yourself, Kisa."

Her eyes flicked to my face but then looked away. She didn't say anything.

"You do not want to tell me? It is a long way to the airship. How are we to pass the time?"

"Relieving your boredom is not my job."

I stifled a smile at her resurged irritation. "What is your job?"

She pursed her lips.

"If you will not give me more information about you, shall I make it up myself?"

Turning her face from me, she watched the trees as we passed. "Why did you not kill me?" she murmured so softly I barely heard her.

"Hmm," I hummed more to myself than her. *Because I do not kill anymore.* "How could I kill such a beautiful woman? I could not live with the guilt had I so robbed the world."

Her cheeks turned pink. "You could not have seen me in the dark," she grumbled.

That is true. "The fact remains."

She snorted. "Mistress Yuliya warned me about you. She said you were charming."

I allowed myself a gratified smile. "You think I am charming?"

Her blush deepened.

"I believe that may be the kindest thing my sister has ever said of me. It is even more flattering from your lips. Remind me to thank her for such a wonderful gift."

Her eyes flashed as her embarrassment turned to anger. "You are worse than she said: arrogant, infuriating, licentious—"

"Licentious—!" I cut myself off, swallowing my fury. "Careful, Kisa. For someone who does not know me, you are making assumptions," I warned coldly.

She paled at my outrage, and I relented, hating myself for the fear behind her mask of defiance.

"My sister has never much understood matters of the heart," I explained vaguely.

She opened her mouth to no doubt come to her mistress's defense, then closed it without speaking.

Neither of us felt much like talking after that, and we walked in silence until we reached the edge of the city.

It was not yet dawn when we came to the dockyard. The wooden airships creaked, lined up on either side of the central dock with their envelopes nearly touching. Most of the cloths stretched over the metal frames of the envelopes were limp, outlining the many squares of their frames as if the fabric was being sucked in. But there were a few that were puffed out, the minte-fueled boilers providing the steam that would soon propel them into the sky.

"Excuse me, sir," I called to the dockmaster, getting his attention.

I was surprised when a bespectacled woman looked up from her logbook.

"Oh, I am sorry, miss," I corrected, smiling at her. "Do you have any ships leaving for Saint Petersburg this morning?"

"There's a cargo ship leaving at first light but no passenger vessels."

"Would you mind telling me the dock number? I am positive the captain and I can come to some arrangement."

"Dock seventeen."

I gave her a warm smile, and her eyes widened slightly. "Thank you, miss."

She dipped her head in acknowledgment, and I felt her gaze on me as I followed her directions.

Liza frowned, trailing after me.

The crew of the airship to Saint Petersburg was loading cargo into the hull when we approached dock seventeen.

"Hurry it up, lads," a man with a clipboard called to the crew. "We'll never leave if you keep working at this pace."

"Excuse me, sir," I said, tapping the captain on the shoulder. "Is this the airship to Saint Petersburg?"

"It is," he answered shortly.

"We would like to buy passage if we could. We are in a hurry to get home."

"There's only enough room for crew and cargo. No passengers," he stated with finality.

I pursed my lips and watched the crew, who were barely making a dent in their load.

"It is only a few hours until first light," I commented. "You look like you could use some help. We could make all the difference."

His eyes studied my build. "You have experience?"

"I do."

Then his gaze lingered on Liza with a look I recognized only too well. I stiffened.

"What about you, sweetheart? You got experience?"

She squinted at his tone, and her eyes flashed in the gaslights of the dock. As much as I wanted for her to let him have it, nothing she said would make him change. And we needed on that boat.

I placed my hand gently on her shoulder. Her head snapped in my direction as she prepared to snarl at me.

"She can handle herself. Believe me. She is likely stronger than half the men on your crew and twice as deadly as the lot," I said, staring directly into the captain's eyes.

He clicked his tongue. "You get us out of port on time, and you can ride along. But you're paying for meals."

I nodded and released Liza's shoulder, urging her forward. "I apologize," I whispered under my breath while we moved toward the waiting cargo. "I assure you that I do not normally act thus. Unfortunately, possession is the only thing men like that understand."

She was silent as we hefted boxes into the hull. With our efforts, it didn't take long for the cargo to be loaded, and the airship was underway at first light as scheduled.

It would be more than half a day's flight to Saint Petersburg, and I hadn't slept in twice as long. Finding an out-of-the-way place to rest, I sat at the stern with my back against the solid, wooden taffrail.

I closed my eyes against the rising sun as Liza sank down beside me.

"If I am asleep when it is time to eat, do not wake me."

I expected her to maintain the silence she'd kept since I'd apologized.

"Did you mean what you said?" she whispered.

I raised my eyebrows without opening my eyes. But when she didn't elaborate, I pried my tired lids open.

Her grey eyes searched mine, pleading for the truth. "Do you really believe I can handle myself? Do you think I am deadlier than all the men here?"

I smiled internally. "All but one, Kisa," I murmured, closing my eyes again.

She didn't say anything, but a quick peek showed me her smirk as she settled in beside me.

4

The evening meal bell woke me from my sleep. My neck and back cracked as I stretched, stiff from sitting in the same uncomfortable position for too long.

Realizing Liza was no longer beside me, I scanned the deck for the wayward assassin. When I located her, I tensed in alarm. A man with curly, black hair smiled as he had his arms wrapped around her from behind.

Clenching my teeth, I took a stride toward them and then froze when she let out a delighted giggle. I looked closer and saw he was showing her how to tie a rope into a proper knot.

My anger drained out of me, and my gaze softened as I watched her carefree eyes alight with curiosity and laughter. *I am glad Yulya has not robbed her of her smile.* Not wanting to disturb her fun, I tried to sneak past the pair to the stairs that led below deck.

"Aleksandr," she called, surprised.

I looked back to see her smile gone as she squirmed from the deckhand's arms.

"Good evening, Kisa. Have you eaten?"

"I ate this afternoon, but I was just heading down to dinner." She moved toward me without looking back.

"What about you?" I asked the deckhand in English. "Are you coming to dinner?"

The young man smiled easily. "I have work to finish. Perhaps I will catch up."

I nodded.

"Hasta luego, señorita," he added to Liza.

She tilted her head.

"He says, 'see you later,'" I told her.

"Ah, yes, see you later, Carlos," she answered slowly in English as if practicing every word. "You know Spanish?" she asked me in Russian while we went to the mess hall.

"Yes, I learned many languages in the time I have been away."

She nodded slowly.

Our evening meal wasn't worth the money we paid for it, but almost anything is palatable to a hungry man. I thought about Reilley and how the food at my previous job had gotten remarkably better once he'd joined the crew.

That thought reminded me of all the comrades I'd lost. Indulal, Nick, all the many people who'd worked on the ship, wiped out in moments by the pirate captain's whim.

I'd long gotten used to the sting of loss. Family, friends, enemies, we all went in the end. We could go screaming and bloody or with a soft, sleepy sigh.

But we went. It was the way we lived before then that was truly important. *Who will I be today? The vessel of the righteous who bring pain and death? Or will I forsake that blood-soaked path and bring beauty and love?*

Liza's steady gaze pulled me from my thoughts.

"Yes, Kisa?" I asked, raising my eyebrows.

She averted her eyes indifferently.

I smirked. "I know you have heard tales of my prowess. Are you in awe at being in my presence?" I teased. "Or perhaps you are surprised at my dashing good looks?"

She scoffed. "I knew what you looked like already. I have seen your photograph."

"Yes, but I was but a boy then. Now, I am a debonair man."

"Pff, debonair my ass. Where does this confidence of yours come from, I wonder?"

With her eyes bright and her cheeks pink with irritation, she stabbed a boiled potato on her plate.

"You really are attractive, Kisa," I commented, smiling.

She squinted at me. "Do not try to sweet talk me, Aleksandr Sergeyevich. I am not like other women."

"No woman is like other women," I answered.

She paused, curiosity drawing her eyes to my face. She would find no lies there.

"You are serious."

"Of course I am."

"But if we are all unique, does that not make us all the same?"

"Not at all."

"It does not matter anyway. Your opinion cannot be trusted."

"Because I am a man?"

"No, because you are Aleksandr Sergeyevich."

"Ah, Yulya must have taken great care in turning you against me."

She didn't respond.

"My sister is not as forgiving as I. You should consider not returning with me," I quietly suggested.

Her eyes flashed as she glared at me. "Mistress Yuliya is the most generous woman I have ever met. She will see the wisdom in my choice. I will not hear words against her, especially not from the likes of you."

"The likes of me, eh?"

"Yes, a man who deserts his family and duty."

I nodded, sucking my teeth. "I see... Well, it is your choice to return, Kisa."

The rest of the flight to Saint Petersburg was quiet and tense as Liza put a lot of effort into avoiding me. She tried so hard that it seemed to produce the opposite effect as if ignoring my presence focused all of her energy directly at me.

Carlos noticed the change and was clearly disappointed. As the airship sailed toward the glittering lights of Saint Petersburg, I felt bad for the deckhand. He had no idea why Liza's smiles were no longer forthcoming.

We did not say goodbye to the captain as we disembarked.

On the ground, I paused to breathe in the city of my birth. It seemed Russia's capital had benefited from her wealth of natural resources, saulht in particular. The city sparkled in the night, a beacon as bright as any of the great cities of Europe.

Not so much had changed in the last decade that I did not recognize my old home. Still, a well-travelled man sees things differently than a runaway youth.

The cold wind off the Gulf of Finland seeped into my soul, greeting me like a mother's caress. I had left the pleasant autumn of the west behind. Nothing warmed the heart quite like the promise of a Russian winter.

Sighing, I smiled to myself and strolled in the direction of the river. A line of small steamboats with black and yellow striped canopies patiently waited on the river's edge. Their smoke stacks, which stuck up through the canopies, puffed white water vapor, telling us they were ready at any time.

After we'd hopped into a taxi, I asked the driver to take us to Volonov Manor.

We chugged up the Neva, and I watched the grand palaces and mansions drift by. I could still remember the names and faces of their boyar residents, those I'd grown up with. Their salons and drawing rooms, the many balls and parties, the dinners and concerts: the gilded façade that was my youth. I also remembered their cellars and basements: prisons for the creatures of the night, poor souls who were only kept alive to torture for information and study to find better ways of killing others of their kind.

Of course, not all of the noble families were members of the Ubyzniki, just the trusted few. Five families, still favored by the empress, made up the

Ubyzniki. Five families with their many branches filled the ranks of "monster" hunting assassins. They lurked in forests, alleys, and ballrooms alike, stalking their supernatural prey and keeping the unknowing citizens of the Russian Empire safe.

I scoffed at their hypocrisy, their righteous hubris, as all the contentment I'd felt upon landing in Saint Petersburg drained out of me.

5

I clenched my jaw painfully the closer the steamboat got to my childhood home. It turned from the Neva into the Fontanka River. *Nearly there now.* I forced myself to relax, letting out a slow sigh as the boat moored at the dock.

I couldn't see the house beyond the road and the trees of the well-kept park.

As the taxi puffed back toward the Neva, I stood rooted on the dock, unwilling to get any closer to my past.

Liza waited quietly at my side, giving me the chance to move forward on my own. *The funeral will be tomorrow. All I have to do is attend and renounce my claim to the title, and I can move on with my life.*

Taking a deep breath and squaring my shoulders, I strode across the street with more confidence than I felt. A little way up the wooded path, an iron gate blocked any farther progress. Beside it, there sat a warmly-lit gatehouse. I smiled softly at the home I'd spent so many happy hours in as a child and youth.

My knock at the cottage door elicited a series of insistent warning barks from inside. It didn't take long for someone to answer. The dark eyes of my childhood friend widened in recognition.

"Hello, Petya." I smiled sheepishly.

For a moment, I was uncertain whether he would embrace or strike me. But he let out a shout and stepped out to hug me.

"I thought we would never see you again, Sasha."

Pulling back, I rested my hands on his shoulders. "About that, there seems to have been some complications regarding my father's wishes."

Petya nodded solemnly. "I do not get involved in what is going on up at the house, but I am sorry you had to return under such circumstances."

"Thank you, my friend."

"Petya, what is it? Boris was barking," a woman called from inside. When she reached the threshold, she gasped, covering her mouth.

I dipped my head at her. "Hello, Tanya."

"Sasha," Petya's sister whispered.

The girl I'd known so well ten years ago had grown into the beautiful woman I'd always known she would be. Only her tired eyes spoke of the hardships she'd seen. Had I not gazed into those eyes for countless hours, I doubt I would have marked a difference.

"Mama?" a small voice called from farther in.

"Not to worry, malyshka. I am coming," Tanya answered as she turned to go.

I frowned when she looked back at me wistfully.

"Your sister..." I began, looking to Petya once Tanya was out of earshot.

Petya returned my frown. "A lot has happened since you left, Sasha," he said quietly. "But now is not the time to discuss it. You must be wanting to head up to the house. I will unlock the gate for you."

I nodded.

"And how was your trip, Liza?" Petya asked while we walked to the gate.

My eyes flicked to Liza's face, half expecting her to snap at him for his familiarity.

"It could have gone better, Pyotr."

Ouch.

"You were sent to tell Sasha about Master Volonov?"

Liza shrugged noncommittally.

I watched Petya with interest as his gaze clung to Liza's every movement. I'd never seen him so interested in a woman though I hadn't seen him in quite some time. Liza's smooth expression spoke of her indifference or her ignorance. I pitied my friend, but I would not be home long enough to help him express his interest.

After he'd let us in, Petya locked the gate behind us.

"Come by for a visit once everything calms down," he told me.

"I will," I promised.

"And, of course, you are always welcome as well, Liza," Petya added.

She dipped her head in acknowledgment.

We wished each other a goodnight, and Liza and I continued up the winding path—the drying leaves clinging to the surrounding trees—toward the main house.

The grief from my father's death hung heavily over the manor. The glow of electric lights illuminated the cream-colored stone and columns but did little to present a warm welcome. The many windows were dark with heavy drapes.

Holding my head high, I strode to the front door and opened it without knocking. Liza followed like a shadow, swift and silent.

The lights in the foyer were dimmed, and the parlour doors were closed. Past the grand staircase, the door to the dining room opened, and a teenage girl in pajamas and robe exited. She froze upon seeing me, her blue eyes wide with fear. Inhaling deeply as if to scream, she then noticed Liza.

"Good evening, Mistress Maria," Liza greeted.

Staring at the young woman with long, golden hair, I couldn't reconcile her with the child I'd known. "Masha?" I asked in wonder.

She squinted at me in the dim light. "Brother?"

I smiled at her and nodded once. With a squeal of delight, my baby sister threw herself at me, and I wrapped her in my arms.

"Sasha, I cannot believe you are finally home! Where have you been all this time? I have missed you so much."

Pulling back, I cupped her face in my hands, her joyful tears wetting my palms. "Masha, you have grown so well."

She grinned up at me.

A sound on the stairs drew all of our attentions. The icy eyes of Yulya glared down at me, her dark, loosely-bound hair falling in waves over her robed chest. Anyone who saw Yulya and I together would know we were siblings. We had the same dark hair though the waves were not so distinguishable at my shorter, tousled length. And despite the daggers she glared at me, we had the same light eyes.

"Sasha," she accused. "You are here."

"I am certain you are surprised, dear sister."

Her hard gaze found Liza, who bowed her head. "I am indeed."

A tense pause sucked the air from the room.

"I will see that your room is prepared," Yulya pronounced finally. "After that, I would like to speak with *you*, Liza."

"Of course, Mistress Yuliya," Liza answered.

"She has been like that since Father died," Masha murmured once Yulya had disappeared.

"Where is Adrik?"

"Yulya sent him on some errand for the Ubyzniki. He should be home soon."

"And Father?"

Masha nodded toward the parlour and squeezed my hand. "I am glad you are home," she whispered.

I kissed her forehead and smiled down at her. Then I went into the parlour to greet my father.

6

At the center of the candle-lit parlour, my father lay on a table dressed in white. I crept toward him as if not to disturb his sleep. His wavy, grey hair was held flat by the headband across his forehead. His deep frown held none of the sternness that used to shake my heart. His expression was empty and unnatural.

Nodding at a maid—a pistol in her hand—who was presently keeping watch, I asked her to wait outside with a look.

"I am home, Father. Just as you wanted," I said once we were alone.

I fell silent as if waiting for him to answer.

"Stubborn to the very end, I see. Well, you will not get your way this time. I will renounce my claim and name Yulya heir. It was wrong of you not to recognize her. She is much better suited to uphold the traditions of the Ubyzniki than I."

The flames of the candles flickered as if a breeze blew through the room, though I didn't feel one.

I smiled softly. "Hello, Granddad," I said to the unseen domovoi. "I hope you have been behaving yourself while I have been away."

The spirit of our forefather did not give a sign one way or the other.

From outside the parlour, a door slammed, and I went to see what was going on, telling the maid she could go back inside with a wave. I heard Yulya's harsh tone from across the foyer in the ground-floor library.

I didn't feel guilty as I eavesdropped at the door. Yulya had sent Liza to kill me, and I had the right to know why.

"He said he was going to renounce his claim and leave after the funeral," Liza explained.

"You stupid, half-wit. You should have just followed my orders instead of trying to think for yourself. He cannot renounce the title even if he wants to, and now I have to find another way to take care of the situation, which will be that much more difficult now that he is here. I knew I should have just left you in Khomyne where I found you."

Liza didn't argue. She took Yulya's abuse as though she deserved it.

"You have failed your mission. The Ubyzniki do not tolerate disobedience. You will never be a member. Pack your things and leave. Your apprenticeship is over."

"Mistress Yuliya, please," Liza pleaded contritely. "I have no family and no money. This is my only home. I will do anything to continue to serve you. Please do not send me away."

Yulya was silent, and I could imagine her icy

glare. "Very well," she relented. "I will give you one more chance to redeem yourself."

"Thank you, Mistress. What must I do?"

Yulya's voice was just above a whisper, and I had to strain my ears to hear her. "Thanks to you, my brother knows I was trying to kill him. He will be on guard now. But he did not kill you. Perhaps he has a soft spot for you. I could use that to my advantage. I want you to follow him. Do not let him out of your sight. We need to find an opening to end this for good."

"Would you like me to try again when I see one?"

"No, you are only on surveillance this time. Follow him and inform me of his movements. I will make other arrangements."

Feeling their conversation come to a close, I sneaked back to the parlour and shut the door until there was only a small slot to peek through. After a few minutes, Liza left the ground-floor library. When she'd disappeared toward the kitchen, I crossed the foyer and joined my sister.

Yulya glared out the window with her arms crossed tightly around herself.

"What worries you, sister?"

"Your sudden arrival for one," she muttered.

"Well, worry not about that. As soon as the funeral is over, I will renounce the title and leave."

Yulya sighed and looked over her shoulder at me. "Still so naive, are you not, little brother? You cannot renounce the title."

"Of course I can. I will name you heir, and all this nonsense will end."

She rubbed her temples and closed her eyes. "No, Sasha. Father made it impossible for you to do so."

"How is that?"

"He and that fool, Maksim Igorevich, worked a spell with the mage."

My muscles tensed. "What kind of spell?"

"One not easily broken," she snapped. Then she sighed again. "They got it in their heads that you and Nika should marry and lead the Ubyzniki's next generation. They used your hair from Mother's locket to bind you together."

"Der'mo."

A book from a shelf across the room fell to the floor with a loud thump.

"Sorry, Granddad," I apologized to the domovoi for cursing. "But who holds the spell then?"

"Father and Maksim both, in case something should happen."

I held in my curse, not wanting to upset the spirit. "Father must have known he was ill," I muttered.

"He did," Yulya agreed.

I sighed. "Still, you took things too far this time, Yulya. Was it really worth trying to kill your own brother?"

"Yes," she answered without hesitation or further explanation.

"At least let me try to convince Maksim to release me from the spell before you attempt to assassinate me again. Yes?"

She neither agreed nor disagreed.

Wonderful. "I am sure Maksim will come to the funeral and reception tomorrow. I will clear this up."

She gave me a hard stare. "Do you really think it will be that easy?"

I shrugged.

She was quiet for a while and then said, "You must still have your ability since you were able to beat Liza. She is the best I have seen in a long time."

I kept my expression smooth.

She scoffed. "Still, I cannot believe you let her live. I see you are even weaker to a pretty face than before. I should have sent Dima to do the job. Perhaps he would not have been such a disappointment."

"Does he still follow you around like a lovesick puppy? And Adrik has nothing to say about that?"

"Adrik knows I would never defile our marriage bed. I have self-control. I assume you have not learned that skill in the last ten years? Still sticking your cock into any woman who is warm, are you?"

Another book fell from the shelf, but Yulya didn't apologize.

"It is so nice catching up with you after all these years, dear sister. I cannot fathom why I stayed away so long."

"Yes, the house was so empty without you, thank God."

I smiled politely. "Is my room ready?"

"Grigori should have alerted the maids, yes."

"Goodnight then, Yulya."

"Too late," she muttered.

Upon leaving the library, I found Liza waiting just over the threshold. "What can I do for you,

Kisa?" I asked as though I knew nothing of her mission.

She bit her lip, then sighed. "I just wanted to thank you for sparing my life." The words seemed to be dragged out of her. "You are not going to be here very long, and I would like to show you my appreciation. So I will be helping you until you leave."

I lowered my eyelids at her as if considering her proposal. "Kisa, sooner or later you will have to be honest."

Her eyes widened slightly, alarmed that I'd seen through her lie. "What do you—"

"If you want to get closer to me, you only have to say so. There is no need to hide behind thinly veiled excuses. You only have to ask."

She sputtered on cue. "I never said anything of the sort!"

I smirked and headed toward the stairs. Stopping at the bottom, I looked over at her. "Well? Are you not coming? I have just the place for you to sleep."

7

I had to hold in a laugh as Liza followed me upstairs, her face red either in anger or embarrassment or both.

Halting before a door at the end of the third floor, I turned to her with a smirk. "Well, here we are, Kisa," I said, low and hushed.

She squared her shoulders and dipped her head in a single nod.

I reached out and turned the knob. The door swung open with a quiet creak. She stared into the small, dark bedroom, sparsely furnished with just the necessities.

"This is your room?" she asked, eying the small bed.

I could hold back my chuckle no more. "No, Kisa. This is *your* room. My room is through there." I pointed at the door beside hers.

She pursed her lips, and I half expected her to suggest she sleep in my room. *I do not care how beautiful she is. I am not letting a snake in my bed. I only have to keep her just close enough to keep an eye on her and convince her she is carrying out her assigned task. There is no need to put myself at more risk than necessary.*

"Well, goodnight then, Kisa. I hope that I might expect an assassination-free rest this evening?"

"I told you I wanted to help you, did I not?" she demanded.

I met her gaze and held it for a while. "You did. Though I never expected such a response when I gave you your life."

She averted her gaze.

Yulya said Liza was one of the best she has seen in a while. She is either not as good as my sister gives her credit for, or she is so good that I do not even know she is playing me.

"I pay my debts," she answered quietly. Breathing deep, she turned back to me. "Goodnight, Aleksandr."

"Goodnight, Kisa."

She watched while I walked to my bedroom and closed the door behind me.

As I entered, Masha looked up from a chair by the fire. Her legs were tucked under her, and she had her arms full of a grey tabby cat.

"I have brought someone to see you." She smiled, standing and moving toward me.

"And who is this?" I asked, taking the cat she held out to me.

"Do not tell me you have forgotten her? Not when she was so sad when you left."

"L'vitsa, is that you?" I questioned the purring animal.

Masha nodded with a smile. "She cried so much. She used to stand outside your door and just howl for you to let her in."

I looked into the cat's grey eyes. "I am sorry, L'vitsa. But you have grown so much. You were just a kitten when I went away. I see Masha has taken good care of you."

My sister reached up and scratched L'vitsa's ear. "It took a while for her to trust me. But with food and cuddles, I bought her affection."

After a few silent moments, she added, "You know, I do not remember a lot from before you left, Sasha. But I will never forget the fights you and Yulya got into. I guess some things will never change... You are leaving again, are you not?"

I met my little sister's eyes and smiled gently. "I want to hear all about you when we get the chance, but I am travel-weary tonight. Can we catch up later?"

After kissing my cheek, she said, "Thank you for all the birthday and name-day presents you sent me over the years. It was a comfort to know you had not forgotten us."

"You are most welcome, Mashen'ka."

"Goodnight, brother."

"Goodnight."

As she left the room, L'vitsa squirmed from my arms and padded after her.

I was almost certain Yulya would wait to see how I handled the situation with Maksim before attempting to kill me again, but I locked my chamber door just in case.

Though I knew I should rest before the sure-to-be exhausting following day, I had slept so much on the airship that I wasn't tired.

My room looked the same as I had left it from the books on my table to the assortment of weapons on my walls. And everything was kempt. The blades were polished and sharp, and there seemed to be no accumulation of dust anywhere.

The thick, crimson curtains were soft and lush as I opened them to view the moonlit gardens behind the manor. Memories of glittering parties on warm summer evenings, hushed trysts on moonless nights, and hunt-bloodied weapons dripping onto the paths in dawn's glow danced before my eyes.

"It seems another lifetime," I murmured to the empty room. "I was so certain of what my future held back then: heir of the Volonovs, leader of the Ubyzniki, husband, maybe father."

I shook my head. "When had it all changed? That night, the night of my failed mission? Yes, I suppose so. But had it really been a life-changing realization, or was it more a slow shift over time?" I sighed. "It does not matter. It is not my life anymore. I rightfully cast aside the path chosen for me and seized my own fate."

A sense of dread clenched my stomach.

"No, I am my own man. No amount of ancestral obligation can force me to pick up the sword and spill the blood of the innocent."

Turning my back to the garden, I closed my eyes and thought of all the beauty I'd given the world. I'd changed lives, one by one. And in so doing, I'd made the world better.

Every woman I'd met had something I could give

her. Lily had needed someone to have confidence in her. Cassandra needed someone to listen. Monique needed to laugh. Emily needed to cry. Mirabel needed protection and Shivani something to protect. I could remember them all.

I remembered their smiles and laughs. I remembered their skin as they trembled and called my name in the heat of passion. But most of all, I remembered when they had left.

A hug, a kiss, a soft goodbye, and the sound of footsteps fading into the distance.

But my bruised heart could not mourn for the lost potential because I knew they'd found their joy. Whether it was Yvette embracing her art or Ember embracing her emotions, I knew my short time with them was worth something.

And though they'd left me with only memories to keep me warm, I wouldn't have it any other way.

8

I had laid down just to rest my limbs, but the familiar scent of the bed linens lulled me to sleep. Of course, every noise shook me awake. The wailing of the domovoi, mourning the death of the head of the household, had not been easy to ignore. I felt more tired than I would have if I'd stayed awake all night.

A quick look in my closet told me none of my old clothes would fit. Sighing, I pulled on the clothes I'd arrived in and unlocked my door to face the day.

I stopped short when I found Liza waiting in the hall. She wore a plain, charcoal dress with a scarf over her dark, unbound hair.

"Good morning, Kisa," I greeted.

She nodded, eying my choice of funeral attire.

"Yes, it is unfortunate that I have grown since I was home last."

"Perhaps Master Adrik will allow you to borrow some of his clothes," she suggested.

I thought of the last time I'd seen my brother-in-law. "Has Adrik put on weight? I recall him being rather lean."

Her eyes evaluated my build, trailing my shoulders and chest, and I found myself straightening my spine under her gaze. "Hmm. You are probably right. You are broader in comparison."

"It cannot be helped then," I muttered.

Liza followed me downstairs to the dining room, where my family had gathered for a light breakfast before the long day ahead.

"Good morning, sisters, Adrik," I stated, taking a seat beside Masha.

"Good morning, Sasha," my younger sister greeted immediately.

A quick glance at Yulya told me she was pleased I hadn't taken Father's seat at the head of the table. She nodded at me, acknowledging my presence.

Taking the cue from his wife, Adrik addressed me. "Good morning, Sasha. I was surprised to hear from Yulya you had arrived last night. My apologies for not being here upon your arrival."

Always the deceitful diplomat, Adrik was both Yulya's perfect match and her exact opposite.

"Do not concern yourself, Adrik. I know Yulya and the Ubyzniki keep you busy."

His smile stiffened. "You are right, of course."

Glancing back the way I'd entered, I saw Liza hesitate. *She has probably never eaten with the family before, but she was told not to let me out of her sight.* I frowned at the uncomfortable look on her face.

"Do not hover, Liza. Take a seat," Yulya snapped.

Liza ducked her head. After creeping to the seat

across from me, she sank slowly into it as if she would find a pin there. "Thank you, Mistress Yuliya," she murmured.

Liza gazed down at her lap.

I clenched my teeth at her change in demeanor, so different from the contentious spitfire who'd cursed me to Hell as she'd tried to murder me.

Reaching out, I placed a slice of bread on the plate before her, ignoring her wide-eyed surprise in favor of serving myself.

After I'd claimed bread and cheese, my elder sister deigned to speak to me. "You cannot attend Father's funeral dressed thus. You are too muscular to fit into Adrik's clothing. But I think perhaps one of Father's old suits would fit you."

"You are right, Yulya. Sasha looks just like Papa from old photographs," Masha added.

I fought the shiver that unpleasant thought provoked and suppressed a sigh. "That is a good idea, sister. Thank you for the suggestion. I want to show my respect by being presentable."

Yulya nodded and beckoned to a maid standing by. "Tell Grigori to wait in my father's room for Sasha," she instructed.

The maid dipped her head and scurried away to her task.

The rest of breakfast was solemn and silent. Liza didn't look up from her plate until I rose from the table.

"I will go change." I excused myself.

Liza stood to follow, and I silenced a snort.

My father's chambers were on the second floor. The story was made up of his bedroom, bath, and private study as well as my mother's apartments. The conference room and secondary library, which housed the special collections we didn't want just anyone stumbling upon, were used primarily for Ubyzniki purposes.

As with many great houses, the walls were lined with the portraits of the bloodline. Volonovs from centuries past glared at the failure who represented the last male of their name. I did not shrink from their disapproval but squinted back at the bloodthirsty butchers in disgust and defiance.

Liza shadowed me in quiet reverence.

"I bet you think of them as great men," I scoffed. "Protectors of Russia and the people who make up her glorious empire."

"Do you not?" she asked.

Is the angel of death and destruction to be loved or hated? I stopped and turned back to Liza. She was the Ubyzniki's perfect weapon: faithful, obedient, lethal. *She believes too deeply to understand my views.* "Fear is a darkness that consumes the light of truth, causing nothing to grow but hate."

She listened to my words, staring into my eyes as if they would decipher the meaning. Dropping her gaze, she answered hushed. "The light of truth can reveal the things we should fear and hate the most."

Thinking of the truths I'd discovered the night of my failed mission, I could only agree with her. *But what truths does she know, and what fear and hate have they caused?*

The door beside us opened to reveal Grigori, our family's aged butler and my father's valet. He smiled kindly at me. "Master Aleksandr, I am pleased at your return. I know, if nothing else, Master Volonov would have been relieved to have you back in your rightful place."

I held in my sigh at my father's trusted confidant. "How are you faring, Grigori?"

His smile saddened. "At my age, I have said goodbye to quite a few friends. But your father had a good death, and I have faith he will be happier with Mistress Volonova than he would be here with us."

"That is likely true," I agreed. "Do you think any of my father's clothes will fit me?"

Grigori analyzed me, his old eyes still sharp. Then he nodded with a smile. "Follow me, sir."

My father's bedchamber was much the same as my own: heavy drapes and weapons on the walls. Though it had been inhabited far more in the last decade than mine, it projected a cold emptiness that made us speak in hushed voices; even the clock was silent and still. The bed curtains were closed as if someone were still sleeping. Grigori crossed to the dressing room and ducked inside. A few minutes later, he emerged with clothes folded over his arm.

"I am sorry there are not many choices, Master Aleksandr. Most of Master Volonov's clothes that would fit your younger frame are inappropriate or too faded and worn. After the funeral, I will contact the tailor to come to measure you."

"Do not worry about it, Grigori. I will be leaving again tomorrow."

His answering silence was laced with disappointment.

Glancing over my shoulder at Liza, I smirked. "Are you planning to help me undress, Kisa?"

Her face flushed as she glared at me. After turning sharply, she stomped from the room.

I chuckled under my breath and faced Grigori, who raised an eyebrow at me. Sobered, I dropped the smile.

Grigori had chosen black trousers and a black waistcoat with a buttoned, grey shirt; the matching jacket with silver embroidery was much too flashy for a funeral, so I left it behind. It felt strange to have a valet again after so long of dressing myself.

"How does it look?" I asked, seeing the mirror had been covered with a dark cloth, like all the mirrors in the house.

"You are very much your father's son," Grigori answered as if it were a compliment.

I frowned, looking even more like my father no doubt.

A gentle tap on the door drew my attention as Masha peeked her head in.

"It is time," she murmured.

I nodded and offered her my arm. She took it gently and allowed me to lead her toward our father's funeral as Liza trailed behind, her head bent in respect.

9

The parlour candles shined steadily, illuminating my father's body and the family who had gathered to say goodbye. While I'd been changing, my father's three living sisters and their families had arrived. They greeted me with quiet nods and silent tears.

The main ceremony would begin once we reached the church, but we were permitted a private farewell. Father Strovanash, the same priest who had baptized my sisters and me, said his prayers before motioning to a handful of men who waited outside the parlour—there to avoid the taboo of family members carrying the coffin. They carried the casket outside and put it on the hearse cart.

It seemed appropriate to give Grigori control of the horses as he had always been father's driver.

We stood, waiting in the cold autumn morning for the echo of the cannon from Peter and Paul Fortress. Ten minutes passed in silence while I strained my ears for any sound beyond the nearby birds. As the reverberation of the noon church bell faded, a distant boom sounded from the citadel.

The daily signal to synchronize the clocks of Saint Petersburg complete, we began our walk to the church. As we followed the hearse cart—the horses' hooves clop clopping rhythmically on the cobbled road—down the path toward the church, Masha handed me Father's nice overcoat.

The wind was refreshing as if it cleared out the stale air in my lungs. I would have called the long walk enjoyable had it not been for the occasion.

The procession to the church took no more than twenty minutes by Panteleymonovsky Bridge.

The cathedral was grand and imposing. The green domes, the yellow façade, it was just as I remembered it from my youth. The Turkish cannons and iron chains that made up the fence—the perfect example of that Russian military pride—never ceased to strike awe in my heart, no matter how many sabbaths I'd spent standing at attention, staring at the elaborately gilded, white walls.

After reaching the few front steps, the casket was lifted, carried inside, and placed on a wheeled table.

Once my father had been moved to the front, Father Strovanash began the funeral service.

It was all golden icons, chanted songs, and pleading prayers. The room was crowded with Russia's elite as if my father was already a saint. The entire production became a blur, and I found myself answering the priest's calls out of habit though I hadn't attended Divine Liturgy since the last time I'd been in that church.

With one final plea, Father Strovanash asked

that everyone approach and kiss my father goodbye. As the only remaining son, everyone looked to me to begin the proceedings.

Approaching a vase of white roses, I plucked two and then stopped before Yulya. Offering her a rose, I said, "Bid our father farewell, sister. You are the eldest child. It is your right to go first."

Ever the stoic, Yulya didn't react. She took the rose from me without a word. After circling our father's coffin anticlockwise, she bent down and kissed him. Then she placed the rose on his chest and stepped aside.

I also circled the coffin and kissed my father. The smooth coldness of his skin was the solid proof that this was the last I'd see of him, or so we all hoped.

Masha followed our lead but with far less composure. After placing her rose, she rushed to my arms and buried her face in my chest. I gently patted her covered, unbound hair until the priest let a handful of soil slip through his fingers into the coffin. With a soft thud and a shah like fat raindrops on loose earth, the sound echoed through the silent church. Then he covered my father with his shroud and dismissed everyone.

The lid was put into place and the casket was wheeled out, where it was loaded back onto the hearse cart. As Grigori again took control of the reins, mourners began lining the streets.

While we followed the cart once again, the mourners threw fir and juniper boughs behind us, covering our tracks as we returned home by the Belinskogo Bridge.

The family crowded the spiked iron fence

surrounding the small chapel building at Volonov Manor as Adrik opened the rusted iron gate. The modest size of the chapel did nothing to reduce its aged grandeur. Below the blue onion dome of the chipped white building, a stone slab declared the name of our forebearers and bore the crest presented by Peter the Great himself. Volonov it proclaimed with a zhar-ptitsa proudly flaunting its full plumage. Though the red, orange, and yellow paint of the bird had long worn away, everyone there knew its likeness.

As we filed into the chapel, the oppressive eyes of the icons bore down on me. Not an arshin of wall or ceiling was left undecorated inside. Even the floor gave no relief as the names and dates of all the Volonovs interred in the vault below pressed heavily on my shoulders. The family members gathered to speak their piece.

My father waited on the altar to be laid to rest with our ancestors and his departed wife, and he would wait for forty days before his body was cremated and entombed below.

Before I could even offer my place, Yulya faced those gathered. "As you all know, my father believed in two things: service to the empire and family. We Volonovs may not have the numbers we once did, but we still have the strength and influence to protect our place. My father was a stubborn, ruthless man when it came to doing his duty. And you can trust that his legacy will not be neglected or forgotten."

The aunts and cousins looked at each other, confused by Yulya giving a speech that should have been mine to give.

Adrik bit his lip as he gauged their reactions, but Yulya stood steadfast with her chin up.

I will never be able to leave if the family does not accept her leadership. Feeling the time was right, I stood beside my sister and put an arm around her.

"Well said, sister," I began as she stiffened under my hand. "As you all know, Father named me the next heir of the Volonov family." I paused as they nodded. "This was not just of him. I neither deserve nor desire this distinction. Yulya is more experienced and more qualified to lead the family the way Father would have wanted."

"But Sasha," my aunt Evelina protested. "Sergei named you heir even after you left. He must have had a reason to do so. And besides, a woman has never led our family before."

I frowned. "Aunt Evelina, how could you, as a woman, say such a thing? It is the 21st century, a woman leads our great empire. Would you say that to the empress? You have all known Yulya her entire life. You know she is more than capable."

"But she is not nearly as skilled as you are, Sasha," my cousin Vasili countered. "You are legendary, by far the best in generations."

Yulya shook with rage beneath my hand.

I sighed at my cousin. "I do not want the title," I stated. "Who here would force it upon me? Would you not prefer to follow someone who wants to lead? Yulya is the eldest of the eldest. It is her place, not mine."

Releasing my sister's shoulder, I left the chapel and my shocked family.

10

I stood outside the chapel door, then peeked around at my family. They chattered in hushed whispers, discussing the decision I'd thrust upon them.

After a while, Yulya announced the reception would be held at Volonov Manor. I moved to the side of the building so they wouldn't notice my presence as they began walking toward the main house.

Once my last cousin was out of sight, I returned to the chapel and stood staring at the iconostasis.

Is this truly the path God wants for us? If God created this entire world and all the beings in it, why would he want them to kill each other? I do not believe he would create magical creatures only to have them slaughtered. No, there is no God. And if there is, I will not worship such a heartless being.

Logically, I had long ago abandoned religion and faith. But I could never truly escape the reflexive motions my parents had instilled in me at such an impressionable age.

Sighing, I closed my eyes. "God, if you are out there, grant my father peace, and grant peace to all the many beings whose lives he took, whether they deserve your love or not. Amen."

Having spoken my mind, I shoved my hands deep into my father's overcoat pockets and started to follow my family. Not ten steps from the chapel, I stilled.

"You can come out now, Kisa. There is no need for you to follow so far behind," I called.

Liza stepped out from the shadow of the chapel without a word. I'd expected her to purse her lips in frustration at being so easily found. But instead, she peeked up at me, all silent curiosity.

"What is it?" I asked.

She looked away. "What, what? I did not say anything."

"You looked like you had something to say."

She pursed her lips. "What could I possibly have to say to you, Aleksandr Sergeyevich?"

"Would I have asked if I knew? You know, Kisa, you do not seem to understand the difference between servant and stalker."

She choked on her fury. "I am not your servant, and I am certainly not stalking you."

I suppressed a laugh. "So why did you not head back with everyone else?" I prodded, not being able to resist.

She fell silent, and my ears strained in anticipation of her answer.

"It is difficult losing a parent. A quiet presence to watch over you is a blessing," she murmured.

My eyes flicked to her downcast face, and a

gentle warmth bloomed in my chest. Then the cold autumn breeze blew it away. *She is following me because Yulya ordered her to. But she is quite convincing. Perhaps Yulya was right about her skills. Perhaps they are not so straightforward as an assassination in the dark.*

The thought gave me a newfound respect for Liza. Though I didn't agree with the Ubyzniki's mission to eradicate all supernatural creatures, I could still appreciate the abilities they cultivated in their apprentices. Still, I was a little surprised. Yulya had never been very good at subtle manipulation, but just because she couldn't do it didn't mean she couldn't teach someone else.

As we approached the manor, the path crowded with carriages of people come to pay respects to our family. The gates were wide open, Petya not bothering to ask why people were there. Nevertheless, he stood by, watching as they came and left. I veered toward the gatehouse, and Liza followed.

"Petya, have you and Tanya gotten a chance to go up to the house yet?" I asked when we neared him.

"No, I hesitate to leave my post. What if there is an accident or someone who should not be here tries to sneak in?"

I patted my friend on the shoulder. "Come, Petya. You and Tanya have known my father all your lives. Come to the house. You have enough time to get a blin or some kutya."

He thought for a moment, looking at Liza, and nodded. "All right. I will fetch Tanya and Mila."

After a few minutes, Petya returned with his sister and a little girl of five or six.

I smiled down at the blue-eyed child in her little red wool coat. Crouching, I addressed her. "Hello there. My name is Sasha. I have known your mama and uncle for a long time. It is very nice to meet you."

She placed her little hand gently in the one I held out to her, smiling and blushing.

"I heard Uncle and Mama talk about you. And Mama calls for you a lot. I am happy you finally came," Mila chattered.

The smile slipped from my face only momentarily as I glanced at Tanya—who was crimson with horror—then back at Mila.

"Tell me. Do you like blini?" I asked the child.

"I love blini!"

"Of course you do. So how would you like to come up to the house with your mama and uncle and eat all the blini?"

Mila's bright eyes turned to her mother. "Can I, Mama?"

"Yes, Mila. We are all going to get blini now," Tanya answered.

With a squeal of delight, Mila grabbed her mother's hand and ran toward the house.

Turning to Petya, I raised an eyebrow, asking for an explanation for the child's unexpected words. Petya's gaze flickered toward Liza.

"Everyone is probably wondering where you are, Sasha." Petya pointed out that now was not the time.

I nodded, putting away my questions for later.

The silence between Petya, Liza, and I was

palpable as Petya searched for something to say to the assassin.

"I know you prefer the stiletto, Kisa. But Petya is quite the accomplished marksman." I bragged about my childhood friend.

"Oh?" Liza asked, giving Petya her full attention. "I did not know you had much weapons training, Pyotr."

"Well, yes, but Sasha—"

"Do not be humble, Petya. You were always better at distance weapons than I. You know, Kisa, with your smaller stature, you may benefit from distance weapons training. Yulya always preferred hand-to-hand, so I am certain that is all you learned from her. Why do you not ask Petya to teach you?"

Liza listened to my words carefully.

"Liza, do not listen to him. You do not have to—" Petya started.

"No," Liza interjected. "I think it is an excellent idea. Will you teach me, Pyotr?"

Petya paused, blinking his wide eyes, then smiled. "If that is what you wish, Liza. I would be happy to teach you what I know."

"Thank you." Liza nodded, her straight face determined.

I internally congratulated myself. *Show her what you are capable of, Petya.*

11

The house was already crowded by the time we arrived. I hadn't even managed to remove my coat before I was stopped by people offering their condolences. It seemed everyone from the owner of my father's favorite restaurant to the governor was in attendance. But most troubling of all was the overabundance of Ubyzniki slithering through the rooms.

I didn't waste any time. Making my way through the multitude, I searched for Maksim Igorevich Ivashkin. I marked Yulya talking with the leader of the Rostavich family as Dima stood by, hanging on her every word. Masha and a young man around her age who I didn't recognize fed Mila treats and chatted with Tanya.

Finally, I reached the ground-floor library, where Maksim was deep in discussion with Vladimir L'vovich Raskoliev, the Ubyzniki's mage.

"Am I interrupting?" I asked, closing the door behind me.

Maksim's eyes lit up, and a smug smile graced his

battle-hardened face. "Sasha!" he greeted. "It is good to have you home."

"Please, call me Aleksandr."

Maksim's smile stiffened.

"I hear you two and my father have been making plans," I said coolly, glaring at the pair.

They flinched, then Maksim squared his shoulders. "We should discuss this another day, Aleksandr. It is your father's funeral after all."

"I disagree. Today is the perfect day to end this farce. Let me make myself clear, Maksim Igorevich. I do not care what you and my father had planned. I will not marry Nika, nor will I lead the Ubyzniki."

Maksim frowned. "I think you will come around."

"What makes you think so?"

"The sword hanging over your head." Maksim looked to Vladimir, and my gaze followed.

"What have you done, mage?" I demanded.

"Only what was asked of me. I serve the Ubyzniki for the glory of the Church and the Russian Empire. I do as I am bid," Vladimir answered simply.

I clicked my tongue. "My sister told me you worked a spell with my hair. What were the spell's conditions?"

"Simple," Maksim started. "To compel you back into the fold, Vladimir cast a glaz smerti."

My heart stopped, and a shiver ran through me. "You cast the eye of death on me?"

Maksim smirked and nodded. "You have a little less than a year before you die. Your father and I are the only ones who know the words to break it. But now, dear Sergei is gone. So only I can save you from an untimely doom, Aleksandr."

My heart pounded in my chest as my mind raced. *Yulya was right. I cannot overcome the glaz smerti. No wonder she tried to kill me. My only choices are to marry Nika and become heir or die.*

I gritted my teeth, suppressing my internal quiver of fear. "Why?" I growled. "Why are you doing this? Would not the Ubyzniki only benefit from a leader who wants to lead? And what of Nika? She is your daughter. Would you condemn her to a loveless marriage just to realize your vision?"

Maksim waved his hand at me, dismissing my concerns. "You are the best, Aleksandr Sergeyevich. No one can match your skills as an assassin. You were born to lead the Ubyzniki. As for Nika, she wants to marry you. If my daughter wants you, I will do what I can to join our houses."

"I may have been the best ten years ago, but what makes you think my skills have not slipped? I have not killed a supernatural being in over a decade."

Maksim eyed me, pursing his lips. "Even so, Nika wants you."

"What if I decide I would rather die than play my part in your sick game? What then? No one wins."

Maksim squinted at me, trying to decipher my resolve. "Very well, Aleksandr. I would be willing to sacrifice my daughter's happiness if you consent to a union between Masha and Kostya instead."

My face heated with rage. "You think I would sell my sister to you? I would never condemn her to a life of unhappiness just so you can lay claim to a Volonov," I spat.

Maksim shrugged. "Then you will marry Nika," he said simply.

Trapped, I cursed my father. *How could you do this to your own son? After ten years of freedom, I thought you had let me go. But no. Once you are in, you can never get out. Is that it? Is this what it means to be born a Volonov?*

Fury shot through me. *No, I will not allow them to choose my destiny without a fight. They think they want to join our names? I will show them just how wrong they are even if I have to burn our prestigious reputation to ash to do it.*

"When did you cast the spell, mage?" I murmured.

Maksim's smirk widened in his beard.

"On the last dark moon," Vladimir answered.

"We have almost a full moon now. So two weeks ago?"

The mage nodded.

I have just under a year then. That is more than enough time. "Fine, Maksim Igorevich. I agree to marry Nika, but only if she consents to it."

Maksim nodded. "I am glad to see you can be reasoned with. When should the wedding be? The sooner the better, I think."

"Not too soon. Out of respect for my father's death, do you not think we ought to wait until the memorial period is over?"

"Forty days?" Maksim mused. "All right. I think Nika can wait that long."

"That is, unless she has a change of heart. Obviously, you would not kill me just because your daughter no longer wants to marry me."

Maksim waved his hand. "Of course, I would not be so low."

I smiled to myself. "Shall we go tell the bride-to-be the good news? It has been some time since I have seen dear Nika."

As I opened the ground-floor library door, I saw Liza leaning against the wall to one side. Her eyes flicked toward me, then back at Petya, who stood near her.

I followed Maksim to the dining room, hearing Liza excuse herself from Petya behind us. Near the door, Masha still cooed over Mila with the golden youth. The boy's blue eyes widened as we entered.

"You remember my son, Kostya. Do you not, Aleksandr?" Maksim asked, directing my attention to Masha's companion.

I glared at the teenager and held out my hand. He hesitated but took it. I was not ashamed when I squeezed his fingers a little too hard. *I know your scheme, Konstantin Maksimovich. But it will not happen. Stay away from my sister.*

Kostya averted his gaze but did not wince at the pain.

"There she is," Maksim cheered.

I turned in the direction he'd indicated, dismissing the whelp.

For those who didn't know better, Veronika Maksimovna Ivashkina likely looked the pinnacle of beauty. Her golden hair was long and unbound, its gentle waves falling to her slim waist. Her full lips smiled to reveal straight teeth. But it was her eyes that gave her away. Her almond-shaped eyes, so dark they were nearly black. They would have been beautiful too had they not reflected the twisted darkness that dwelt in her soul.

"I have excellent news, Nika," Maksim started.

"Yes, Papa?"

"You will soon be a Volonova."

12

Nika grinned, her black eyes hungry for either me or the power I represented.

As I stifled my instinctive shudder, I realized the room had frozen along with me. Everyone but Mila, who happily ate her blin, stared at me in stark silence.

Masha's and Kostya's eyes were wide, and Tanya cast hers down at her hands in her lap. Liza made no sound as she slipped from the room.

"You do not know how happy this makes me, Sashen'ka," Nika simpered.

The sound of her using my pet name was as sweet as sugar of lead.

Play the part, Sasha. Unclenching my teeth, I assumed an indifferent expression. "It has been a long time, Veronika. I am not the boy you once knew."

"Of course," Nika agreed, sauntering up to me. "But I am not worried." She reached up and rested her hand on my cheek. "I can get to know you again."

You will not like the new me. I nodded and stepped out of her reach. "But not today. Today is my father's funeral, and I must see to our guests."

She solemnly agreed, reminded that she must at least maintain appearances.

I had barely left the room when I found Yulya blocking my path, murder in her glare. "Follow me, brother."

I sighed, marking Liza over her shoulder; her attention was seemingly on whatever Petya was telling her.

I complied with my sister's request and followed her upstairs to our father's study. She managed not to stomp as she went ahead, but her shoulders were tense.

The room we entered was completely different than what I remembered from the few times I'd been permitted admittance. The large, dark desk with its leather armchair was the same as was the fireplace with the colorful painting of the zhar-ptitsa above the mantle. The small bookshelf, even the inkpot, everything in the room seemed exactly where it had always been. Still, it was a foreign place to me. Without my father's imposing presence, it was as though I'd never been there at all.

Yulya rounded on me the moment I closed the door. Her icy glare froze me in place. I couldn't remember a time I'd seen her more furious, and I'd seen her angry a lot.

"Give me one reason I should not kill you right now," she snarled in a low voice.

I showed her my palms. "Just listen, Yulya."

"No, Aleksandr!"

I flinched at her formal address.

"I made that mistake once before. You told me you would 'clear this up.' And what did you do? You agreed to marry Nika!"

"I had no choice. They cast a glaz smerti on me."

"I know, and I also knew you would agree to it all if you found out."

"But I have a plan," I argued.

Yulya clicked her tongue. "I do not care."

"Sister, wait. Maksim has agreed to lift the eye of death if Nika no longer wants to marry me."

"She will never do that. She has always wanted the power of the Volonovs."

"They agreed to postpone the marriage until after the memorial period. I can easily get Nika to call off the marriage before then." Seeing Yulya was still unconvinced, I hurried to finish. "Besides, you cannot kill me right now. Everyone would know it was you, and then you would never get what you want. Give me forty days. After that, even if Nika does not let go, I will still leave. I will not allow Maksim and Father to dictate my life. I would rather live out my last year in freedom."

Yulya paused, squinting in thought. "No promises. Out of respect for our father and because you kept your word about naming me heir to the family, I will give you today. But that is all."

"My plan will work, Yulya," I reiterated.

She waved her hand at me, dismissing me in a gesture that echoed our father perfectly.

Sighing, I complied and left our father's study. *I had hoped Yulya would see reason. I suppose I will just have to stay on guard for any other assassination attempts from that direction. Oh, who am I kidding? That is every direction.*

"Forty days. Forty days," I muttered to myself. "Concentrate on the mission."

Looking up from my musings, my eyes met Liza's as she waited at the top of the stairs. *She did not hesitate to immediately report me to Yulya even if she would have found out anyway.*

When Yulya did not appear, Liza's eyes widened, a hint of fear behind her gaze.

I smiled bitterly. "Worry not for your beloved mistress, Kisa. I left her well. She will be out as soon as she regains her composure."

Her relief showed as her shoulders dropped ever so slightly with a silent sigh.

I didn't feel much like playing the good host after all that had passed, but the guests didn't give me much of a choice. Only family had been there when I'd said I wouldn't be taking over, so everyone who passed through the front door felt it was only right to greet me. It didn't help that I'd been gone a decade, and those not involved with the Ubyzniki were curious as to what I'd been doing all that time. I politely told them I was traveling and turned toward the next person.

The members of the Ubyzniki were far less warm in their greetings. They met my eyes coolly, likely only greeting me at all because they thought I would be the next head of the Volonovs.

I took a break from the chaos and slipped into the kitchen. Sneaking past the staff as they filled their serving trays with more food, I snatched a glass and a piece of bread and went downstairs to the cellars.

The cellars, like the rest of the house, hadn't changed much in the last ten years. I paid no mind to the first few rooms, where the cooks stored the meats and cheeses. At the end of the hall, I pushed open the sturdy wooden door to the wine cellar. Past the dusty, aging bottles—at the very back—were shelves of other spirits.

I reached up and grabbed a bottle of vodka, uncorking it with my teeth and spitting the stopper back toward the way I'd come. Liza stepped aside to avoid the projectile.

13

I didn't say anything and neither did Liza. I knew why she was there. *Not even a moment alone.* I sat with my back against the wall and poured vodka into the glass. Then I set the glass on the floor beside me and put the piece of bread over it for my father.

After taking a sip from the bottle, I held it out to Liza. She hesitated. Then she sat next to me and took a sip before handing the bottle back.

I didn't drink again but rolled the bottle between my hands. I had been foolish to think I could have a quiet drink. *This is no place to let my guard down.*

Tilting my head, I directed my attention at Liza. "You disappeared when Maksim announced my engagement," I pointed out.

She stiffened, no doubt trying to think of an excuse other than she ran to tell my sister.

I smirked. "Did the thought of me marrying another upset you that much, Kisa?"

Liza clicked her tongue and squinted a glare at me. The expression only made me grin wider.

"Why would I care who you marry, Aleksandr Sergeyevich?"

"Why did you follow me down here if not to be alone with me?"

She averted her gaze, seeming to find the shelves of wine bottles particularly interesting. "You lied to me," she murmured. Then she turned to meet my eyes. "You said you were going to leave after you named Mistress Yuliya heir. You told me you would leave after the funeral."

"How was I to know Maksim would offer me his lovely daughter in marriage?" I asked.

She frowned. "Mistress Yuliya is not pleased."

"When is she ever?"

She pursed her lips but didn't argue.

We sat in a heavy silence, too unfamiliar with each other for it to be companionable.

"I imagine there are a great many who will be sad at hearing you are getting married."

"You mean as licentious as I am?" I asked bitterly.

She looked away.

"I doubt anyone will care very much," I muttered. Then I thought of Tanya's wistful gaze, her frown at hearing Maksim's announcement, and Mila's assertion that she often called for me. *Well... perhaps one.*

Liza looked at me sidelong, a distinctly disbelieving glint in her eyes.

"Except you, of course, Kisa," I added. "I can see your heart is quite broken."

Liza clicked her tongue again and rose to her feet. "Had you better not go upstairs and receive the condolences of those who loved Master Volonov? What are you doing down here anyway?"

I stood up, looking at her with a steady gaze. "I was waiting for you, Kisa. I did not want to disappoint you. You never did tell me why you followed me."

She reached around me to the shelf of spirits and grabbed a bottle of vodka by the neck. Wiggling the bottle for emphasis, she said, "They were running out upstairs."

We both knew she was lying. I sighed internally, steeling myself to re-enter the throng of assassins and well-wishers.

"Sooner or later you will have to be honest, Kisa. You are only making it more difficult on yourself."

She turned and left without a word, and I followed, smiling.

As soon as I exited the kitchen, I was assaulted by the hostile glare of Dmitri Stepanovich Zhdasky as he blocked my path. The last ten years had hardened him. His mouth was creased from frequent frowning, and his eyes told of many sleepless nights. Still, it was clear to see he was stronger, his body lean and lethal under his funeral clothes.

I raised an eyebrow at him, appearing unconcerned by his obvious malice. "Dima," I greeted with a nod. "It has been a long time. You are looking well."

"I hear you are staying with us for a while, Sasha," he said, his tone deep and barely restrained.

I tilted my head at him. "You seem upset, Dima. I hope I am not stepping on your toes by marrying Nika." We both knew Dima had never loved anyone but Yulya, and he was only upset because Yulya was.

He pursed his lips with a squint and changed the subject. "My condolences on your father. He had a good death."

I nodded.

Dima showed no indication that he was going to move from my path.

"Is there anything else?" I asked him.

He didn't respond but didn't budge either.

Farther down the hall, Liza's eyes watched our exchange. She made no move to intervene. Petya approached her, and she turned her attention toward him in such a way that she could still keep an eye on us.

"If you have nothing else to say, Dima, I am afraid I have other things to attend to."

"We will be seeing each other again soon, Sasha," Dima threatened.

"I am certain that is true. Now, if you will excuse me."

Dima reluctantly stepped aside for me to pass.

As I approached Liza and Petya, I heard the end of their conversation.

"I am supposed to be helping Aleksandr," Liza said with a frown. "But I think if we meet early in the morning, it should be all right."

"Early tomorrow morning then," Petya said. "I will meet you at the training grounds."

Liza nodded her agreement.

I smiled to myself. *Good luck to you, my friend.* I swept the foyer with my eyes. Tanya was helping Mila into her little red coat. I approached them.

"You are leaving already?" I asked Tanya.

She met my gaze, and I recognized that guarded

look she wore when she was hurting. "Yes," she answered without further explanation. "Thank you for allowing us to pay our respects."

"Of course."

She bowed her head slightly and took Mila's hand to leave. As she turned and led her daughter out the door, I watched her go, ignoring the echo of my racing heart from so many years before.

14

The rest of the day blurred together in a disorienting yet overly focused mixture of talking to guests and watching assassins glide from room to room of my ancestral home. By the time the last visitor left—I was not at all surprised it was Dima —I was exhausted. A quick look around the quiet dining room table told me my sisters felt the same.

"I am going to bed early, I think," I told my family and Liza.

Yulya didn't even acknowledge I'd spoken. Adrik nodded, and Masha looked around bleary-eyed as if startled awake by the sound of my voice.

"Elizaveta," I addressed the still-alert woman across from me. "Would you help Masha to her room? She is so tired that I am not sure she will make it alone."

Liza frowned but looked to Yulya for guidance.

Yulya tilted her head in assent, indicating that Liza could momentarily abandon her quarry in favor of keeping up appearances that she was working for me.

"Come, Mistress Maria," Liza murmured softly, touching Masha's arm.

As I followed them out of the dining room, Grigori approached me.

"Are you preparing for bed, Master Aleksandr?" he asked.

"Yes, but I do not need any help changing. Thank you. However, since I will be staying for a while, you should call for the tailor tomorrow as you initially suggested."

He dipped his head in acknowledgment and turned to leave.

I called out to stop him. "Grigori, who is keeping watch tonight?"

Grigori frowned in disapproval. "I believe Dmitri Stepanovich is watching until Master Rostavich is finished with supper. Then he will take over."

I analyzed the man's expression. "You do not think it proper for Dima or Adrik to keep watch?" I guessed.

Grigori shook his head. "It is not that."

"Then what is it?"

"If I might be so bold?"

I nodded, giving him permission to voice his opinion.

"This tradition your family has: watching the body for forty days instead of burying it immediately, and cremating... It is against the Church's teachings, sir. I worry for the soul of my friend."

I sighed. "I understand your concerns. But as

members of the Ubyzniki, they not only have knowledge of magical beings, they are also often exposed to them while they hunt. Cremating the bodies assures none of our family members return from the grave in any number of inhuman forms. And keeping watch for the memorial period gives the soul time to get used to being dead while still ensuring the body does not rise in that time. It is to protect us all."

"But the Church..." he trailed off, not wanting to argue.

I nodded. "The Church has long given us special dispensation to cremate our dead rather than bury them."

Grigori hung his head. "I know," he relented, stifling his misgivings.

I patted the elder on his shoulder. His strongly held beliefs were causing him anxiety on my father's account, and nothing I said would relieve that.

Once in my room, I removed my waistcoat and unbuttoned my shirt. The fire had not yet been lit, and a pleasant shiver gave me gooseflesh as I made my way to the fireplace.

Bending before it, I unlatched the door and opened the glass; the ashes from the previous night's fire hadn't been removed as there was no cleaning on the day of a funeral. Still, there weren't so many that I couldn't build another atop them. From a chest nearby, I pulled out a match and some kindling.

I lit the kindling and placed it into the fireplace, watching flames consume the small bundle of sticks.

The kindling lit easily in my hand, and my heart leapt as I watched the flames spark to life.

"Now put it in the fireplace, Sasha," Yulya instructed, coming up behind me and guiding my hand by the wrist. "You have to do it quickly, or you will get burned."

I nodded silently, glancing over at my sister, her dark, unbound hair still covered by the kerchief she'd worn that day. Her black dress had a small stain on the chest where Masha had spit up on her as she'd tried to get the infant to sleep.

"Where is Papa?" I asked her, flinching at the brittle tone in my voice.

Yulya's gentle eyes met mine, and I could tell my sister was trying very hard not to show me she was just as upset as I. "Papa is in his study."

"Can we see him?" I murmured, pleased my voice sounded stronger.

Yulya frowned. "You know we should not bother him while he is in there."

"But surely today, of all days, he will let us in," I argued.

My sister nodded slowly. "Perhaps. Let us go knock softly and see if he answers. But if he says he does not want to be bothered, we must not argue."

I agreed to her stipulation.

As we left the room, I reached out and took Yulya's hand. It was cold and small even for someone much more grown than I. But feeling her pulse through her fingertips gave me comfort nonetheless.

We crept down the stairs to the second floor. The portraits of the Volonovs that came before us stared down at us as we passed, and I stood straighter to show I was worthy of the name.

When we reached our father's study, Yulya tapped lightly on the closed door. "Papa?" she called softly.

"What is it?" our father's low, gravelly voice demanded.

"Papa, can we come in? Sasha wants to say goodnight."

"Very well," he answered.

Yulya turned the knob, and we stepped into the space that was normally out of bounds.

Our father placed the pen he'd been writing with into the inkpot as he looked up from his desk. His light eyes showed neither the sternness they usually held, nor the sadness one would expect from the day of a funeral. They were just tired, dull and soft with weariness.

"Is Masha asleep?" he asked Yulya.

She nodded.

"Good." He tilted his head. "Had not you better be on your way to bed, too, young man?"

I thrust my shoulders back under my father's gaze.

"You should get a good night's rest," he continued. "Your training resumes tomorrow morning."

"But, Papa, can I not take a short break—"

He shook his head firmly, cutting off my protests. "I thought you liked to train. You were so eager before. You are very good at it, the best in generations. Why the sudden reluctance?"

I cast my eyes down, not knowing how to articulate my fears.

"Come here, Sasha," my father ordered though his voice held a gentleness I rarely heard from him.

I obeyed, leaving my sister where she stood, and rounded the desk to stand beside his chair.

He turned to face me and placed his hands on my shoulders. "I am only going to say this once, so I want you to listen carefully. People die. It is inevitable. And as a member of the Ubyzniki, you will see much death, both from your enemies and your comrades. It is a feeling you must get used to. Your mother might not have fallen in battle, but she lived a fierce life. It is up to you children to carry on her spirit. One day, you will lead this family; one day you will burn even me to ash."

My vision blurred as the tears I'd been holding back all day forced their way to the surface.

"None of that," my father softly scolded. "We can, each of us, only hope for a good death. We can only hope that we will be remembered by those who survive us."

I nodded, wiping my tears away with a hard sniffle.

"Now off to bed with you both," he said with a nod.

I hesitated. "Papa?"

"What?"

"Would...would you sing us a song? Mama always sang us a song before bed."

My father fixed his steady gaze on me, and I bit my lips.

"You are nearly twelve years old, Sasha. You still need someone to sing you to sleep?" he asked.

I knew the answer he wanted, but I pushed for

just a little more warmth. I lowered my head again. "Just this once? Just this once, and I will never ask again."

He sighed. "Very well."

———

A crack from the kindling pulled me from my memory. The fire was bright enough that I could add some wood. I did so as I softly sang the song my father had sung to me some eighteen years before.

"Oh, Cossack girl, fierce and brave,
You wield your sabre like a dance.
On the battlefield, none are your match.
Your dark eyes burn like fire coals.

Oh, Cossack girl, tender and true,
Put down your sabre and kiss me.
In my arms, no one is sweeter.
Your dark eyes are deep and pure.

My Cossack girl, fearless and faithful,
Pick up your sabre once more.
And though apart, you are with me,
Forever haunted by your dark eyes."

Finally, as the wood reached the appropriate heat, I took some minte from the bin and threw it into the fireplace before securing the door.

15

The room didn't take long to warm up once the minte was thrown into the fire. I took a deep breath, closing my eyes only momentarily in an attempt to calm my mind and body. *How long do I have before Yulya sends someone to kill me again? How long before she tries herself? Can I even trust the food or drink in this house? I need to get rid of Nika quickly. The faster she gives up on the idea of marrying me, the faster I can leave.*

I sighed heavily and made my way toward the bed, too exhausted to think through the problem completely. It had been a long while since I'd been in a situation that needed constant vigilance. But I trusted my instincts would carry me through as they always had.

A firm knock sounded on the door just as I was unfastening my borrowed trousers. I buttoned them again and made my way toward the disturbance.

As I unlocked and opened it, I met Liza's grey

eyes. Her gaze traveled over my body, taking in my bare feet, my only recently replaced trousers, my still unbuttoned shirt. *Are her eyes lingering on my exposed abdomen?* Finally, she took in my grin. I knew she was only there to make sure she knew where I was, but that didn't stop me from provoking her.

"Did you miss me, Kisa? Could not bear the thought of not seeing me until morning?" I opened the door wider and added heat to my tone. "You could join me if you like."

Her face flushed, and her eyes sparked like sharpened steel as she squinted at me. "I just came to see if you needed anything before I went to bed."

I tilted my head at her. "Are you certain that is all?"

She stood up straighter and sucked in air, her nostrils flaring in irritation. It took a great deal of effort on my part not to laugh.

"What else could I possibly want from you, Aleksandr Sergeyevich?"

I shrugged lightly. "Women have wanted a great many things from me. How will I know if you do not tell me, Kisa? Tell me what you desire, and I will give it to you. I am very accommodating."

She just stared at me for a few silent moments. "Goodnight, Aleksandr," she stated firmly before turning on her heel and stomping to the door beside mine.

"Goodnight, Kisa," I called sweetly, chuckling under my breath.

Relocking my door, I removed my shirt on the

way to the bed. Then I took off my trousers and climbed between the cool sheets. Smiling to myself, it didn't take me long to fall asleep.

The sound of soft footsteps outside my door woke me the next morning. Making my way over to the window, I looked out at the gardens. A faint morning mist hung close to the ground in the predawn light.

I smiled as I recognized Liza's smooth gait while she strode toward the training grounds, her lean yet lethal form set the fog to swirling as she cut through it.

Inhaling deeply while I stretched, I breathed easier knowing Liza's watchful eyes wouldn't be fixed on me for at least a little while.

"A morning walk," I mused. "Yes, that sounds nice."

Having made up my mind, I pulled on the clothes I'd arrived in and silently left my room. The maids were up and about their morning chores. But the family was not, and I easily slipped out the front door without incident.

The chilly morning air stung my lungs in the most pleasant of ways. *Autumn in Saint Petersburg, nothing quite like it.*

In the distance, I saw a faint light from the chapel, telling me Adrik was likely still inside keeping watch. But as the horizon to the east continued to lighten, I knew he wouldn't be there for much longer. I lengthened my strides to get off the property and out of sight.

I hoped Petya had left the gate unlocked when he'd headed in to meet Liza; I didn't know whether my old way of sneaking out was still an option.

Just as I reached the gate, I heard a bark. I froze, my eyes sweeping the direction the sound had come from. Some three sazhens away, in the park on the other side of the gate, a reddish brown laika chased a pair of birds, its tail wagging happily.

"Boris," Tanya scolded the dog lightly as she came into view.

I easily opened the unlocked gate and closed it shut behind me. At the sound, Boris's head swiveled in my direction, his ears pricked up.

His tongue hanging out to one side, the dog ran toward me at full speed. I smiled as he skidded to a halt at my feet. I held my hand out for him to sniff me. His tail wagged, telling me I could pet him.

"What a good boy," I told him as I stroked the soft, thick fur of his head and ears.

I glanced up at Tanya while she watched us, her dark eyes warm yet holding a sadness that would have pained my heart so long ago.

"Good morning, Tanya," I greeted, with a polite but soft smile.

"Good morning, Sasha." Her voice was barely above a whisper.

"It is very early to be up."

She dipped her head in agreement. "Petya got up early to meet Liza. Boris was restless, and I did not want him to wake Mila, so I took him outside."

A strained silence settled between us. It was foreign and strange. It had no right to separate me from the girl I'd once been so open with. But much had changed since then.

"Tanya, could I talk with you for a moment?"

She frowned but nodded. "I can see you have many questions. Come inside. I was just about to make breakfast."

I agreed and followed her into the cottage, Boris running on ahead.

16

Petya and Tanya's home had hardly changed since I'd been there last. The front room had a sturdy, square table and chairs; shelves along the back wall held cookware and jars of various preserves. Most of the main room was taken up by a large masonry stove and oven, which pleasantly warmed the space. A rumple of blankets and pillows told me that someone—Petya if I were to guess—called the top of the stove his bed.

"Would you like coffee?" Tanya asked, the sound of her soft voice filling the room like a third occupant.

"Yes, thank you."

She nodded and fetched a jar of coffee beans and a grinder.

"May I help you?" I asked, offering to take the items from her.

She hesitated, then bowed her head. "Thank you," she murmured. "I will get started on the rest."

I sat down at the table facing her as she set a pot

of water on the stove to boil. Then she lifted the lid of another pot, looked inside, and placed that pot on the stove as well.

"Petya built up the fire before he left this morning, so it should not take long to heat up the porridge and boil the eggs," she told me. "Do you still like your boiled eggs soft in the middle?"

My eyes met hers as she looked over her shoulder at me, the heavy silence lasting only a second. "Yes," I answered.

For the minutes that followed the only sounds were the grinding of beans as I turned the handle of the coffee grinder and the soft scraping of the wooden spoon in her cast iron pot as she stirred the porridge.

After I was finished grinding, I stared at Tanya's back. Her shoulders were tense. I sighed. "What happened, Tanya?" I asked.

She didn't look back at me. "Too much, Sasha. I am not the girl you knew. Sometimes...sometimes I wish I could go back and make the right choice. How much different would my life be now?"

My heart squeezed at the strained quality of her tone. I knew what decision she now called a mistake. I had spent many sleepless nights wondering, dreaming, what my life would be like if she had chosen differently. I rose from the table and approached her at the stove. Standing at a familiar but polite distance, I held the coffee grounds out to her.

"What happened, Tanya?" I repeated softly. "Where is your husband?"

She took the grounds from me, not meeting my eyes. "Gone."

"For how long?"

Tanya shook her head. "I was still pregnant with Mila when he left. He went to work one day and never came home."

"Is he...alive?"

She curled her lips. "Oh yes, he is alive. He sent me a letter after a few weeks telling me he would not be back." She sighed. "So I came home. Petya and Mama took care of Mila and me. But now that Mama is gone, it is just the three of us."

She moved away from me, grabbing the turka to start making the coffee.

She is lost. She has forgotten herself.

"Do you remember, Sasha, our last time together?"

How could I forget? I nodded, not giving voice to my old grief.

"Do you remember when I told you that you had taught me to love myself?"

Of course I remember. It only shaped the rest of my existence; it only gave me direction when I wanted nothing more than to bring beauty and love to this world. Again, I nodded silently.

She turned to me, her dark eyes fragile and pleading. "I wish...I wish you could do it again."

I froze, staring at the woman who at one time had held complete dominion over my heart. I didn't breathe as her words echoed in my mind, reaching back to a primary part of myself, back to a younger Sasha who was still a part of my foundation.

"I should have followed my heart, Sasha. You knew, you had to know, I loved you. That I only chose Zhora because I thought he was the smarter choice. The safer choice. I did not expect that you would leave home because of my decision, that you would give up your entire future, the future I was trying to preserve for you, because of what I did."

I blew out a heavy breath, understanding that it was guilt that made her act this way. *Yes, guilt. Not some longing for me.* "That is not why I left home, Tanya. The timing was a coincidence. You would have left as soon as you were married. That was no reason for me to leave. So, all of this, you need not fret about it. You have nothing to feel guilty about."

"Guilty? Sasha, do you think that is why I say these things? No. After this much time, I know that not marrying you was the mistake that started my life down this path. We were so happy together. We could have been that happy all this time."

I shook my head. "Perhaps. Perhaps we could have been happy, but our lives would not have turned out as you think. I still would have left home."

"But I would have gone with you!" Her voice raised in a passionate plea for understanding. "No matter where we had gone, I would have been happy if we were together." Her dark eyes lit with desperation, an appeal to the one man she had loved, had trusted, the man who she had been with when she was happy, confident.

I couldn't pull away from that supplication in her gaze. *What is this feeling that draws me to her? Would I still feel it if she were not Tanya? Is it because she is pleading for help? My help? Or have I held on to some far-off hope all this time?*

I lifted my hand to rest it on her flushed cheek

and caressed her face with my thumb. She closed her eyes and sighed, leaning into my hand.

My unease receded at her contented expression. Still, I felt no warmth. I felt no relief. All those nights dreaming of a moment like this, where Tanya would tell me she'd made a mistake, that she wouldn't forsake me, I had not expected such a lack of reaction in myself. Had I not longed to hear these words? When had I moved on?

"Sasha," she murmured, shining a smile that reflected hope and promise. She looked ten years younger. And then it was gone. "But...I guess it was truly not to be." Tanya stepped away from my comfort. "After all this time, you finally come home. And now...you are to be married."

My stomach dropped as she reminded me that my life was on the line if I didn't find a way out of this marriage. "Yes," I muttered.

Tanya tilted her head, squinting ever so slightly as she took in my expression. "You...do not want to be married..." she said.

Debating whether or not to confide in her, I decided she had enough problems without worrying about mine. "I am also not the boy you knew," I stated, telling her that she could not read me as well as she used to.

She frowned but nodded slowly.

17

It was not long before Mila shuffled out of the bedroom, her hair still tangled from sleep. She was pleased to have me there for breakfast. With Tanya's words still fresh in my mind, I wondered if that warm and pleasant meal together could have been my everyday had things gone differently so many years before.

But as I strolled back toward the manor, I knew that it was not the warmth and pleasantness of home and belonging. It was merely an echo of my past feelings, my past desires, too far off to be anything but a bow of courtesy to what we used to have.

The sun was just lighting the face of the manor, its morning glow accentuating deep shadows behind the columns and in the eaves.

No, this is not my place anymore.

Movement to the left of the deceptively frank façade drew my attention to Petya and Liza as they rounded the building. Liza's dark hair was threaded with streaks of golden red in the soft blush of dawn-light. She smiled at Petya as they talked. I could see the easy way she walked beside my friend, and Petya grinned at having her attention. I mentally congratulated myself for suggesting they train together.

I knew there was no avoiding their notice in the open space I was in, so I stopped walking and watched them until Liza saw me.

"Aleksandr," she said in an accusatory tone.

Petya followed her squinted gaze, perceiving my presence only after she'd spoken. "Sasha." Petya's greeting was far warmer. "You are out early this morning."

"As are you, my friend."

"Liza wanted to train early so she would be available to you when you awoke."

"Did she now?" I smiled easily as I met Liza's eyes.

She flushed but didn't say anything.

"I guess you got up earlier than she expected."

I didn't respond but smiled wider.

"Where have you been, Aleksandr?" she demanded quietly.

Petya's eyes widened as his head snapped in her direction.

Her tone and manner didn't bother me in the least. "I just went for a little walk," I told her, still smiling. "Then I met up with Tanya, and she made Ludmila and I breakfast."

Liza cast her eyes down.

"Breakfast is ready then? Good. I am hungry after our work." Petya turned to Liza. "Would you like to meet again tomorrow?"

Liza watched me as she answered. "I do not think so. I will let you know when I have time again."

Petya frowned at her rejection.

"But thank you for this morning, Pyotr. You were a great help. I hope to meet again soon."

Appeased, Petya smiled easily once more. "Anytime, Liza." Saying his goodbyes, Petya patted me on the shoulder as he passed to return home.

I watched my friend go, grinning to myself at the spring in his easy gait. But when I turned back toward Liza, I found her staring at me rather than Petya.

"Do you normally get up this early?" she asked.

I wasn't going to tell her it was her sneaking steps outside my door that had awoken me from sleep. I shrugged.

"You should have sent someone for me," she urged.

Her insistence chafed like shackles around my ankles. I knew why she wanted to stay close to me, but her servant disguise was only vaguely covering her actions. "Did you follow Yulya around every moment of every day, Kisa? Is that how she taught you to be of service?"

She pursed her lips ever so slightly. "Grigori always knew where Master Volonov was when he was not with him."

That is because my father trusted *Grigori.* "What qualifications do you have to be that level of service? What have you done for me thus far that I would rely on you so heavily?" *Does Yulya believe she really has a chance to become an effective member of the*

Ubyzniki without even knowing the basics of maintaining a cover?

She squinted in thought, and I could practically see her cursing herself for choosing such an explanation. A servant's job is to carry out the master's orders. *Why had she not thought of that before she had used that reason for why she follows me?*

Liza blew out her cheeks in an exaggerated sigh. "Fine," she snapped. "I did not want to help you. I wanted to keep an eye on you. You swore to me that you would leave after your father's funeral. And I told you if you were lying to me, I could take you down here as easily as there."

I stared at her, keeping my expression bland. "Was that so hard, Kisa?"

"You knew?"

"You really should learn how to lie. You will never be a good assassin if you cannot even do that."

She clenched her teeth and growled. "Why did you go along with it if I am so bad at lying?"

"Hmm," I hummed, tilting my head and starting back toward the manor.

She rushed to catch up and keep my face in view as she waited for my answer.

"Because it amused me."

She did not look pleased, which only amused me more. I chuckled in the face of her annoyance.

"You are intolerable, Aleksandr Sergeyevich."

I smirked. "How should I treat someone who tried to kill me and plots to do so still? Since I did not kill you, you might as well provide me with some entertainment."

"I am not your personal jester," she snarled.

"What are you then, Kisa?"

She stepped into my path, and I halted so as not to run into her. Then she glared up at me, fury sparkling in her grey eyes. "I am not someone to be taken lightly. You may have thwarted my initial attempt. But you will not win, Aleksandr Sergeyevich. In the end, it is *you* who will be looking up at *me*. It is *you* who will beg *me* for mercy. It will be *my* voice and *my* command that will determine your fate. And my name will be what you whisper with your dying breath."

As I watched her turn on her heel and stomp into the house, a shiver ran up my spine, despite my confidence that I could best her in any situation.

I entered the foyer and found Liza being reprimanded by Yulya.

It seemed she must have been interrogating her as to where I'd been because she stopped as soon as she saw me, her jaw stiffening as she clenched her teeth.

Without another word, Yulya turned and headed toward the dining room.

Liza saw me as her gaze swept over the room behind her, but her eyes didn't fix on me as if I were some inanimate object like a lamp or stool.

I frowned when she turned away and started to follow Yulya. My hands prickled, and I twitched my fingers to relieve the feeling. Refusing to watch her retreat, I went to the stairs.

"Are you not coming to breakfast, brother?" Masha asked when we met on the staircase, heading in opposite directions.

"I already ate," I told her.

She nodded and went on her way.

A heavy sigh from the foyer told me Liza had heard that I had no intention of eating again. My shoulders tensed as I felt the weight of her presence behind me, following me as her orders demanded.

"Get something to eat from the kitchen," I murmured, not looking back at her. "You trained this morning. I am certain you are hungry. Yulya will never know you did not follow me if you eat there."

"But—"

"I will not go anywhere, Kisa. Go eat," I urged, interrupting her protest.

I felt the weight on my shoulders ease, and I glanced behind me just as she slipped out of sight.

I didn't feel the least bit guilty as I quietly but confidently strode into the secondary library and closed the door behind me. I had just as much right to be there as anyone else, which is exactly what I would say if Yulya found out for she would be suspicious of me sneaking around without Liza.

Like everywhere else in the house, the secondary library hadn't changed. The glass doors of the cedar bookshelves were still clear and dusted. The handrail of the stairs that led up to the gallery was still polished and smooth. Even the bust of Peter the Great—his wavy marble curls artfully rendered, his well-trimmed mustache atop his Cupid's bow lips— wore the same bored expression as if he'd rather be in any other room but the one he was stuck in.

Still, a glimpse at the books on the shelves told me some things had changed. At least the selection had been updated over the last ten years.

I hope he still has the book.

After climbing the stairs, I scanned one of the top shelves, remembering where it had been before. My chest squeezed when it wasn't there.

I sighed, shutting the glass door. "It probably would not have helped anyway," I muttered.

Biting my cheek, I pursed my lips and wondered if any of the new additions could help me.

I searched the shelves to my left, looking for the beginning of the books on all things magic. Spotting the copper bust that marked the front of the section, I moved toward the dead eyes of the mage Grigori Rasputin.

My shoulders twitched in a shiver as I faced the statue straight-on. I'd never met the man, but my father had when he was quite young. He'd once told me that Rasputin had eyes that could see directly into a man's soul, that it was impossible to lie to him. But it was said that he'd been very kind and affectionate toward children.

I stared at the face of the man who'd kept Emperor Alexei II alive to the age of thirty, a massive feat in the life of a hemophiliac. His reign may not have been very long, but it had been long enough for his nephew, Mikhail II, to reach an age where he could reasonably govern.

The Ubyzniki had enjoyed a great deal of power while Rasputin had been the mage, a power that had only slightly waned in the many years since his death.

I squinted as the corner of my eye caught a hint of gold behind the copper bust. Leaning closer, my eyes focused on the faded gold leaf spine of a book shoved behind the likeness. I reached carefully in and pulled out the volume.

I read the title I'd been looking for: *A Field Guide to Curses.*

My brow furrowed. *Why is this here? Was someone trying to hide it?*

Opening the weathered cover, I flipped through the alphabetical entries to the page on the glaz smerti.

A slip of paper fluttered out of the book onto the floor when I reached the page. As I bent to retrieve it, I hadn't even touched it before I recognized my father's handwriting.

My breath rushed out of my lungs, and my fingers tingled as I picked up the bookmark and read it:

> *Black-and-white in equal measure.*
> *Acrobats, Justice, golden treasure.*
> *The knife's edge cuts more than your foe.*
> *The wisest mind this truth does know.*

I groaned aloud. I'd always hated riddles, likely all the more that my father had forced them on me. He thought they kept the mind sharp. I just thought they were unnecessarily complicated.

"Why would he stick a riddle in here?" I muttered. *Was he training Masha the same way he had trained me? Hiding little hints everywhere just to discover the most basic information. Who knows why? Maybe it was just a scrap of paper used as a book-*

mark. Perhaps Masha even likes riddles. "On the other hand..." I folded the paper and put it in my pocket. "A riddle on the exact page of the exact book I wanted? A book that was hidden? It could prove important."

Turning my attention back to the field guide, I read the short entry on the glaz smerti:

The eye of death is a timed death curse. From casting date, expiration is anywhere from one month to nineteen years, matching moon phase determining the shortest of periods.

The eye of death is a powerful curse cast only by the most experienced of mages. If done incorrectly, it will blow back and kill the magician who cast it.

The curse requires something of the person to be cursed; hair, nail clippings, or bodily fluids the most preferable. Therefore, to protect oneself, it is important to keep careful track of one's sheddings.

Built into the spell is a cancellation order: a word or phrase that can remove the curse anytime during the period before expiration. The call-off words will be known by either the mage who cast the curse or the curse holder, the person who hired the mage to do so.

The cancellation order is the only known way to break the curse.

"Yebat'," I swore.

The glass doors covering the shelves beside me rattled, telling me the domovoi was not pleased with my choice of language.

19

I reshelved the book where it belonged instead of behind the bust of Rasputin and pulled the watch from my pocket. *Maksim said only he and my father know the phrase to break the curse... But knowing Vladimir, I find that hard to believe. Perhaps I could get it out of him. But that will be tricky.*

After leaving the secondary library, I descended the stairs, thinking about when the best time to pay Vladimir a visit would be. I was halfway through the foyer when Grigori answered a loud knock at the front door.

"Good morning, Grigori," Nika said from the other side. "I am here to see my future husband."

The hair on my arms stood on end, and adrenaline gave me the necessary boost I needed to speed from the room before Grigori admitted the intruder. I raced toward the nearest exit, which was down a servants' hallway and into the kitchen.

I hardly registered Liza's wide eyes as I burst into the room.

"Aleksandr," she called from a small table in the corner.

Ignoring her, I went straight for the door, only stopping when she blocked my exit.

"Where are you going?" she demanded.

"Out," I said, not really having an answer myself.

"What is your rush? I have not even finished breakfast. You said you were not going anywhere."

I sighed heavily, my limbs shaking with restrained effort. "Get out of my way. Either come with me, or stay here. I do not care, but I am leaving now."

She stared into my eyes for only a second before she stepped aside, and I launched myself out of the door. I quickly made my way along the side of the house to the back gardens, the gravel skittering after my hurried steps.

Liza rushed to catch up, pulling her jacket on, a hunk of bread hanging out of her mouth. "Where are we going?" she asked after she took the bread from between her teeth.

"I do not know yet," I told her. I made my way toward the garden wall, which was hidden by vines, while keeping my eyes on the parallel, red gravel path.

"Then what is the rush? If you do not know where you are going, then you have no specific time to be there."

"Can you not read the situation?" I grumbled. "Time is of the essence. I will explain when I have a moment."

She didn't protest but followed me in silence.

When we were lined up with the fountain at the

center of the garden, I turned to the wall beside us. Pushing back the vines, I grinned at the iron spikes driven into the bricks. *Still here after all this time.* My body repeated the movements it had executed so many times in my youth. I easily scaled the garden wall, using the evenly-spaced spikes as hand and foot holds until I straddled the top of the tall wall.

Liza was already climbing up after me when I looked back at her. I lowered myself down to the other side, dropping the last arshin. Liza followed suit. And though she had to fall farther than I due to her height, she barely made a sound as she landed.

Hunching my shoulders against the wind, I stuffed my hands into the pockets of my too thin jacket and headed through the woods toward Inzhenernaya Street. I turned east upon reaching the road, Liza silently following close behind.

"What now?" she asked softly when we'd reached the Fontanka River.

I glanced over at her. She stood passive and patient; her expression saying she didn't really care where we went. *Should I visit Vladimir now? Liza will tell Yulya whatever is said, but that should not be a problem since I am trying to break the curse that keeps me here.*

"Now, a water taxi," I told her.

It didn't take long to find one, and we were soon chugging toward the Neva. I stood near the smoke-stack, trying to get whatever warmth I could as the wind bit my nose and the tips of my ears.

"You really were in a hurry," Liza pointed out. "You did not even bring your coat." She watched me, blinking slowly in expectation of the explanation I'd promised.

I sighed. "I was avoiding an unwanted visitor," I muttered.

She snorted with a smirk. "Who could make the great Aleksandr Sergeyevich Volonov flee thus?"

I glanced at her sidelong, keeping my thoughts to myself.

She raised an eyebrow.

"Veronika," I murmured.

She tilted her head. "Mistress Ivashkina, your nevesta?"

"Do not call her that," I snapped, the temper in my voice surprising even myself.

Liza was unperturbed. "Call her what? Your nevesta or Mistress Ivashkina?" she asked.

"Neither."

"What would you have me call her then, Aleksandr?"

"Bes," I said in a moment of true mean-spiritedness.

Liza didn't respond, but I felt her eyes on me. After we'd disembarked on the bank of the Monastyrka River, I heard her murmur, "Why would you agree to marry her if you hate her so much that you call her a demon?"

If she'd wanted me to answer her muted question, she didn't push me to do so when I ignored it.

The white and brick-orange wall surrounding this part of the Aleksandr Nevsky Monastery was rather inconspicuous and unassuming compared to some of the other entrances. There were no grand arches with inlaid mosaics here, just simple wrought iron gates blocking the road and sidewalks.

Upon reaching the closed gate, I tried the latch to no avail. With a sigh, I leaned to one side, looking to see if there was anyone nearby who could let me in.

"You are not going to break into a monastery, are you?" Liza asked doubtfully.

I smirked at her. "You sound awfully squeamish for an assassin."

Just as I leaned to look the other way, I caught sight of movement. "Oi!" I shouted.

My quarry halted before heading toward the gate. I smiled pleasantly at the grisly bearded monk in his black cassock when he approached us. "Good morning, Father," I greeted.

He nodded his acknowledgment, his serious, dark eyes holding no hint that the morning was indeed good.

I kept my smile in place. "I am here to see Vladimir L'vovich Raskoliev."

I was amazed to discover that my good monk's frown could deepen further.

"Vladimir L'vovich has not resided at the monastery for some years." He turned to leave without another word.

"Wait, Father," I urged.

He stuttered to a halt and turned back.

"Where is he now?"

The monk shook his head. "I know not. Only Archimandrite Ostrovsky knows."

I did not try to stop him when he walked away. I sighed.

"Why do you need to see the mage?" Liza asked.

I shifted my gaze to hers and smiled smoothly. "Still so interested in everything I do, Kisa?"

She may have already come clean about following me to spy and plot my death, but I found teasing her too amusing to stop now.

She snorted. "Do not get ahead of yourself, Aleksandr Sergeyevich. I know where the mage now resides."

"You do?"

She nodded.

20

"Where is he then?" I asked, fully turning to face Liza.

"Perhaps if you had communicated where we were going when I asked, we could have saved the trip," she said, ignoring my question.

"Why would I be so open with someone who has professed her determination to kill me?"

"Perhaps you are not so confident in your abilities as you appear, Aleksandr Sergeyevich." She smirked. "Otherwise, you would not be so secretive."

I blinked, taken aback by her suddenly playful tone. *Does she think she can beat me at my own game?* My smile widened, and I took a step closer to her, dropping my voice to one low with intimacy. "Perhaps you do not want to kill me as much as you claim, Kisa. Otherwise, you would stop talking about it and do it already."

Her grey eyes met mine for only a moment before she looked away. "You have such an imagination. I wonder what part of your muddled brain these ideas spring from." Her tone was just short of biting.

Warmth spread through me as I internally celebrated having an impact. I knew Yulya had ordered her not to make a move, and it was fun to watch her scramble for a response to point me in any other direction.

"So are you going to tell me where the mage is?" I asked.

"He was moved to the Peter and Paul Fortress so his laboratory would have better security."

I nodded.

"But he is not there today. I overheard him yesterday talking about some rare book he has been looking for. He heard a rumor it was nearby, so he was going to see if the rumor was true."

"I guess your spying can come in handy sometimes," I commented.

"I was not spying. I just overheard."

I shook my head and sighed dramatically. "Poor Petya. Did you even hear anything he said to you at the reception?"

"Pyotr?" she asked, tilting her head.

I nodded. "Yes, Pyotr. Surely, you are not so oblivious, Kisa. You have to know."

Liza frowned and didn't meet my gaze.

Yes, she knows. Well, it is not as if Petya was trying to hide it. "You do not like Petya?" I guessed.

"It is not a question of whether I do or do not like him," she responded.

"Then...?" I trailed off, waiting for her to continue.

"Do you have anywhere else you need to go? Or

can we go home? I am sure she has left by now, and did not Grigori want you to meet the tailor today?" she asked, changing the subject entirely.

I shrugged. "I do not want to go back yet," I said simply.

Liza sighed. "Okay, then where are we going? Or are we just going to stand outside the monastery all day?"

"All right, Kisa. I have just the place." I turned from the monastery and began walking along the Monastyrka embankment back toward the Neva, where we could more easily find a boat. Once on board, I murmured our destination to the driver.

"Where are we going now?" Liza asked as we headed north on the Neva.

"It is a surprise," I told her.

"I do not like surprises, Aleksandr Sergeyevich."

I smiled pleasantly. "Well, then use your superior powers to figure it out."

After following the curve of the Neva, we turned onto the Great Nevka River then followed it to the Little Nevka.

"Any ideas?" I prodded Liza as we passed Tikhiy Otdykh Park.

"We have trees at home," she said. "And it is too early for the theatre."

As the tree-line gave way, an iron structure loomed over us. Its square base artfully supported its seven floors, each smaller than the one below it. The overhanging eaves of the pagoda were painted red with gold accents.

"Kurino Tower?" Liza asked, her head tilting

back as we approached the small dock for the building.

I nodded. "Have you ever been?"

"No," she answered. "I have seen it, of course, but I have never been inside."

"There is nothing quite like it," I said fondly. "I remember when it was being built. I was even at the opening ceremony in 2004."

"Sometimes I forget how old you are," Liza said as we walked toward the tower. "I would have been eleven."

I scowled at her. "I am not that much older. I was only sixteen."

My petulance slipped away as her eyes twinkled while she tried to suppress a smile. *Is this a new side to her? Is this who she really is peeking through her assassin's mask? Or perhaps this is an act as well. Is she trying a new tactic?*

The warmth that had bloomed in my chest was snuffed out. Liza must have changed her mind about her new approach because when I glanced at her again, she wore the unperturbed exterior once more.

"Let us go to the tearoom," I said. "It will warm me up."

After climbing the stairs to the entrance of Kurino Tower, we were greeted by a large portrait of Emperor Nikolai II shaking hands with Emperor Meiji. The Russian-Japanese Friendship Museum took up all of the first floor. And while the room itself was decorated to look like simple yet elegant wood, it had the strength and sturdiness of iron and steel.

The museum told the history of relations between the two great empires from the 1700s through the 1904 treaty all the way to present day. I started straight for the center, spiral staircase though I slowed when Liza wasn't following close behind. She walked with halting steps, her gaze drawn by the various historical displays.

She stood before the daishō Emperor Shōwa gifted to Nikolai III upon his ascension to the throne in 1970 for a good five minutes. She just gazed, her eyes wide with awe, at the golden bears intricately painted onto the black sayas of the swords.

And I watched her study the weapons. *Surely, this is a real emotion in her. This wonder, this appreciation, could be fabricated, but for what purpose? No, this is my first honest glimpse of Liza...*

"What is your name, Kisa?" I asked quietly.

She blinked, her brow crinkling. Then she turned toward me. "I have told you my name is Elizaveta."

"And the rest?"

She frowned, more internally than at me. "Elizaveta Yurivna Zaporozhnaya."

"Zaporozhnaya...is that a Cossack name?" I asked.

She nodded once.

"Is your father a soldier?"

She turned and walked the rest of the way to the spiral staircase. Then she paused—her hand on the railing—before mounting the first step. "My great grandfather was. My father was a baker," she answered quietly, her back to me. Then she began climbing without another word.

21

I followed Liza up the staircase, climbing past the language, traditional arts, and cultural centers. We passed the conference center and finally reached the tearoom on the very top floor.

Beyond the entrance shōji, the tearoom—as the floors before—was sturdy iron decorated to look like wood. There were chabudai in two rows along the center of each of the four sides of the room, with private rooms separated by decorated shōji at each corner.

The hostess, an obviously Russian woman in a kimono, bowed to us in greeting and asked where we would like to sit.

"Is the sakura room available?" I asked her.

She nodded.

"Then I would like to sit there, please."

"Of course," she said.

We followed her to the room at the southeast corner. After sliding the shōji open, the hostess gestured for us to take our seats on the zabutons, placed on the floor around the circular chabudai.

"Would you like Japanese or Russian tea?" she asked politely.

I glanced at Liza, tilting my head to ask her preference.

"Russian," she answered.

I nodded at the hostess. "Russian is fine with me as well."

With a bow, the hostess closed the shōji.

As Liza took a seat on a cushion, I looked around the space. It hadn't changed much though I thought the table might be new as polished and unmarked as it was.

I glanced at the maiden—the hem of her pink kimono peeking from below her large parasol—standing under the raining cherry blossom tree painted onto the shōji.

"I wonder if it is really made of rice paper," Liza murmured, staring at the shōji.

"No," I answered though she hadn't really asked a question. "Sometimes they are made from washi paper, but these are made from white silk."

"Do not tell me you have also been to Japan," she responded with a hint of sarcasm.

I smiled down at her. "I have been many places, Kisa."

She huffed through her nose and redirected her gaze out the large window beside her.

Following suit, I stood before the other window, looking out over the Little Nevka.

The autumn sun glistened off the water, its easy

waves and ripples accentuated as steamboats traveled up and down.

My eyes focused on the sun's reflection off the freshly frozen Little Nevka. A tingle ran through me when slender fingers slipped between mine.

I smiled over at Tanya as she leaned against me. "Do you like it?"

Her dark eyes lit up, and her smile was all the reward I needed. "I love it. I did not think there were any tickets left for the grand opening." Standing on her toes, she kissed me on the cheek. "Thank you," she said, hugging me around the neck as I fully turned to her.

I wrapped my arms around her waist, pulling her closer. Her soft warmth pressed against me, stirring heat within me.

"How did you convince Mama and Papa to let you bring me here alone?" she asked, amused.

"I am not that capable, Tanyukha," I chuckled. "I convinced Petya that there was nothing we could do in such a large crowd."

She pulled slightly back, her eyes sweeping the private—and empty—tearoom. Her smile heated as she gazed up at me. "Always so clever, Sashechka."

"I love you," I whispered just before I pressed my lips to hers.

Her body's reaction was enthusiastic. "Sasha..." Her breathy invocation between kisses was all the encouragement I needed.

"Aleksandr?"

My mind resurfaced from memory, and I looked down at Liza. Her grey eyes were lit with concern though her brow was unfurrowed.

"I am fine, Kisa." I answered the question she did not—and likely would not—ask. "Just thinking of times long passed."

"The last time you were here?" she guessed.

I shook my head. "No, the first."

She gazed out at the Little Nevka. "It was a good memory?" she murmured after a moment.

I didn't answer right away, waiting for the old feelings swirling inside me like a small dust devil to quiet down. Liza didn't look at me, perhaps she didn't care enough for my answer to show that much interest.

"At one time, it was a good memory. Now...it is tainted by what came after."

She nodded slowly.

Does she understand that feeling?

We both looked toward the door when a waitress opened it, wheeling in a cart with our order.

I joined Liza on the floor as the waitress placed the samovar with teapot atop, glasses, and podstakanniks on the chabudai. She also set out spoons and tea sweeteners along with an assortment of cookies, biscuits, and tarts. With a bow, the waitress left.

"How do you take your tea?" I asked Liza as her eyes traveled over the bounty.

"With sugar," she answered.

I moved the bowl of sugar closer to her.

"Thank you," she murmured as she took the teapot down from the samovar and poured dark zavarka into the glass in her podstakannik.

I dipped my head in acknowledgment of her thanks.

Then she reached out and turned the samovar's valve, releasing boiling water into her glass and diluting the zavarka to suit her tastes.

When she was finished, I did the same, filling my glass with zavarka and then water from the samovar.

"Do you take it with sugar?" she asked, offering the bowl.

"No, thank you." I picked up a small bowl of raspberry jam and stirred a spoonful into my tea. It was surreal to have the action not seen as an oddity. I had been away from home for so long that I was used to others viewing the choice as strange. But Liza didn't react as she took a lump of sugar between her teeth and lifted the glass to her lips.

I breathed deep the earthy scent of black tea as I lifted my own glass. The bitterness of the brew was undercut by the sweet fruitiness of the jam. I smiled softly at the simple joy of a warm glass of Russian-brewed tea as I gazed out the window at the sparkling autumn scene.

22

Glancing over at Liza, I tilted my head and smirked when I saw that she'd been watching me.

"It seems the idyllic scenery Kurino Tower offers cannot compare to my allure," I said.

Liza didn't react to my comment but kept her expression smooth. "Why did you leave Russia?" she asked.

I frowned.

"From what I can see, you seem to have missed it here."

"What makes you say that, Kisa?"

She shrugged. "There have just been a few quiet moments where you seem to be breathing in the atmosphere as if it was a scent you had forgotten and do not want to forget again."

I masked my expression as I met Liza's eyes. *She certainly has the surveillance part down. Returning has brought back a lot of things I thought I had long left behind. Some of them pleasant like the taste of*

Russian-style tea and the scent of the breeze off the gulf and some...less than pleasant.

"Surely, my father, Yulya, the Ubyzniki have some sort of explanation as to why I left," I said, breaking the silence.

She nodded slowly. "Everyone has a different explanation."

"And you would like to hear mine?"

Liza didn't respond but stared expectantly back at me.

"The Ubyzniki are not as infallible as you believe them to be," I told her.

"How do you know what I believe, Aleksandr Sergeyevich?"

"Because I was once like you. I was trained by them my entire life. I know how they think, what they say, how they manipulate the truth to support their own means."

My words made no impact on her demeanor. "What happened?" she asked.

Images flashed in my mind. A dignified manor on a modest estate, torches flickering in the distance, a young girl with pale eyes and hair as dark as the moonless night. My heart squeezed in the echo of memory. I don't know how long I sat silently, my eyes staring unfixedly, seeing nothing.

"What happened, Aleksandr?" Liza repeated, her soft voice calling me from far away.

"You would not believe me if I told you," I murmured. "After all," I added with a bitter smile. "I am Aleksandr Sergeyevich, and my opinion cannot be trusted, yes?"

She frowned at me reciting the words she had previously used against me.

But before she could come up with a response, I rose from my cushion.

"Where are you going now?" she demanded with a sigh.

"Volonov Manor," I answered. "Grigori made me an appointment with the tailor, remember? Honestly, Kisa, I did not think you would be this forgetful."

She bared her teeth at me in a soundless growl, and I didn't bother to hold in my merriment.

When we returned to my ancestral home, Nika had already left. As I reached the second-floor landing, in search of Grigori, Yulya exited the secondary library and headed toward our father's study. She stopped, book in hand, when she noticed Liza and me.

"Nika was here," she informed.

I tilted my head. "Was she?"

"You will never get her to give up if you only avoid her," she pointed out, not acknowledging my feigned ignorance.

"I did not think she would come so soon. I will be ready next time."

Yulya stared blandly at me, entirely unconvinced.

"Where is Grigori?" I asked.

"Do you not think I have better things to do than keep track of where each servant is at any given time?" And without another word, she entered our father's study.

"It is Thursday," Liza said once Yulya was gone.

"Grigori always makes the staff's schedule at this time on Thursdays."

I glanced over at her. "You know, Kisa. If you were not constantly plotting my demise, you would make a good assistant."

She didn't react to my praise.

Returning to the first floor, we went to Grigori's office, a small room off a narrow hallway near the kitchen. I knocked at the door and was greeted by Grigori not a moment later.

"I just wanted to let you know I have returned, Grigori. I have not missed the tailor, have I?"

"No, Master Aleksandr, he is not due until this afternoon," Grigori informed.

I nodded and turned to leave. But then I halted and looked at Grigori again. "Do you happen to know where Masha is at the moment?" I asked him.

"I believe Mistress Maria is taking her turn at your father's watch, sir."

"And who is scheduled for watch tonight?"

"Pyotr Danilovich is supposed to watch tonight."

I quirked my mouth. "I will take over Petya's watch," I told Grigori.

"Would you like me to inform him of that, sir?"

"No, thank you. I will just let him know when I see him."

Grigori dipped his head in a slight bow. "Then I will inform you when the tailor arrives."

I nodded. "Thank you... Grigori, you answered the door when Nika visited earlier?"

"Yes, sir."

"Was she angry when she found I was not here?"

Grigori tilted his head in thought. "I would not say angry, sir...more frustrated."

"Did she say when she would return?"

"She mentioned to Mistress Yuliya that she would like you to stand with them at Divine Liturgy Sunday. But she did not say whether she would make another unannounced visit or not."

I frowned. "All right. Thank you, Grigori."

"Of course, sir."

I left Grigori to his work, Liza following silently behind as I went back upstairs to my room. I needed to think, needed to form a plan about how to make Nika give up on the idea of marrying me. And I needed to do it alone, without Liza ever present, ever watching my every move, ever noting whatever I said or did so she could tell my sister later.

As I opened my bedroom door, I turned back to my personal spy. "As much as I enjoy spending time with you, Kisa. I need a rest. I cannot give you the attention you deserve in my current state. Can you forgive me?"

Liza leveled an annoyed glare at me. "Could you not just say you are tired and need a nap like a normal person, Aleksandr Sergeyevich? Must you always be so outrageous?"

I gave her a wink. "Until we meet again, my sweet kisa."

She sighed and leaned on the wall opposite my door, crossing her arms over her chest.

23

The tailor's visit didn't take long. I answered his questions about fit preference as he measured me. He promised to send some premade necessities over before evening with more to come the following week. He boasted that I would have the latest styles of shirts, waistcoats, jackets, and trousers. It had been a long time since I was so well dressed, and I hoped I wouldn't feel confined by so many layers. After all, an airship deckhand didn't have to be as presentable as a boyar. Then again, this was the Ubyzniki's tailor, so I could be fairly certain that I would be able to move freely in whatever he made for me.

After a quiet and uncomfortable supper, I made my way to the chapel. Liza, of course, was at my heels as always.

The inside of the chapel was hushed, the wispy flickering of candles the only sound. The abundance of light from the many flames danced on the gold paint of the wall icons. Beside my father's coffin, Masha sat in a simple wooden chair, a loaded crossbow in her lap. Her eyes were raised, unfocused and staring as some daydream played before them.

I shuffled my feet on the threshold to announce my presence. Masha jumped at the sound, swinging the crossbow in my direction.

I raised my hands with a smirk. "Be careful, Mashen'ka. Those are dangerous."

Masha's startled blue eyes softened, and she lowered her weapon. "You scared me," she said with a sigh.

"I see that."

Frowning, she tilted her head. "Are you here to keep watch? I thought Petya was after me."

"I am relieving him."

Masha nodded slowly, then rose from her chair, carefully placing the crossbow on the seat.

Her jumpy reaction made me wonder how well Masha was being trained though I was certainly glad her fingers weren't so twitchy. The thought reminded me of the riddle I'd found, which was still in my pocket.

"When father was training Yulya and me, he used to leave riddles for us all over the house. He would hide everything from candies to my shoes, and I would have to figure out the riddle to find whatever I was looking for. Did he do this to you as well?"

Masha scrunched her eyebrows. "He hid your *shoes*?" She giggled, the sound echoing off the walls of the chapel. "He never did something like that to me. Sometimes at supper he would challenge me to a riddle contest, but that was just for fun. I never went barefoot if I didn't figure out the answer."

"I see." *That makes it unlikely the riddle was for her then.*

"Why do you ask?"

I frowned, very aware of Liza standing just behind me. "No reason," I answered. "I have just been having a lot of memories."

She smiled sadly and nodded.

"Are you tired?" I asked her, changing the subject. "We could catch up now if you would like."

My little sister met my eyes, glanced over my shoulder where Liza lurked, then looked back at me. "I am a little tired," she said, stretching her arms above her head for emphasis.

"I understand." I nodded slightly. "Get some rest. We can talk later."

As she left, she stood on her toes to kiss me on the cheek. "Goodnight, brother."

"Goodnight, Mashen'ka. Sweet dreams."

She smiled, then moved past me. "Goodnight, Liza," she added pleasantly.

"Goodnight, Mistress Maria," Liza answered softly.

After Masha was gone, I crossed the room and retrieved the weapon she'd left behind. I'd always preferred the shashka, but I had been trained in many weapons.

I examined the mechanisms. "When you were training with Petya this morning, what weapons did you use?" I asked Liza, who stood in one corner.

"Today, we practiced with a recurve bow," she answered.

I smiled to myself, picturing Petya helping Liza adjust her stance. I completely understood why my friend had chosen a bow instead of a firearm. Standing close to her, her long hair caressing my cheek as I corrected her aim. My fingertips trailing the lean lines of her arms to improve their placement.

At that moment, Grigori entered the chapel, a solemn expression on his face and a wooden box in his hands. "Master Aleksandr," he beckoned.

I approached the man. "What is it?"

"Master Volonov asked me to give you this when you took your first watch at his side." He offered me the box, and I accepted it.

Without another word, Grigori dipped his head and left.

Lifting the lid of the box, I saw a sort of rounded oblong object nestled in velvet. It had the shape of a matryoshka doll, but it didn't have the painted face and clothing. Its markings were seemingly random.

I took out the object and tucked the box under my arm. As I handled the mysterious bequest, I realized the thing was separated into rows, bands that slid and moved when pushed. *A puzzle?*

I frowned at yet another riddle my father had left behind. *What could possibly be in this that will be worth all the effort of solving the puzzle?*

As I sighed at the doll, its shape and size reminded me of the last time I'd held one.

———

I smiled down at the blue-eyed matryoshka doll in my hand. *Today is the day.* My heart sang with every passing moment.

The late summer sun was warm, but the breeze brought the scent of dirt and autumn. It was refreshing, not the breeze of summer that just moves hot air around.

Every time the wind blew, a few early colored leaves fell lazily to the ground.

As I waited, leaning against a tree in my family's park, an acorn narrowly missed my head, whizzing past me and then thunking as it met earth.

I watched a squirrel skittering along the ground, already preparing for winter.

Crickets chirped earnestly all around me, their calls overshadowed only by the soft brush of approaching footsteps.

I stood up straighter, facing the sound. Tanya arrived, her unbound hair swirling around her as a gust played with it. She smoothed it, then halted when she saw me.

"Tanya," I said like a prayer, smiling as I met her.

"Sasha." Her tone was soft but lacked the warmth it usually held.

"I know you have been busy lately. Thank you for meeting me. I have something to say...something to ask you."

Tanya nodded seriously, her dark eyes staring into mine. "Yes, we need to talk, Sasha."

I smiled. "We have known each other our entire lives," I started. "And I have loved you for as long as I can remember." I took a deep breath, steadying my nerves. "Tanya, will you marry me?"

I held my breath, anticipation clogging my throat as my heart pounded in my chest. The matryoshka in my hand felt warm, the ring within its innermost crevasse seemed to pulse with its own heartbeat.

Tanya's cheeks paled. "Sasha," she murmured. She reached out and took my hand, holding my gaze with her unwavering one. "Sasha, you are an angel to me. You have loved me and cared for me for so long. Most importantly, you taught me how to love myself. I cannot tell you how important that is. I would not be who I am without you, Sasha. You made me able to face the world with pride."

She frowned, and my smile slipped as dread squeezed my heart.

"Sasha, my family serves yours. I do not think we can truly live in the same world."

"I know you are worried about our difference in station," I said reasonably. "But that does not have to define us. It is the 21st century. Such things do not matter anymore."

Tanya shook her head.

"Tanya, please. Do you love me?"

She sighed, then met my eyes again straight-on. "I cannot marry you, Sasha. I am marrying Zhora."

The blood drained from my body. I couldn't breathe as her words kicked me in the gut. When I finally sucked in a breath, it was shallow and raw. "Who is Zhora?" I found myself asking in a voice not my own.

"You do not know him. He is an engineer," she said, so far away I had to strain my ears to hear her.

My head spun, and I blinked to steady myself. *Is my heart still beating?* I reminded myself to breathe again, and my chest ached at the expansion.

"Sasha, I..."

"Sasha?" Petya wondered, pulling me back to the present. He tilted his head at seeing us there. "I thought Masha was keeping watch before me."

I took a deep breath, steadying the shakiness that the memory had brought on.

"I decided to take over your watch tonight," I answered, glad my voice held none of the regurgitated remorse. "You were up early this morning after all." My eyes flicked significantly toward Liza in the corner.

As always, Petya picked up on my meaning. "Right. Thank you, Sasha. We were both awake quite early. Are you tired, Liza? Would you like me to walk you back to the house?"

Liza glanced at me. "I am not tired, Pyotr. But thank you for the offer. Perhaps next time."

Petya smiled sadly but nodded. "All right. Then I wish you both a good night."

Liza and I said goodnight to Petya and watched as he headed back into the darkness.

"You could have gone with Petya, Kisa. Where am I going to go? Someone has to keep watch here. Are you certain you do not dislike him?"

"I told you it is not a matter of whether I like him or not."

"Then what is it a matter of?" I pushed.

"I am not like you, Aleksandr. I do not have the luxury to love. Why would I try to get to know Pyotr if I have no real control over my destiny? It is better to not start to begin with."

I frowned, glancing sidelong at her as she

continued to watch Petya walk away. *She does not appreciate herself.* "Are you sure you will not regret letting a chance at love slip away, Kisa?"

Her smooth expression stayed the same as if I hadn't said anything.

24

The rest of the night was long and uneventful, as one would hope when keeping watch at a grave. Sometimes I sat, and sometimes I stood and wandered around the chapel. Mostly I tinkered with the puzzle box my father had left me. I twisted the bands, trying to match up the lines into some semblance of order. Quite a few times I thought about hurling it at the wall or crushing it underfoot, but I knew the painted metal wouldn't yield to such an attack.

Shortly after dawn, my watch relief arrived in the form of a golden youth, whose blue eyes widened when I turned toward him. After a moment of hesitation, he straightened his spine and strode farther into the chapel. "Good morning, Aleksandr Sergeyevich," Kostya greeted with a formal nod.

I frowned at the boy. "What brings you here, Konstantin Maksimovich?"

"It is my watch today," he explained, gesturing at the butt of the revolver on his hip.

I stared at him blandly. "Are you not a little young to be in the Ubyzniki?"

He took in a deep breath, offended by my challenge. "I am nineteen. I have been a full member for nearly a year now."

I glanced over at Liza, twenty-four and still just an apprentice. "I guess a pedigree is really all they care about," I mused, brushing him off.

The boy frowned but didn't defend himself. After a tense moment with him glancing around the floor as if looking for something, he said, "Masha seems happy you are home. She was worried you would not stay long, but now with you and Nika—"

"That is Maria Sergeyevna to you. And do you presume to know how my sister feels?"

Kostya flinched as if I'd slapped him. "N-no, I do not presume, Aleksandr Sergeyevich. Mash—Maria Sergeyevna and I..." He sighed heavily. "We are to be brothers. Are we not? Surely, we can come to friendlier terms."

I admired the youth's calmness under pressure, his straightforwardness, his perseverance. But that didn't mean I was going to make things any easier for him.

"I have known your family my entire life, Konstantin Maksimovich. I have grown up with your sister. I was at your baptism. Do not think that I do not know what it means to be an Ivashkin. You have heard of my accomplishments in the Ubyzniki?"

He nodded sullenly.

"Then you know what I can do, what I have done to those who are a threat to me and mine. Do you understand what I am saying to you?"

He nodded again, his expression even more sullen.

"Good. Then I will leave you to your watch."

Brushing past him, I didn't look back to see if Liza was following me or not. But after a few steps into the chilled morning air, I didn't need to wonder. I could feel her gaze on me, her eyes silently reproaching me for my behavior.

"You think I was being unkind to the boy?" I challenged.

"I said nothing, Aleksandr Sergeyevich."

I stopped, halting my progress to the main house, and turned to her. "Maksim Igorevich tried to bargain my happiness for Masha's. He offered to dissolve my commitment to his daughter if I would promise Masha to Kostya. And I have every right to believe that he has been manipulating Masha to that end for some time. That is how Ivashkins work, how Ubyzniki work."

Liza was silent for a moment, and I took a deep breath to steady my nerves.

"Mistress Maria and Konstantin Maksimovich have known each other their entire lives. They have played together, trained together. Do you not think it possible they are friends?"

I wrinkled my nose but then sighed. "Yes, it is possible. But Masha is so young. She has an entire bright future ahead of her. I will not see her forced into a loveless marriage. I will not see her end up like Yulya."

Again, Liza paused, and I was beginning to realize that it was standard for her to think carefully before she spoke, that all of the outbursts I'd seen thus far were unusual and out of character.

"Mistress Yuliya said something yesterday about Mistress Ivashkina giving up."

I looked at her sharply.

"And you have asked me to refer to her as Bes," she continued, ignoring my censure. "It is clear you do not want to marry her. So why did you agree?"

I hesitated. *I suppose there is no reason to keep it from her. It is not as if Yulya does not already know.* "How knowledgeable are you on the subject of curses, Kisa?"

"I know enough."

"Do you know of the glaz smerti?"

Her eyes widened. "The eye of death?"

I nodded. "My father and Maksim Igorevich cast a glaz smerti on me. If I do not marry Nika and take over the Ubyzniki, I will die."

Liza's brow crinkled in confusion. "Why would Master Volonov do that?" she murmured.

"Because he was a stubborn old man who would do anything to get what he wanted."

"No, that cannot be right," she argued. "Master Volonov loved you. He would not put you in such danger."

I stared at her hard. "Such faith, Kisa. If you are so certain of your convictions, then explain to me why my father would cast such a curse on me."

She frowned and was silent for what seemed a very long time. "I cannot explain it. But I am sure he had a reason. He must have."

"Blindly loyal to the very end," I said with

disgust, shaking my head. "Do you think you know my own father better than I do?"

"I think you have been gone for a very long time, Aleksandr Sergeyevich," she shot back. "And while you seem to think very highly of yourself, perhaps you do not know as much as you think you do."

Fury pumped through me, and I stomped toward the house. *Who does she think she is to tell me these things? She does not know what my childhood was like. There is no excuse for casting a curse on your own son. And even she has no explanation for that. But still she sides with him, sides with* them.

I didn't bother to go to breakfast. I just stormed upstairs and shut myself in my room.

25

I paced the length of my room, anger injecting energy into my tired limbs. My thoughts were tangled like a chaotic mess of threads. Any end I grabbed became jumbled before I could reach the other end. I was frustrated. And so I paced, my boots thumping heavily on the floor.

And then, a flash of light shined off the window. I glared at the distraction and halted. I did not recognize my own reflection in the glass. His complexion was flushed. His eyes were intense, his brow severe. His lips were slashed down in a deep frown.

I started at the face, jumping at the change in my features. My brow smoothed out, my eyes widening slightly. But my frown stayed the same.

"What is happening to you?" I asked my double. I shook my head, disappointed in my own lack of control. "Not a week back and you are already slipping into your old self."

I thought about all the times I'd been angry since Liza had tried to kill me. I hadn't let that particular emotion get the best of me in some years. Even when I'd killed the pirates I hadn't been angry.

I sighed heavily. "You are letting them change you, Sasha," I told myself. "You are better than this. Have you learned nothing in the last ten years? Your life was peaceful overall in your snatched moments of beauty. You were a bamboo raft on an easy flowing river."

I gave myself a hard look. "This is not who you are. This is who you used to be," I said sternly.

I thought of Liza, of Yulya, of Maksim and Nika, and I gritted my teeth. "Forty days," I told myself. "Forty days and you will be free either way."

After forcing myself to lay down and close my eyes, I unclenched my jaw and regulated my breathing. I imagined the slight sway of my cot in the deckhands' quarters on the airship. I could almost hear the wind whistling at the high altitude. I could almost hear the creaks of the wood. I could almost hear Mac's soft snoring. I drifted off to sleep.

I awoke midafternoon hungry as a bear. As I left my room to go to the kitchen, I was a little surprised not to see Liza waiting outside my door. A strange thrill of disobedience prickled across my skin at the thought of sneaking around without supervision. I chuckled at the sensation.

As I reached the second-floor landing, the timbre of Yulya's voice filtered down the hall from our father's study. I paused for a moment, weighing my choices, and sneaked down the hall to listen in on her conversation.

"No," she said sternly. "No, I do not need to

consult my brother before making this decision. *I* am the new head of the family."

She paused as if listening to someone speak, and I realized she must be on the telephone.

"Despite what my father may or may not have wanted, my brother has made it clear he does not want the title. He acknowledged my claim immediately after the funeral."

Another pause.

"This is unacceptable!" she stated as if the very phrase would shame whoever she was talking to into complying.

Her words, her tone, her impotent rage, brought back a memory from years ago.

"This is unacceptable!" Yulya said, taking a rare tone of defiance.

I could just picture Father's stern, nonverbal reproach as I stood listening from the hall. But Yulya didn't let that stop her.

"After all I have done, you are still going to name Sasha heir?" she demanded. "I have trained harder; I have sacrificed more. I even married Adrik when you told me to, and you know how I feel about Dima."

"Dmitri Stepanovich Zhdasky was not as advantageous a match as Adrik," Father stated without emotion.

"Dima is in the Ubyzniki. His family is one of the five. There was no reason for us not to marry. We love each other," Yulya argued heatedly, for once not backing down.

"Even the Ubyzniki has a hierarchy as you well know."

"I do know, which is why I did as you asked of me. As I always do. I have proven what I am willing to do for this family. Sasha has done nothing to earn the title. He is probably rolling in the hay with some peasant's daughter right now."

I looked down at my disheveled appearance. Nataliya had been particularly enthusiastic that evening, ripping all the buttons off my shirt. But she was no peasant's daughter.

"He is a young man. He will settle down when it is time," my father reasoned.

"That is my point, Father. I have never been so wild, so undisciplined. Yet you pass me over without a thought."

"You also have not your brother's skills, Yulya."

"His skills," she scoffed. "What good are they if he is not a proper leader?"

But Father had clearly reached the end of his indulgence. "Sasha is my heir, Yulya," he said flatly. "There is more to this position than you can imagine. I am head of this family, and I decide who will replace me when I am gone. You have thus far been a good and obedient daughter. I would not like to see you otherwise."

I flinched at the steel in his voice even though it was not directed at me. My heart sank at the pain I knew his words caused my sister. Yulya and I had had a friendly sibling rivalry for some years, since the first time I'd beaten her while sparring. But she was my older sister; I loved her, and she loved me. She had practically raised both Masha and me since our mother had died. But the more our father didn't recognize all she did, the colder she became toward me.

"Yes, Father," she said softly, her tone brittle.

Her quiet footsteps announced her approach, and I stood waiting to comfort her. She silently shut the door of our father's study and turned around.

Her eyes swam with tears. They trailed down her face as she blinked. My chest tightened, and I reached out to embrace her.

"Yulya—"

"Do not touch me," she growled, her eyes icy daggers.

I let my arms fall to my sides helplessly.

"I hate you," she said quietly, and every syllable stabbed me right in the heart.

Yulya slammed the telephone down, the sound bringing me back to the present moment. My heart still ached at her pain, at the antipathy she felt toward me. My very existence was a threat to her every happiness.

My stomach growled though I felt too nauseated to eat anymore. Casting my eyes to the floor, I continued my way to the kitchen, thinking a cup of tea might be just enough.

26

The cooks were surprised and flustered when I showed up in the kitchen unannounced. I managed to calm them with assurances that a sandwich and a cup of tea were more than enough to satisfy me. I ate quickly, realizing too late that my presence at the kitchen table distracted them.

After I'd downed the last of my tea, I thanked them for the meal and was about to leave when one of the kitchen boys hauled a basket of apples into the room.

I eyed the fruit. "Could I have a few of those?" I asked.

"Oh, I am sorry, sir," he said with a bow. "These are bad apples. I just sorted them from the good apples in the cellar. I can go fetch you a good apple if you would like."

"Even better. What are you planning to do with them?"

"I was just taking them to the compost."

"May I have them? I can take them to the compost when I am finished."

The boy hesitated, looking around for help from the cooks. They must have given their encouragement because he handed me the basket with a nod.

I thanked him with a smile and headed out the kitchen door. After passing through the gardens, I followed the dirt path into the trees until I reached the armory.

I placed the basket of apples outside and opened the heavy door. Various weapons lined the walls of the armory, everything from firearms to long bows, sovnyas to shashkas. I passed the cabinet of ammunition—sterling silver, exploding bullets, casings soaked in holy water and etched with prayers—and pulled a shashka down from the wall. I frowned at how familiar it still felt in my hands even after all these years.

Leaving the armory, I placed the sheathed sabre atop the basket and carried the lot to the training field.

Of all the grandeur afforded to the Volonov house, gardens, and grounds, nothing compared to the training field. It wasn't even fair to call it a field at all; it was more a facility. There were shooting ranges, obstacle courses, a room that let no light in to train assassins in complete darkness.

I didn't need anything so over-the-top at the moment, so I made my way to the simple outdoor sparring ring. The ring was fenced by a corral with wooden posts.

Setting down the basket, I took one apple and put it atop one of the posts. Then I turned and faced it. Unsheathing the sword, I threw the scabbard aside. I tested the weight of it, the feel of it, in my hand. I twirled it once with my fingers, and it spun effortlessly at my command. I did it again, once backward and then forward. I slashed it on my left side and then swung it back to the right, slicing the apple neatly in half. The bottom half still sat on the post as the top half skittered into the grass.

Another apple, another strike, another enemy down. The motions were natural, so long ingrained into my body. I didn't even have to think about what I was doing. Any remnant anger leftover from my argument with Liza, from the life-threatening situation I was in, was released in the soft whistle of steel slicing through air.

I was just building up a sweat when the sound of clapping called my attention to a visitor. I turned toward the noise and faced a smirking Dima.

"Very good, Sasha. Those apples are no match for you."

"You can laugh all you like, Dima, but you have never won against me."

Dima squinted a glare at me. "I am not the boy I once was. While you have been out on your little adventures, I have been training every day. I have killed countless monsters since I saw you last."

I shrugged, dismissing his claims.

"Why do we not put it to the test, eh Sasha? Let us see who is the better man now."

"Winning a fight does not make one the better man, Dima."

"Only a coward would say such a thing."

I glanced at Dima, not truly provoked by his

words. But his smug grin did irritate me, and I wanted nothing more than to wipe it off his face.

"All right," I said with a nod. "But do not complain when I beat you again."

"Pff." Dima blew a disbelieving sound through his lips. "I will fetch a shashka from the armory."

While Dima went to retrieve a weapon, I began removing my shirt.

"You did not tell me where you were going. *Again*," I heard Liza's voice complain as I finished pulling my shirt over my head.

I glanced in the direction of her voice; she stood inside the sparring ring an arshin from where I had been slicing apples, the evidence of my efforts littering the ground by her feet. I met her irritated gaze and walked toward her.

"You should have kept a closer watch on me, Kisa." I moved nearer, reaching behind her to hang my shirt on the fence.

Her cheeks flushed at the proximity of my body to hers, or perhaps it was my criticism that she had somehow failed in her task. But her eyes widened ever so slightly, and her ample breasts heaved with heavy breaths, drawing my attention to the round cleavage that peeked out from the neckline of her shirt.

I wet my lips and smirked down at her as her gaze took in my bare chest, settling right around my collar bone. "I see you are not having a problem watching me closely now," I said low and intimate.

Instead of responding with a flash of fury and a snarky comment as I expected her to, she raised her eyes to mine. Her lips were slightly parted, her grey eyes were clear as smoky quartz, and her freckles dusted her pinked cheeks in such a way that I felt compelled to reach out and brush my thumb over them. But before I could decide whether to act or stifle that impulse, the look was gone. Once again, Liza squinted her displeasure at me, frowning and glaring as she stepped out from the space I'd created with my body and outstretched arm.

"Knock him down a peg or two," she told Dima as he re-entered the sparring ring.

Dima smiled at her encouragement, eager to finally prove himself against me. "With pleasure," he said, removing the scabbard and throwing it aside.

27

I smirked at Dima as I took a lazy stance in the middle of the sparring ring, my shashka pointed in his general direction. He glared, much more serious as he crouched, ready to strike.

And I let him, analyzing his progress, his change in technique.

He lashed out, bringing his blade down from above in a powerful slash. I brushed it aside with my sabre and stepped to one side. Next, he swung upward, and I smacked his sword down with mine.

As he continued to retreat and advance, his attacks became more sophisticated, less easy to predict. I found that I had to pay close attention to avoid the cut of his blade.

"Very good, Dima," I praised. "You have greatly improved since we last met."

"Do not play with me, Sasha. Fight me," Dima growled.

I grinned, adrenaline singing in my veins. "All right."

And so, the real bout began. I had to admit, Dima truly had improved. He avoided my strikes, deflected my attacks—not effortlessly but with grace. My limbs were strong from the work I'd been doing for the last ten years, but they were out of practice. I was building up a sweat, and I recognized the deep burning in my muscles that said I would be sore later.

But despite what Dima had gained in experience, he still could not overcome what I had in talent and muscle memory.

With a grunt, Dima thrust his shashka at my middle, I knocked his blade aside, spun along his outstretched arm and brought my sword to the edge of his neck.

He froze, not even daring to breathe.

"You lose again, Dima," I said with an easy tone.

His eyes burned with fury as he glared at me, his mouth twisted in a scowl.

After a tense moment, I disengaged and released him. He let forth a string of obscenities as he stormed from the ring. He snatched up his scabbard and stomped past Liza, who sat atop the fence. He didn't head toward the armory to return the shashka but instead went into the surrounding trees.

I turned toward Liza, smirking smugly at my victory. Her expression remained unmoved.

"What was that you said about knocking me down a peg, Kisa?" I prodded.

She just stared blandly back at me. "You are out of practice, Aleksandr Sergeyevich. You were sloppy and undisciplined. It is clear you have not trained since you left home."

Irritation rose within me, but this time I recognized it before anger got the better of me. I let the cool autumn breeze blow it away as it chilled the sweat on my bare skin. "Would you mind handing me my shirt, Kisa? Unless you prefer me half naked like this."

She scowled and threw the shirt into my face. I chuckled. *Yes, I like this arrangement much better.*

After redressing, I retrieved the scabbard and returned the weapon to its place in the armory.

We went back to the house in silence. Upon reaching my room, I told Liza I wanted to bathe before supper. I offered for her to join me, but she did not accept.

As I soaked in the warm bathtub, I thought of the last time Dima and I had sparred. So much had changed since then.

"Oof," Dima grunted as he fell on his back, my shashka at his throat. After a moment, he smiled. "I should have known I had no hope of winning."

I reached out my hand and helped him up.

"You really are a wonder, Sasha," he said, shaking his head with a chuckle. "I have never seen your equal."

I grinned at the older man, three years my senior at twenty. "Perhaps you should spend more time training and less time with my sister," I teased.

"I would rather let you win every time if those are my choices."

I laughed.

"And look at that," he added. "Here she comes, right on cue."

I turned toward where he indicated and saw Yulya's smile brighten when she noticed him.

"Dima," she said delightedly surprised. "What are you doing here?"

"Is that the greeting you give me, Yulen'ka?" he asked.

Her smile grew as she reached him. She wrapped her arms around his neck. "Of course not," she said. "I just came down to tell Sasha Father wants him up at the house. I did not expect you."

Dima leaned down to kiss her, and she met his lips with a love and devotion I felt from sazhens away.

I smiled at the pair. I had never seen two people so in love, and it brought me warmth to see my sister so happy. I knew they were secretly engaged, that they were only waiting for Dima to be accepted into the Ubyzniki before they asked permission to marry.

"Would you like some tea, Dimochka?" she asked. "I was just about to have some, and I would like to spend a little time with you."

"You know that I will always be by your side when you want me, my love," Dima said.

Yulya beamed at the promise. "Come, Sasha. You better get back before Father grows impatient."

"All right. I will just put our swords away first."

After I'd completed my task, I followed behind Yulya and Dima, giving them space as they walked hand-in-hand toward the house. Their love was beautiful, and it gave me hope that one day Tanya and I could be so happy. One day, we would be beyond these teenage restrictions and we could marry and start a family.

I stared unfixedly at my wet skin as it glistened in the low bathroom light. My heart was heavy at Yulya's loss, at Dima's continued devotion.

"So many rules, so many restrictions we put on ourselves," I muttered. "So much love and happiness lost for power, for appearances, alliances and greed."

I sighed, my breath sending the steam from the water swirling in an elegant dance.

"This is no way to live."

The next morning, I awoke early and returned to the training field. Though I wasn't planning on taking part in any hunts, I'd found that the motions of training had quieted my mind the day prior. For that short time, I wasn't thinking about my impending doom and what I was going to do about it.

Besides, my fight with Dima had shown me that I was sorely out of practice. And I didn't know if I would need those skills again to survive my visit. I had a strong suspicion I would.

I practiced the movements I'd done countless times in my life, following the rhythms that were still so familiar, the techniques that had saved Ubyzniki lives for generations, the techniques that had condemned so many to death.

After I'd finished, I returned to the house, showered, and dressed. When I left my room again, Liza was waiting for me in the hall, none the wiser that I had already been up and about that morning.

I smiled at my accomplishment. "Good morning, Kisa. Did you sleep well?"

She eyed me suspiciously but didn't say anything.

"I slept well. Thank you for asking," I continued.

Breakfast was not as uncomfortable as it could have been since Yulya was keeping watch at Father's coffin-side.

"Are you busy today, brother?" Masha asked, looking up from her coffee. "I would like to have that talk you mentioned. We seem to keep passing each other."

I glanced over at my younger sister, such a young lady now, one whom I still barely knew.

"I have something to do this morning, but how about this afternoon?"

"All right. We can have tea together. Just you and me." Her tone was warm and inviting, and I looked forward to finally chatting with her.

I nodded. "Sounds good."

This time as Liza and I left the manor, I had a chance to grab a coat.

"Will you tell me where we are going?" Liza asked as we began making our way toward the front gate.

I glanced over at her with a smirk. "That is right. You do not like surprises."

"Certainly not from you, Aleksandr Sergeyevich."

Yet again, I'd managed to provoke her into overriding her default caution. I smiled wider. "You know, Kisa. I think you have not given me a fair chance. Perhaps if you did, you would find that you actually like me."

"Why would I need to like you? Do you have a complex? Can you not handle when people do not worship you?"

I shrugged. "I just think you are set against liking me is all."

"Then why do you keep trying?"

I frowned. But before I could even think of a response, we had reached the front gate.

We slipped through and were already several sazhens away when Petya called out to us.

"Sasha, Liza, good morning," he greeted with a smile.

We returned his sentiment.

"Are you free today, Liza? They are opening the gardens to the population today. I promised Mila I would take her and thought you might like to join us."

I had to admire my friend's perseverance. He didn't seem dissuaded by all the times Liza had turned him down, though I could see how one might find his diligence tiresome, even irritating. Liza glanced at me, and my stomach quivered; I coughed to relieve the sensation.

She shifted her weight from one foot to the other, and I could see her hesitation as she wet her lips. "I..." She frowned.

"I will be with Masha this afternoon," I offered softly when she glanced at me again.

"All right, Pyotr," she stated more firmly than seemed necessary. "The gardens are only open to noble families during the summer, and it will be nice to see them before it gets too cold."

Petya smiled broadly, a victory at last. "Wonderful. Come by this afternoon when you are ready."

Liza nodded. "I will."

We bid Petya goodbye and walked through the park. I glanced sidelong at Liza. Her expression was smooth, but her right hand rubbed at her left wrist.

"You have decided to take a chance at love after all?" I asked.

She scowled at me. "Do not be so dramatic. A walk in a garden means nothing."

Perhaps it means nothing to you. But to Petya, it certainly means something. But I didn't say anything. It was clear she was nervous about her decision, and I didn't want to make it worse.

Once we'd crossed the road, we walked along the Fontanka River until we found a water taxi.

"Peter and Paul Fortress," I told the captain once on board.

Liza settled on the bench beside me as the boat headed for the Neva. While we passed under the low Panteleymonovskiy Bridge, Liza's voice echoed when she murmured, "What will you do if you cannot convince the mage? If Bes does not give up the idea of marrying you?"

I did not wonder at her figuring out that I wanted to get the cancellation order from the mage; she had all the information to come to that conclusion. But my heart warmed a little at her calling Nika Bes.

"Let us hope it does not come to that, Kisa."

Liza didn't respond, but I felt her gaze on me. And after we'd disembarked on the Commandant's

Pier, I heard her murmur, "Will you be all right, Aleksandr Sergeyevich?"

My eyes flicked to hers, and my heart gave one hard thump at the heavy moment that passed between us before Liza glanced away.

If she'd wanted me to answer her whispered question, she didn't push me to do so.

As I turned back to the task at hand, my gaze was naturally drawn to the golden spire of Saints Peter and Paul Cathedral above the Neva Gate's peaked stone roof. The copper angel clinging to the cross on top pointed east, indicating the direction of the wind. Through the tunnel, we followed the cobbled path straight to the side portico of the yellow cathedral.

29

O nce inside the cathedral, we passed six marble coffins on our right, marking the locations of the Romanovs entombed in the crypts below. The three coffins in front represented Peter the Great, his wife Catherine I, and their daughter Yelizaveta Petrovna. I paused before the elaborately crafted, golden holy doors of the iconostasis.

Flanking the doors were the archangels Gabriel and Michael. Gabriel held a branch of paradise aloft, his shining lantern in his other hand, while Michael battled the serpent with his flaming sword.

As I stood there, I found my gaze pulled toward Gabriel and his lantern. I blinked at the carved golden flame as it seemed to flicker. The experience was not foreign to me. The last time I'd been in the church, Michael's flaming sword had similarly entranced me. But it was no wonder for a boy of twelve, a boy training to be an assassin, to fixate on such a magnificent weapon.

I'd stood between my father and Yulya during

the funeral of Emperor Nikolai III. Masha, only a year old, had been left at home with a fever.

Because Masha was ill, Yulya and I did not accompany Father to Moscow for the later coronation of Empress Alexandra I. But I got to see her at her father's funeral. I'd been struck by how serious and wise she'd looked, and I couldn't believe when my father told me she was a year younger than Yulya. I'd wondered if a girl of sixteen could really lead such a great and vast empire.

Standing yet again in this hushed place, I wondered why it was Gabriel's lantern that held my attention this time.

"May I help you?" a deep, gentle voice asked.

I glanced over at the priest who exited the door opposite the one we'd entered.

"Yes, Father. We are here to see Vladimir L'vovich Raskoliev."

The priest frowned, and the expression seemed to make his beard longer. "You are one of them?" he asked.

"I am Aleksandr Sergeyevich Volonov," I told him, hoping my name would be enough.

The priest nodded seriously. "Follow me," he instructed.

We did as he bid us, walking under the ivory chandelier said to be carved by Peter the Great himself. Near the front entrance, we turned right, passing the coffin grave markers of Mikhail Pavlovich and his wife Elena, three of their daughters Maria, Anna, and Alexandra by their side. I couldn't ignore the two smaller coffins of Anna and Alexandra Mikhailovna, so young when they'd died.

Through the door across from Mikhail and his family, Liza and I followed the priest into a study. The desk and chair were entirely ordinary. In fact, the only oddities of the study were the staircases on the left. One set led up, presumably to the belfry. We took the set leading down.

By the time we'd reached the lower-floor landing, the light from above was already gone. If it weren't for the lanterns, hanging on hooks every few feet, I wouldn't have been able to see the tunnel stretched out before us.

Our shoes made soft scuffling sounds on the bricks of the tunnel as we passed crypts on each side.

What would Vladimir be doing down here?

For a church that housed the royal ancestors, the keepers didn't seem to care about cleaning the actual tombs. While the coffins upstairs were smooth and polished, the place where they physically rested was dusty and covered in cobwebs.

At the very end of the tunnel, we turned right, entering a smaller room with plain stone coffins on either side. To our right was Peter the Great with his wife and daughter, and to our left was Catherine the Great, Pyotr III, and Anna Ioannovna.

Pausing before Catherine the Great's coffin, our guide took down the lantern that was hanging on a hook above it.

"Hold this, please," he requested, handing me the lantern.

Then, with two hands, he grabbed the large hook and tugged with great force.

A loud clicking filled the room as the wall on the far end slowly slid to one side. The priest took the lantern from me and nodded in the direction of the revealed hallway.

I glanced at Liza before going on ahead.

After we'd both entered the dark, narrow tunnel, the clicking returned and the wall shut behind us. A soft glimmer of light flickered ahead. Looking back over my shoulder, I whispered, "I guess we can only go forward."

Liza didn't respond, but I could feel the tension in her like a tightened spring.

At the end of the hall, I reached out and pushed at a partially opened door of thick oak.

The large, stone room that lay before us overwhelmed my senses in its sheer disarray. It was the lair of a half-mad alchemist. Its shelves were laden with old tomes, bottles, and jars, some of which I would swear wiggled with whatever living things they housed. There were bones and preserved creatures that I couldn't even identify.

As I squinted at what looked like a deformed, hairless dog with strange spikes along its spine, Liza nudged me with her elbow.

I glanced over at her before following the tilt of her head. Vladimir L'vovich stood before us, a pointed, fur hat in his hands. He wore a long, black coat—buttoned to the neck—and thick leather gloves.

"Where did you come from?" I asked, certain he hadn't been there before. I eyed the hat again; it had a bright red stone on it. "Is that—?"

"Chernomor's hat, yes."

I blinked, taken aback. "How could you possibly have found a thing like that?"

Vladimir raised an eyebrow. "Why are you here, Aleksandr Sergeyevich?"

I guess we are just going to ignore that he has a magical dwarf's invisibility hat. "I want to talk to you about the glaz smerti you cast on me."

Vladimir calmly, indifferently, placed Chernomor's hat into a box on the shelf beside him. "What about it?"

I frowned. "Do not toy with me, mage. This is my life we are talking about. I want you to tell me the cancellation order, the words I need to say to break the curse. We have known each other for a long time, Vladimir. I know you are a man of God. Surely, you do not want to have a hand in killing me."

My face flushed with fury as Vladimir stared blandly back at me.

"I do not know it. Only your father and Maksim do."

I scoffed. "I do not believe that for a moment. You have always been the slippery sort."

He sniffed as if I'd offended him. "Hypothetically speaking, if I did have it and if I gave it to you, what would you do then?"

I took an angry step toward him, but he didn't react. "I would break the curse and leave, of course."

"You would leave again? You would not take over your family title? You would not lead the Ubyzniki?"

"Yes," I confirmed.

Vladimir frowned and shrugged. "As I have said, I do not know it."

I growled, a low sound that echoed off the stone walls of the room. Closing the distance between us, I grabbed Vladimir by the coat and drew his face close to mine. "I know you have it. And you *will* give it to me."

His dark eyes widened, but his mouth was firmly set. "I have performed my duties as a servant of the Church and Russia's glorious empire. I am prepared to be martyred."

"Oh, I will not kill you, Vladimir," I said, soft and threatening. "If I killed you, I would not get what I wanted. But I will make it hurt. I have been well trained to do that."

I was vaguely aware that Liza was by my side, calling my name. "Aleksandr Sergeyevich," she admonished.

But I didn't acknowledge her; I kept my attention on the mage, glaring into his eyes, willing him to obey me.

"Aleksandr," she said again, her tone a clear warning.

Again, I ignored her, watching as beads of sweat began to form in Vladimir's mustache.

Liza's voice was soft but firm when she rested the sharp tip of her stiletto against my neck. "Sasha, let him go."

The tension in my arms eased, her use of familiar terms much more effective than the edge of her threat. My heart sank as I became fully aware of what I'd done, what I'd been about to do. I released Vladimir, whose chest heaved as he found his footing.

I squeezed my eyes shut for a moment, shame knotting my stomach. "Let us go," I said.

30

I didn't speak to Liza as we exited the crypts, as we left the cathedral, as we walked to the pier and boarded a boat. And she didn't speak to me though I could feel her watching me.

But I couldn't face her scrutiny, her judgment. I was too ashamed of myself.

I was barely aware of our trip up the Neva. I didn't even realize we'd turned into the Fontanka until Liza called for the driver to turn down the Moyka. He followed her directions and stopped at a ladder leading up the embankment wall.

Finally, I glanced over at her. She met my eyes, and the corner of her mouth twitched ever so slightly into a tiny smile. I didn't ask questions as she tilted her head, telling me to climb the ladder.

I did so, then followed her lead and crossed the street. We walked beside the short, grey metal fence of the Summer Gardens, the small gates now open to the public. People crowded the streets and walkways of the park.

Farther down the road, Liza approached an old woman with a kerchief tied under her chin.

"Hello, Katerina, how are you today?" Liza asked with a smile.

Katerina's eyes brightened. "I had wondered what happened to you, Liza. I have not seen you in so many days."

Liza dipped her head in apology. "I know. I am sorry. I have been very busy lately."

Katerina glanced at me over Liza's shoulder. "I can see why," she joked with a grin. "You have brought a friend today."

Liza didn't correct Katerina's assumption. "Do you have any nuts for me today?"

Katerina pursed her wrinkled lips at not being introduced to me. "Of course I do. I always save the best for you, Liza." Then the elder produced a brown envelope from her coat pocket and handed it to Liza.

Liza passed her some coins in return. "Thank you."

Katerina smiled again. "Do not stay away so long next time," she warned.

"I will see you soon," Liza promised.

Their exchange completed, Liza continued farther down the sidewalk, stopping at a group of trees. Opening her paper envelope, she pulled out a fat walnut and crouched down, sticking her arm between the bars of the fence.

"You know the gates are open," I pointed out. "We could go inside."

She shushed me, and I crouched beside her to see what she was doing. She clicked her tongue rapidly. After a few moments, a brown squirrel with long, tufted ears and a bushy tail appeared. After a second's hesitation, it darted forward and took the walnut from Liza's hand.

She smiled broadly and reached into her envelope for another walnut. Again, the squirrel took it from her.

She looked to me over her shoulder, her eyes still sparkling with joy. "Would you like to try?"

I nodded and took a walnut from the envelope she offered. Sticking my arm through the fence, I offered my hand to the creature. I held my breath as it twitched toward me. After one tense moment, I felt its tiny paws on the tips of my fingers as it snatched the walnut from my hand. I couldn't help but smile at the sensation.

Before long, another squirrel appeared, and we were soon out of walnuts.

Without agreeing to do so, Liza and I started to walk, following the stream of people into the Summer Gardens. As we strolled around Karpiyev Pond, Liza glanced over at me.

"People have been living with arranged marriages for thousands of years. Would it be so very bad to marry her?" she asked softly.

The contentment feeding the squirrels had brought me faded a bit. "How well do you know her?" I responded.

"Not well. I have never hunted with her, and we certainly have not had occasion to interact socially."

An image flashed in my mind of one spring evening in the Ivashkin dungeons. Nika smiled gleefully as she stood over a captured rusalka. The creature's long green hair was matted with blood, her pupil-less eyes were wet with tears, and her screams...her screams, high-pitched and echoing like a too close thunderclap.

I shuddered at the memory. "Yes, Kisa. Yes, it will be very bad to marry her." I slowed on the path, stopping near a rosebush with a single rose left. I reached out and caressed the soft petals of the red rose, running my fingertips along its white stripes. "I want to thank you, Kisa," I murmured, keeping my eyes on the last rose. "Thank you for stopping me. I have never tortured anything before, and I do not want to become someone who does."

"I know," she said.

And I believed her. Something in her voice said that she did know, that she truly saw me.

After a long moment, she asked softly, "How long are the terms of the glaz smerti?"

"I have 337 days left."

She was quiet for a while. "The mage knows the cancellation words. But he is not ready to give them up. Still, we have other avenues to explore before we resort to forcing it out of him."

"We?" I asked, raising my eyebrows as I turned toward her. "It is my understanding that you were wishing to kill me this entire time, Kisa. Now you want to help me overcome the eye of death?"

She frowned at me. "No one should die in such a way, not even Aleksandr Sergeyevich."

I snorted. "Such sweet words, Kisa. You know how to set a man's heart to pounding. I find myself charmed to my very depths."

Liza rolled her eyes and scoffed a laugh. "Who would try to charm you?"

I smiled. "A great many, I assure you."

"Well, there is no accounting for taste," she shot back as she started to walk farther into the gardens.

I grinned and jogged to catch up to her.

31

By the time we had reached the other end of the Summer Gardens—wandering the paths with no set course—it was well into the afternoon.

"Are you hungry?" I asked Liza as we exited the garden gates.

She thought about it for a moment, then nodded.

I motioned toward a little green hut down the street. As we neared the kiosk, the scent of fried dough and spices made my mouth water.

The woman behind the glass greeted us and waited expectantly for our order.

"One ground meat pirozhk, and..." I turned to Liza.

"Apple," she supplied.

"And one apple pirozhk, please," I finished.

I paid her for the stuffed buns, and she wrapped them in paper before handing them through the hole in the window. Taking our treats, we looked for a place to sit and eat. There were no free benches in sight.

I crossed the street, and Liza followed. Then I sat on the embankment wall, my feet dangling over the water of the Neva. Liza joined me, her shoulder only a pyad' from mine.

I watched the water drift by as the sun, struggling through the clouds, sparkled off it. The gilded crosses atop the blue domes of Peter's Trinity Cathedral twinkled as they caught the light on the other side of the Neva. I gazed at Troitskiy Bridge as carriages and bicycles crossed the river. So much activity in the heart of the city, so many people going about their lives beside one another—perhaps never to truly meet.

"Are you not going to eat?" Liza asked when I had yet to take a bite of my pirozhk.

I brought the golden-brown bun to my mouth and bit into it. The pleasant chewy texture gave way to discomfort. "Oof, hot!" I complained, sucking in air to try to cool the food in my mouth.

Liza turned to me anxiously. "Are you all right? Did you get burned?"

I waved my hand at her, managing to swallow the offending morsel. "I am fine."

Her features relaxed, and she turned back toward the river.

I blew carefully on the bun before taking another bite. This time the chewy texture mixed perfectly with the warm, savory meat. I sighed contentedly.

"I really have missed this place," I murmured to myself after quite a while.

Almost a minute later Liza asked, "Then why have you not returned before now?"

Does she truly not know why I left to begin with? Does she not know of the penalties for what I did?

"How could I have reached my current level of licentiousness if I had returned, Kisa? The world is a big place. There is much to explore."

She clicked her tongue and sighed. "Can you never be serious, Aleksandr Sergeyevich?"

"Life is too short for that. I would rather have fun and laugh. You should try it sometime."

"Do you not have someplace you need to be? Surely, irritating me cannot be the only thing you have to do today."

I grinned, letting my gaze drift toward the sun, which had dipped lower in the time we'd been sitting there. It seemed to dye everything gold.

"Wait," I said, a thought disturbing my tranquility. "What time is it?" I pulled out my pocket watch and groaned. "I was supposed to meet Masha for tea."

Liza gasped, her eyes wide. "And I was supposed to go with Pyotr."

I sighed and rose to my feet. "Well, it is too late now, but we had better go and try to apologize at least."

It took us only fifteen minutes to walk back to Volonov Manor. I left Liza at the gatehouse to make her excuses to Petya as I went to talk to Masha.

I found my younger sister in the parlour, her legs tucked under her as she stroked L'vitsa by the hearth.

Her golden hair was loosely tied with a pink ribbon as it tumbled over one shoulder, and her eyes wistfully watched the flames.

My chest tightened at the sadness in her face; she was much too young to have known such sorrow.

"Masha," I called out to her softly.

She glanced over at me and smiled, the expression not reaching her eyes.

"I am sorry about tea. I got caught up," I said, without extrapolating on my excuse. "Can I make it up to you? Would you like me to buy you some pryaniki? You always forgave me when I gave you them when we were children."

Masha smiled at the memory, and this time it was sincere. "I should get you to buy me all the sweets since you stood me up," she said in a teasing tone.

"I will if you forgive me."

She sighed, shaking her head. "Of course I forgive you, my unreliable brother."

I grinned. "Since I missed tea, would you like to go for a walk?" I asked.

"It is almost dark," she pointed out.

"Are you afraid of the dark, Mashen'ka? Surely, you have been taught to protect yourself from anything that may lurk in the darkness."

She frowned. "I have, but..." Trailing off, Masha gnawed on her lower lip.

"Do you already have plans this evening?" I guessed, certain that it was not fear that kept her from going with me.

"I—Yes, I am to meet...some friends soon."

I raised an eyebrow as she delivered her excuse in starts and stops. "Oh really? What are your plans then?"

"We are going to a concert," she said without hesitation.

I shrugged. "All right. That is what I get for not meeting you at the appointed time. I suppose I will just stay in...all by my lonesome and reflect on the nature of existence and the inevitability of death."

Masha giggled.

Though I'd said it dramatically, it likely wasn't far from the truth. But given Masha's response, she didn't seem to know about my impending doom. She rose from her chair and handed L'vitsa into my arms.

"Here," she said. "Take this consolation cat. She is very good at comforting people."

I scratched behind the cat's ear. "Is that true, L'vitsa? What a good cat you are. How about I take you to the kitchen, and we have a nice bowl of milk?"

"No," Masha admonished, shaking her head. "L'vitsa is too old for milk. It will upset her tummy."

"Okay, then I will have a glass of milk, and you can have some fish." I glanced over at Masha to make sure that was all right.

She nodded. "But watch her carefully. She will try to drink your milk if you leave it unattended."

I acknowledged Masha's orders and left the parlour with the cat.

32

The next morning, I awoke early again and trained. When I returned to the house, I was sweaty and hungry.

I promised myself a nice hunk of soft cheese and an apple as soon as I showered. But when I entered the dining room for breakfast, no one was there. I tilted my head and went through the back hall to the kitchen. It too was deserted.

With a shrug, I went to the cellars and retrieved my reward. Deciding to take a walk in the park with my meal, I paused at the gathering of people in the foyer, blocking my way out.

My family stood as if waiting, Liza looking down at her feet to one side. They all turned to me when I entered, their eyes wide.

"What are you doing?" Yulya demanded, shock raising her voice in pitch.

I looked down at the cheese and apple in my hands, the focus of her intense glare. "Uh, eating," I said as if it should be obvious.

"You cannot eat before taking communion," Yulya scolded.

I shrugged. "No, *you* cannot eat before taking communion. *I* am not going."

Just as Yulya took a deep breath to respond, a knock sounded on the door. Adrik opened it since he was the closest. Then he bowed his greeting as Maksim, Nika, and Kostya entered.

Nika's black eyes immediately zeroed in on me, and she smiled that predatory smile of hers. It took her only a few slithering steps to reach me.

"I see you are being naughty this morning, Sashen'ka, eating before Divine Liturgy," she cooed with a simper as she looked up at me. "But I will forgive you if you ride in the carriage next to me."

I gazed coldly down at her. "I cannot indulge you today, Veronika, as I am not attending service this morning."

She pouted. "Why not?"

"Because it is inappropriate."

"It is inappropriate for you to attend service with me?" she asked with a tilt of her head that was no doubt meant to be flirtatious.

"No, it is inappropriate for me to attend service because I do not believe in God," I stated.

Masha gasped from behind Nika, but everyone else stood in silence, their expressions ranging from shock to fury.

"Surely, that cannot be true, Sashen'ka," Nika reasoned, ignoring her father's angry muttering. "Perhaps you have just been away too long."

"I told you I am not the boy you knew," I reminded severely. "And if we are to be married, then you better get used to the idea of me being an atheist. There is nothing you can say that will convince me."

We stared at each other silently for a moment, me standing my ground and her not knowing how to react.

"Nika," Maksim called. "We must go now, or we will be late."

Nika frowned but left me.

"Stay here, Liza," Yulya ordered as she followed the Ivashkins out.

A few moments later, Liza and I stood in the foyer alone. She didn't approach me, but I heard her soft question just the same. "Do you really not believe in God, Aleksandr? Or did you say that to put her off? That is a risky play to make."

I glanced over at her, leaning against the wall with her arms crossed, her hair covered with a kerchief.

"My relationship with God, or lack thereof, is nobody's business. But no, I do not believe. Or rather, I refuse to worship such a cruel entity should he exist."

She gazed at me for a quiet minute, her expression neither condemning nor praising. Finally, she nodded slowly, accepting my declaration as my own truth.

"I am sorry you are missing Divine Liturgy though," I said. "Just because I do not believe, does not mean I want to take faith from others."

"I do not usually go with the family anyway. I was only permitted today because I am to keep my eyes on you at all times."

"Where do you usually go?" I asked.

"Sometimes I go with the rest of the servants, and sometimes I just take a quiet walk and connect with God in my own way."

"You ought to be careful, Kisa," I warned with a grin. "That is almost blasphemous."

Her mouth twitched only momentarily into a slight smile, then it was gone.

"If you want to go to service with the servants, or if you want to self-reflect and pray, I will not tell anyone you left me alone."

Her eyes returned to mine. "And what will you do during that time?"

I smirked. "If you want to know, you will have to join me. You are more than welcome, Kisa."

"You attempt to corrupt me with your heathen ways."

I waved my hand at her accusation. "The righteous cannot be corrupted. You are only corrupted if you want to be."

She pursed her lips.

"What will you choose?" I said in a teasing tone. "You have quite the dilemma before you. You can disobey Yulya's orders and go to Divine Liturgy, or you can skip service to follow in whatever debauchery I have planned."

She squinted at me. "Saving this city from your debauchery seems a more sacred duty than attending service."

"Then follow me," I said with a grin.

I could see the tension on Liza's face as she walked upstairs beside me. "Where are we going?" she asked suspiciously.

"You are overeager, Kisa. But anticipation is half the fun."

She scowled over at me.

When I led her into the secondary library, her brows furrowed.

I took a seat in a cushioned chair and glanced up at her. "I am sure you have not been permitted in this room, and there were many books you did not have access to while my father was alive. Go ahead, Kisa. Take your pick."

"Actually—" she cut herself off, and I raised an eyebrow at her. "Is this your idea of debauchery?"

"You are always so ready to believe I will do something inappropriate," I pointed out.

"Because your tone and words always suggest you will," she argued.

I smirked at her. "Maybe it is just your mind that goes to inappropriate places, Kisa."

She frowned but didn't respond, closing the discussion by approaching one of the glass-doored bookshelves.

I smiled at my small victory and pulled the puzzle box from my pocket.

33

A few hours later, the door to the secondary library opened.

"Found you," Nika said as if she'd finally caught the prey she'd been hunting for days.

I looked up from the puzzle box I was still working on. "What are you doing here, Veronika?"

"Masha was kind enough to invite us to lunch after service," she explained. "I have been searching for you for a while. I did not think to find you being so diligent in a library." Her tone was one of praise.

"It was a special treat for Elizaveta since she could not go to Divine Liturgy."

Nika glanced up at the gallery where Liza read just above me. "How considerate of you, Sashen'ka," she said sweetly, slowly making her way to where I sat. "I have to admit, I was a bit surprised to hear your declaration this morning. I was worried about what Papa would say. But I thought about it all through Divine Liturgy. And on the way here, I calmed Papa down." She smiled. "This should not hinder our wedding plans though I do hope you will consent to being married in the Church since I am still faithful. Papa assured me you would."

A flash of rage climbed up my throat, but I swallowed it down. *Does she know about the glaz smerti?*

Upon reaching me, she smiled down at me and unceremoniously sat in my lap. My skin crawled as she stroked the side of my neck. "I came to see you a few days ago," she said, wrapping her arms around my neck. "I was very disappointed that you were not here. But I know how you can make it up to me."

As she leaned closer to kiss me, I turned my head, ignoring my stomach as it rolled. "I do not think this is appropriate behavior, Veronika," I said sternly. I tried to push her away gently, but she tightened her grip.

"Come now, Sashen'ka. You cannot have changed so much. I recall you being very free with your kisses once upon a time. You gave them away to everyone who asked. Surely, your nevesta is worthy of such an expression of affection."

I frowned severely and gave her a cold look. "Not everyone, Veronika." I attempted to release myself again, but she slid her fingers into my hair and tugged. The action didn't hurt, but the warning was clear.

"I do not want to tell Papa that you are being cruel to me, Sashen'ka. I cannot imagine what he would do to you. And I do so want our marriage to start off on the right foot."

I met her black eyes as she threatened me. *She does know.*

Just then, a loud thump sounded on the floor beside my chair. Nika flinched and looked up.

"Watch what you are doing, dura. That almost hit us."

I used Nika's momentary distraction to push her off my lap and stand. She stumbled to catch her footing. She glared at Liza and me in turn, and her black eyes promised retribution. But before she could unload her contempt, Masha and Kostya entered the room.

"There you are," Masha said with a smile. "We have been looking everywhere for you. We had better get to lunch before Yulya grows impatient."

Nika gave Liza one last stab with her eyes, then turned to follow Masha and her brother out.

As she left, my tension eased a bit. I bent down and picked up the hefty book Liza had dropped. "Tolstoy's *War and Peace*," I read the spine. "Good choice, Kisa. Though you ought to be careful. This is a first edition."

Liza's smirk was gone in a flash as she walked down the stairs to where I was. "I do not know what you mean, Aleksandr."

Satisfaction warmed my chest.

"You had better go on ahead," she said, taking the volume from me. "Bes is waiting for you."

I smiled at the mischievous twinkle in her eyes, not at all hidden by the straightness of her face.

"Would you like me to save you a seat, Kisa?" I asked.

She pursed her lips in an attempt to stifle a laugh. "I doubt I will be welcome at the family's table just now. I will eat in the kitchen."

"Abandoning me to the vultures already?"

She raised her hand and rested it on my chest, patting me gently as if to reassure me. A tingle ran through me.

"You are a big boy, Aleksandr. I am sure you can handle it."

And then she walked away as if there was nothing to keep her there, as if she hadn't just helped me, as if she hadn't just touched me, as if there had been no exchange whatsoever.

I watched her go back up the stairs to return the book to its place on the shelf. Her hips swayed smoothly, accentuating the firm roundness of her rear. *Every time I think I understand her, she proves me wrong.*

I didn't wait for Liza to come down but went to lunch with my family and the Ivashkins. It was a tense affair despite everyone's impeccable politeness. Even Masha looked anxious, shooting solicitous looks at Kostya, who frowned and avoided her gaze.

After our visitors left, Yulya turned to me as we watched them go from the front steps. "It did not work. Denouncing God may have upset them, but she still wants to marry you."

I didn't look at my sister but watched their carriage get farther into the distance. I smirked. "I know what I am doing, sister. This has unsettled them. Even Nika acknowledged how upset Maksim was. My plan will work."

Yulya harrumphed and left me where I stood.

She was right about one thing though. Avoidance is not going to deter her. I need to see more of Nika in order to make her not want to marry me.

My stomach knotted at the idea of spending more time with her even if it was to get her to dislike me. I sighed and followed after my sister.

34

The following morning, I went to the training field early, this time to practice my archery.

The grass was still wet with morning dew as I strung my long bow. My mind went back to another morning such as this.

The grass sparkled as the sun's rays reached the morning dew. My stomach clenched while I drew back my bow, and my tight chest protested the movement. My arms shook with the effort it took to hold the bow steady, to maintain the string's tension in the same practiced motions I'd long mastered. I let the arrow fly, and it missed its mark, finding purchase at the very edge of the round target.

I could feel Petya's eyes on me, but I didn't look at my friend. I didn't know how much longer I could keep my secret from him. The words were ever on my lips, keen to be spoken into life yet terrified to be heard. I'd managed to avoid him for nearly a week before he'd finally figured out I was training earlier in the day.

"What is the matter, Sasha?" Petya asked when his persistent gaze was not enough to make me answer.

I shrugged, glancing over at him. "What do you mean?"

Petya frowned and pointed at the target we'd both shot arrows into. "I have never beaten you in a shooting match before. Something must be wrong with you."

"I am tired today. I did not eat yesterday," I hedged.

"Are you ill? Surely, your father would allow you one day to rest if you are unwell."

"No, I..."

Petya's brow crinkled, and he tilted his head when I trailed off. "Sasha, we have been friends our entire lives. Whatever it is, you can tell me."

I met my friend's eyes. He had grown taller than me as of late, his boyhood features just starting to sharpen into the hint of what he would look like as a man.

The feelings that had always been a dull hum in the background, a pleasant and subtle uptick in mood, had recently grown into an unbearable ache. It had never occurred to me that these feelings had actions attached, that one day I would feel the need to do something, anything, about them. What had always been enough was no longer so.

My heart ached, and I feared to open my mouth lest a scream escape merely to relieve the pressure.

Still, Petya's gaze demanded an answer. The words bubbled to my lips without my consent. "Your sister..." I murmured, my voice hushed as if I were speaking a prayer.

"Yes, what about Tanya?"

"I...I am in love with her."

Petya blinked, his countenance not betraying his thoughts. My stomach lurched.

"She has always been special to me," I rambled, the act of speaking calming the storm inside me if only a little. "I did not know it was love then. But lately, I have...wanted more. I have wanted things I have never wanted before. I wanted to reach out and touch her hand. A gesture that I would not have hesitated to do only a year ago suddenly made me tremble. And then other thoughts came to my mind. What would it be like to kiss her lips?"

"That is my sister you are speaking of," Petya interrupted, his warning clear.

My mouth went dry. I'd heard that tone in Petya's voice before, but it had never been directed at me.

Petya's eyes were hard, serious, but not unfeeling. He sighed heavily. "The truth is I am not surprised," Petya said. "I have noticed how your glances at her have changed."

My heart squeezed. *Have I been so very obvious?*

"Sasha, she is my little sister," Petya reasoned. "I do not want to see her hurt. Maybe you love her now, but what of the future? What if your feelings are fleeting? Maybe you only feel this way because you are familiar, comfortable, with her. What happens when you meet a lady of your own station?"

I scowled that he could think my true love so base and fickle. "You sound as if she is the only girl I know. Do not doubt my feelings, Petya. I love your sister more than my own self."

Petya stared at me for a long moment. "Promise me you will never cause her pain."

I placed my hand over my heart. "I would sooner run myself through," I swore.

Petya nodded, seemingly satisfied by my declaration.

Then I sighed heavily. "No offense, my friend, but you are not who I was worried about. What of Tanya? How does she feel? What if I tell her, and she rejects me? Unrequited love seems the cruelest fate to me."

Turning from me, Petya notched another arrow. "Well," he said. "I would not worry about that." Then he let the arrow fly toward the target.

At the thought of the promise I'd made, my heart felt heavy as if it would drag me down with it. She had known sorrow, no matter how I'd tried to protect her, to cherish her. Though I knew Petya didn't blame me, it had been her choice after all. I wondered if it would have been better if I'd never told her of my feelings.

I sighed and drew back the first arrow, then let it fly. With a soft whistle and a fwip it found its mark at the center of the target. An entire quiver later, I made my way across the wet grass to retrieve them.

"Why did you say you were not as good at long

range weapons as Pyotr?" Liza asked from behind me.

I looked over my shoulder at her, wondering when she'd arrived.

"Did I say that?"

"You did."

I smirked. "Perhaps I have gotten better over time."

Her expression told me she wasn't buying my lie. "Have you been coming out here to train every morning?"

I didn't answer but continued toward the target and removed the arrows one at a time, replacing them in the quiver.

"You should have woken me," she censured when I returned to the shooting line.

"Why is that, Kisa?" I smirked. "Do you want me to train you?"

"Yes," she answered without hesitation.

My eyes widened.

"You are always saying you are the best, Aleksandr Sergeyevich. Why would I not want to learn from the best?"

I stared at her, trying to discern her angle. "How do I know you will not use this opportunity to try to kill me again?"

She grinned mischievously. "Are you frightened of little me, oh great Aleksandr Sergeyevich Volonov?"

I snorted. "Come here, Kisa."

Her smile slipped, and she squinted at me. "Why?" she asked suspiciously.

"Do you want to learn or do you not?"

She didn't say anything as she approached me. I handed her the long bow and an arrow.

"Let us see what you know already."

She nodded and stepped up to the shooting line. I analyzed her stance, her grip, making mental notes as she moved. Pulling back the string, she let loose her arrow. It didn't even get close to the target.

She glanced back at me. "What am I doing wrong?" she asked.

"Take your stance again," I told her.

She reached for an arrow.

"Without the arrow."

She nodded and obeyed.

"You worked with Petya on the recurve bow last time?"

"Yes."

"Well, that does not explain your stance, but I understand why you are holding it that way. May I?" I asked, coming up behind her.

She glanced over her shoulder and nodded.

I placed my hands gently on her hips. "You are out of alignment. Place your feet shoulder-width apart with your hips straight."

I felt her hips move under my hands as she modified her stance. I raised my left hand to her wrist, which held the bow. "Unlike a recurve bow, you have to hold a long bow at an angle," I instructed, adjusting her wrist accordingly.

A cool breeze wafted the scent of her hair toward me. She smelled of rose and sandalwood, jasmine and juniper berries. I ignored the pleasant aroma, concentrating on the task at hand.

I ran my right hand under her drawing arm. "Lift up your elbow."

Removing my tingling fingers, I walked around her, making sure she was doing everything correctly. I nodded. "All right. Try again."

She grabbed an arrow and notched it carefully. Then she slowly readjusted her stance how I'd just shown her. And when she loosed the arrow again, it hit the target in the outer ring.

"Good job," I praised.

She smiled at her achievement and reached for another arrow.

After a while, we had to retrieve the arrows again.

"So did Petya forgive you for standing him up the other day?" I asked, pulling an arrow free.

She nodded.

"Did he ask for anything in return?"

She paused, frowning. "Sort of. Not really."

"Oh?"

She didn't look like she was going to take my hint.

"What did he want?" I asked directly.

"He...wanted me to be more familiar with him, to call him...Petya instead of Pyotr."

I raised an eyebrow. "Is that all?"

"And he wanted to take me on a real date, just the two of us."

Seems Petya has finally found the courage. "And what did you tell him?" I asked.

She tugged an arrow from the target and twirled it between her fingers, watching the arrowhead spin.

"I said I was not against the idea, but I could not commit to saying yes for certain."

"Why not?"

She raised her eyes to meet mine. "Because of you, Aleksandr."

My heart thumped in my chest, and I stilled.

"Because I am assigned to keep an eye on you, and I cannot promise to meet him at a certain time and place if I need to follow you around. I do not want to keep him waiting like that again."

My mouth twitched as if trying to smile, but I didn't quite carry it off. "It seems you are open to giving love a chance after all," I suggested.

She gazed down at the spinning arrow again. "Maybe..." she murmured.

"You know, Kisa," I said softly. "You do not have to give him a chance if it does not feel right. Sometimes we do not feel strongly about certain people. It is not that we dislike them; we just do not like them in that way."

She did not react, as if she hadn't even heard me.

35

When Liza and I returned to the house, we walked into an argument between Yulya and Adrik.

"Do not defend her, Adrik. I do not want to hear it. Your cousin has always been unreliable. And now, I have to take her watch when you know I have to prepare for tomorrow."

"Elena is not feeling well. She would come if she could."

Yulya gave him a hard stare. "It is amazing, do you not think so? That Elena always has a *very* good reason for not fulfilling her obligations."

Adrik opened his mouth to argue some more, but Yulya cut him off before he could say anything. "I do not have time for this." Then she turned toward where Liza and I stood on the threshold.

"I can take this watch, sister," I offered. "Tomorrow is the ninth day after Father's death. There is much to do."

Yulya glared her frustration at me, then sighed.

"Fine. Thank you," she said, her tone reflecting that she was reluctant to rely on me. "It is already late. Please go now. I will have someone bring you food in a while."

I nodded and left the way I'd come, Liza following behind as always. When we reached the chapel, we found Petya waiting for us at the door.

"Good morning, Petya," I said. "There has been a change in plans. I am taking the next watch."

Petya snorted. "I should have expected Elena to find some way out of it. Do you need to borrow my weapon?"

I nodded, and he handed over his revolver, loaded with creature-killing bullets no doubt.

"I am sorry for the late relief, I would have come sooner had I known," I told my friend.

"It is all right." His eyes flicked to Liza. "I would not have gotten to see Liza this morning if not for this."

I glanced over at her and did not miss the blush that blossomed behind her freckles.

"Good morning, Pyo—Petya," she murmured.

My stomach clenched at the soft tone in her voice; I didn't know she could sound so gentle, that her whispers could caress thus. I moved farther into the chapel, my eyes downcast, but not before I saw Petya's brilliant smile.

"Would you have supper with me later tonight, Liza?" Petya asked.

"I...I am to help Aleksandr keep watch, so I cannot tonight."

My breath stopped for only a second as she said

my name, so different from the way she'd just said his. *Aleksandr*, I'd never disliked my name so much.

"Surely, Sasha does not need your help to keep watch," Petya argued. "His skills are legendary. I have seen them. Believe me."

Ah, so she has not told him that she is my personal spy. Interesting.

"I know, but I have vowed to act as his assistant for a while. And he had not planned on taking this watch, he could need me to fetch things for him."

I stifled a snort at her lame excuse.

Petya took her at her word. "You are so dedicated, Liza," he praised. "I like that."

There was a moment's silence, then Liza murmured her thanks.

"Well, I better get some rest then. See you later," Petya said.

I raised my hand in farewell without looking back at him.

I felt Liza's approach, her presence getting heavier with every step she took toward me. "You could have eaten with him," I muttered. "It is not as if I could have left my father alone. You would have known exactly where I was."

"I know."

I glanced down at her indecipherable expression. I wanted to know what she meant. Why she didn't go with him when given the chance, but I didn't ask. I just stood there staring at her, and she just stood staring back.

"You did well today," I said finally. "Even in just one lesson, you showed progress."

Her lips twitched into a small smile. "Thank you, Aleksandr."

I frowned. "Do you still not know me well enough to call me Sasha?" I asked quietly.

"I am not your equal, Aleksandr. We are not friends. We could not be. The distinction between us has been made very clear to me over the last ten years. I ate with the servants, slept with the servants."

My stomach rolled, so close were her words to those said to me long ago. "It hurts me to hear you say that, Elizaveta," I murmured. Then I turned away from her and sat in the chair facing my father's coffin.

After a long while, I rose and started to slowly pace the space, stretching my legs.

"I am sorry," Liza said softly. "I did not say those things to hurt you."

I turned to her and took a few steps toward her, studying her eyes to determine her truthfulness. I smiled when I saw that she didn't lie.

"Will you call me Sasha then?" I asked.

"Let us make a compromise," she suggested. "How about I do not call you Master Aleksandr?"

I pursed my lips. "You have not once called me that."

She smirked. "Then I have already kept my word."

I stared at her seriously. "Kisa, I have something I need to tell you. Something I've wanted to say for a little while now."

Her smile slipped as I stepped into her personal

space. "What?" she whispered, not taking her eyes from mine.

"You stink, Kisa. You really should bathe after you train," I said straight-faced.

She clicked her tongue and groaned, pushing me away from her.

I laughed, letting her attempts to move me succeed.

A discreet cough called attention to the chapel door, where Tanya stood with a basket. She dipped her head when we saw her. "Your sister asked me to bring you two lunch," she explained.

The playful mood dissipated.

"You go first," Liza said. "I will watch until you are finished."

I handed Liza the revolver and followed Tanya from the chapel. I sat under a nearby tree, still close enough to come to Liza's aid should the worst happen. Tanya sank down on her knees beside me and began digging through the basket. She handed me a sandwich and poured me a cup of tea from a large flask.

With her task complete, I thought she would leave, but she settled down next to me. The atmosphere was tense, and it was clear I was still not comfortable being around Tanya again. I was two bites into my sandwich before she spoke.

"You are different, Sasha. I have never seen you tease someone like that."

I glanced over at her, swallowing before I spoke. "I do not think I have changed so much."

"You never would have said those things to me. And do not think I did not see you with the women who came after me, at least the ones here. You were charming, flattering. You make women love themselves. I never thought I would see the day when you told a woman to bathe because she *stinks*."

I laughed at the scene as it replayed in my mind. "That is because she is not a woman to me. I am not trying to earn her affections."

Tanya raised an eyebrow at me but didn't say anything. She just turned her gaze back toward the chapel as the wind shook loose a few of the yellow leaves above us.

36

Adrik relieved my watch that evening. His face was drawn and tired, and I wondered if he was going to be able to stay awake all night. Then again, nothing wakes a person from sleep quite like the sound of the dead rising, so I wasn't worried.

The night was quiet, but I had trouble falling asleep. Staring up at the ceiling far above me, I hoped my plan for Nika worked. I'd found over the years that nothing was so hurtful as indifference. And while I was under no impression that Nika truly wanted my regard, I was relying on the fact that she cared about her own image at least.

It was also clear to me that Maksim felt tradition was very important. With a two-fold approach, I was confident I could be free before my forty days were up. I was confident, but that didn't ease the tightness in my chest.

Why now, when I have a solid plan, do I feel uneasy?

I didn't know the answer. But as I willed my eyes

shut, sounds from earlier in the day played back in my ears.

"Good morning, Pyo—Petya...I am not your equal, Aleksandr. We are not friends. We could not be."... *"You are different, Sasha."*

Am I different? I sorted through the women I'd known, and I couldn't recall ever wanting to elicit that irritated glare I found so amusing in Liza.

I chuckled to myself as I pictured Liza's reaction to being called stinky. Then my smile slipped. *"I am not trying to earn her affections."*

Good morning, Petya... Aleksandr, we are not friends.

I rolled to my side and peered into my hushed room, the dim light from the fireplace reflected off the polished weapons hanging on my walls. The glint of light gave me something to focus on, and my mind slowly lulled to sleep.

I was startled awake the next morning by a thumping on my door. My head was heavy from restless sleep, and I thought seriously about ignoring my visitor. But as the thumping resumed, I cursed under my breath and threw my blankets back.

The cold floor beneath my feet only added to my vexation.

"What?" I demanded as I unlocked the door and threw it open.

Liza's grey eyes widened, and she dropped her hand, which was no doubt meant to cause another disturbance. She took in my disheveled appearance, then quirked an eyebrow. "Were you still sleeping?"

"Have I offended you in some way?" I

demanded. "Is that why you disturb me at such an hour?"

"At such an hour? It is nearly ten in the morning. I have been searching for you for hours. It did not even occur to me that you would still be sleeping."

I ran my hand over my face. "When does the family arrive?"

"The gathering officially starts in an hour, but a few have already arrived."

"Where?"

"First in the chapel, then the dining room, and finally the conference room."

"Come in," I said, turning on my heel and making my way toward my wardrobe. I grabbed a clean shirt and trousers.

Glancing over my shoulder, I saw Liza had silently entered and shut the door behind her though she stood near it as if ready to make her escape at any moment.

"Yulya is planning on leading a hunt tonight?" I asked, making my way toward the adjoining bathroom to wash up and change. I left the bathroom door open only slightly so I could more easily hear her response.

"Yes, they are to discuss the specifics in the conference room." By her volume, I guessed that she was right outside the bathroom door.

Not all Ubyzniki who died had hunts hosted in their honor. But with my sister wanting to legitimize her claim, it made sense for her to showcase her leadership. And there was nothing my father liked so well as murder in the dead of night.

"Any idea who she is planning to hunt?" I asked before splashing my face with warm water.

"You mean *what* she is planning to hunt," she corrected.

"I mean *who*, Kisa," I insisted.

There was a long pause from the other side of the door.

"I do not know," she answered.

"How many Ubyzniki will be there?" I asked.

"At least one person from the main branch of each family. But likely more Volonovs than anyone else."

I nodded though she couldn't see me.

"Bes will certainly be there," she added quietly.

I frowned. "Good."

She didn't respond for so long that I thought she'd left.

"Are you still there, Kisa?" I asked before sticking my toothbrush into my mouth.

"I am here," she answered. "It is possible that more of the Ubyzniki will come than expected."

I waited for her to continue.

"You have been away a long time, Aleksandr, and you were already a legend before leaving. Many could come to join a hunt with you."

I spit into the sink and rinsed my mouth before responding. "Then they will be disappointed."

"Why is that?"

I opened the bathroom door, then began buttoning my shirt. "Because I will not be going on the hunt."

She frowned, and I could see disapproval flash in her eyes.

I tilted my head at her reaction. "You think I should go? Why? It will only help Yulya's claim to the title if I refuse."

"But people will think you a coward."

I shrugged. "I do not care if these people think I am a coward or not."

"It is a hunt held in your father's honor," she argued.

"My father knew how I felt about hunting before I left."

She stared at me seriously for a quiet moment. "Sometimes I cannot see the man he said you were."

The disappointment in her tone made me flinch. "And who is it he said I was?" I asked.

She didn't respond to my question. She just lifted her chin and said, "Are you ready?"

I wasn't downstairs twenty minutes before Nika arrived and glued herself to my side.

I pulled my arm from her grasp. "Try to control your enthusiasm, Veronika," I scolded as she smiled broadly at my family and the Ubyzniki who were gathering. "This is a memorial for my dead father."

She frowned, her black eyes heating with indignation, but she didn't make a scene.

I wasn't under the impression that our exchange went unnoticed though; assassins are an observant bunch as a rule.

When it was time, we all went to the chapel. Our little chapel was not big enough to fit everyone. Family was given priority, my sisters and I at the front nearest the coffin. Once crammed in, Father Strovanash said some prayers.

Then we walked back to the house for luncheon.

"What do you like, Sashen'ka?" Nika asked as we approached the table where all the food had been set out on platters. "I would like to learn your tastes so I can be a good wife."

"There is no need," I said. Then I fetched my own plate and filled it with food, not offering her anything.

Nika's expression grew more and more sour as I continued to brush her off. She was not used to being treated thus. Everyone had always given her exactly what she wanted. After all, she was beautiful. And if her beauty had no impact, she used cruelty and fear.

But what could she say against me? I had not overstepped my bounds. Anything I said that could be called rude, could also be interpreted in other ways. And any time I scolded her, it was to keep her following the exact and proper manners for the situation. I couldn't be faulted for that. And besides, I'd been away for over a decade; could anyone reasonably expect me to be the same as I was?

This is only a prelude. What did you think would happen when you and your father threatened me? If you are going to force me into a business-like marriage, then you will not get the benefits of courting. You will be held to the traditional standards that governed such situations.

In the afternoon, once everyone had eaten, some of our guests left. Those who stayed were to join the hunt. I frowned as I looked at the crowd, much larger than what would normally participate. I felt their eyes on me as we climbed the stairs to the conference room.

By design, I was one of the last to enter the long room. Yulya stood before a large map of the surrounding area. Adrik sat at one side and Dima on the other. But everyone's eyes focused on me when I joined the assemblage. I stayed in the back, waiting for the right time.

A look of confusion traveled among the group, but I just focused my gaze on Yulya.

My sister cleared her throat to draw everyone else's attention. "Our trackers have found a volkolak just outside the city—"

"Why is he here?" I interrupted.

Yulya squinted. "We do not know. Perhaps to hunt, perhaps to do its master's bidding. Does it matter?"

She didn't wait for me to answer but continued. "We have weapons enough for everyone: hawthorn stakes, arrows, spears, whatever your preference."

"Have you ever wondered why a person would choose to become a volkolak?" I asked. "And how do you even know he changed himself? It could be he was changed against his will."

Yulya glared at me. "I do not care why or how it became a monster. My duty is to kill it so it does not harm any humans."

"Has he harmed any humans?" I pushed.

"It is only a matter of time," she snapped.

"Is it?"

Fuming, Yulya sighed loudly. "Do you have any constructive questions, little brother? Or can we get back to planning our hunt?"

"Oh, I think the questions I have asked are the most important of all, sister."

Before I could say anything else, Nika stood from her seat. "He is just trying to gauge the level of threat. Are you not, Sashen'ka? Knowing how it became a volkolak could give us insight into its thought processes. And knowing whether it has harmed people can tell us how well it can defend itself against us. Right?"

The group, whose brows had been puckered in confusion, nodded at Nika's words. Her explanation put them at ease in the face of my unusual behavior, though my sisters were not so easily convinced.

"No, Veronika. That is not what I am saying at all. And I would prefer you let me speak for myself in the future. I am saying that hunting these magical beings is wrong. It is barbaric. This person may have had perfectly sensible reasons to want to become a wolf. This person may be a victim, turned into a wolf against his will. He may be no danger to anyone, and you would kill him just because he is no longer fully human? I will not participate in such a practice, and I hope you are all ashamed of yourselves."

Having said my piece, I exited the room. I could hear the uproar I'd left behind all the way down the hall. By the time I reached the stairs, I felt Liza's silent presence trailing after me. I halted on the first floor. Liza stopped too, still on the stairs above me.

"I will be with my father tonight," I told her, not looking back. "Should you wish to join the others."

She was silent for a moment, and my skin began to prickle as I awaited her response.

"I will keep watch over Master Volonov," she stated.

I nodded and took a step forward. Then I stopped again, looking over my shoulder at her.

Her expression was smooth and dignified.

"What say we go to the garden and feed the squirrels before our watch?" I suggested softly.

The corner of her mouth twitched. "I suppose we should get our coats. It is getting cold outside."

That evening, Liza and I again kept watch at my father's coffin-side. I didn't want to think of the havoc the hunt was wreaking somewhere just outside the city. I particularly didn't want to think about my sister, little Masha, taking a knife to some poor soul. So I sat in the chair and concentrated on twisting the tiny bands of the puzzle box into place.

After a few more hours of work, I stared down at the painted matryoshka. Her little white cheeks were dotted with freckles, and her grey eyes stared up at me beneath her dark hair. As I shifted the final row into its correct position, the internal mechanism clicked, and the doll split in half along the middle.

I held my breath and gently removed the top. Then I groaned with a sigh. "What was I expecting?" I muttered to myself as I stared at yet another layer of the puzzle box.

I pulled out the inner matryoshka, its painting as jumbled and confused as the first. Clicking my tongue, I shoved the new challenge into my jacket pocket.

Then I glanced around at Liza. She was leaning against the doorway, looking outside. I stood and walked toward her.

"What are you looking at, Kisa?" I asked, dipping my head to follow the direction of her eyes.

"Just the moon," she answered.

I grunted. "*Just* the moon? What an unromantic way of putting it."

She glanced over at me as I moved to stand beside her. "Who said I was a romantic?"

"More artistic souls have been moved to write poetry, music, on the subject. Surely, the moon is something inspiring."

"You speak as if you were one of them."

"I was...I used to be."

She raised an eyebrow. "Forgive me for not believing that you have given up your frivolous romantic notions."

I smiled softly at her. "No, I have not given up on them. But my days of song and poetry have long since passed. I prefer more tangible beauty these days. Nothing so far out of my grasp as the moon." I paused, reflecting on the statement I'd just made. "Then again, perhaps what I am reaching for is more unattainable than I thought. Maybe I should be more like you, Kisa."

She frowned. "I would not like to see it."

"Oh?" I raised my eyebrows.

"I like to think there are optimists in the world. For if there are not, whose dreams am I fighting to protect?"

I gave her a smile. "Now *that* is a very romantic notion, Kisa."

"Perhaps," she murmured, turning her attention back to the sky.

I sighed and also directed my eyes at the waning moon, hanging just above the trees. "I used to believe that, that I was protecting people."

I could feel her eyes shift back to me, but I didn't face her.

"Will you tell me what happened?" she asked yet again.

After a long moment, I gazed down at her. Her grey eyes shined in the moonlight. "Are you ready to know?" I wondered. "It may thrust unpleasant truths into the light. Those truths cannot be unknown."

She listened carefully to my warning, then nodded slowly. "Tell me, Aleksandr."

I frowned but dipped my head in agreement. "Did you know I was the youngest person to ever become a member of the Ubyzniki?"

"Yes."

"By the time I was nineteen years old, I had killed hundreds of magical creatures, everything from Mara to a zmei. I was given the most dangerous missions and the most important. One such mission, my last, took me to the bleak home of a boyar. Took me to the Minsk Governorate."

I stared up at the manor from the shadows of the nearby trees, its torches casting hardly a glimmer. It was a windy night, moonless and cold. The perfect night to sneak in and take out three high-profile targets.

I didn't know why I was sent for just a few Fae, but it was not my place to question orders, as my father kept telling me. I frowned at the thought and ignored the tension in my stomach.

Creeping closer—silent and invisible—I watched a guard pass on his rounds. After he was gone, not to return for twenty minutes, I approached the side of the manor, where the glass walls of the conservatory rattled in the wind.

At the door, I took out the gadget the Ubyzniki's weapons master had given me. Sticking the pointed end into the keyhole, the mechanism clicked and clacked and then stopped.

I twisted the handle and clenched my teeth when it didn't budge. I'd always preferred the tested solidness of age-old gear, trusting the sturdiness of rope and steel when my life depended on it.

Stifling a sigh, I dislodged a loose brick from a nearby planter and whacked the handle of the door off.

I was in the humid conservatory within seconds, carefully waiting and assessing where to go.

My next task was to reach the noble bedrooms. I knew where they were of course, thanks to our reconnaissance, but getting there without notice was another story.

I opted for approaching through the more official route rather than the servants' hallways. Servants never got to rest on nights such as this, and they were more unpredictable.

The lateness of the hour meant that most

everyone was abed though storms did bring out the restlessness in people. Every creak, every swish, every thump as I crept silently through the halls and parlours of the manor, set my nerves on edge. I moved from cover to cover, never out in the open for too long.

But finally, I had to face the stairs. The wooden stairs, exquisitely carved, wound upward. They were wide, and there was no way of knowing who, or what, may be waiting around the blind corners.

Being a successful assassin comes with a certain amount of luck. As I made my way up the stairs, I was lucky, which meant my targets were not.

The half-breed's chamber was easiest to find.

Standing outside the polished wooden door, I readjusted my grip on my shashka and took a deep breath. Then I quietly turned the doorknob and slipped inside.

And there I found my first target huddled in her bed, her pale eyes wide and reflecting the single candle on her bedside table. The little girl had wrapped her blanket around her like a cloak, the makeshift hood falling down from her dark hair.

"Did Mama send you to protect me from the storm?" she asked, her eyes fixating on my shashka as the blade flashed in the flame-light.

My heart screamed, and my chest felt like it was being crushed. *She cannot be older than five.*

And as my mind swirled in horror, her small voice called to me again.

"Mister, would you tell me a story? The wind is too loud."

I closed my eyes to the unbidden tears. "There is

no need to be afraid of the wind, little Lady," I said softly, my strangled voice barely a whisper. "The wind is but a bear's roar."

Her pale eyes widened. "A bear?"

I nodded. "He has hurt his paw, and he is calling for his mama to help him."

"But why will she not come?"

"She will," I promised. "She is just trying to find the right medicine. She will come, and she will comfort him. And he will stop crying soon."

She smiled. "What is the bear's name?" she asked. "I will tell him not to worry, that his mama is coming soon."

"What is your name, little Lady?"

"Eury," she answered.

"That is a great coincidence. That is also the little bear's name, Yuri."

"Really?" Her tiny voice was all astonishment.

I nodded. "So, worry not, little Eury. His roaring will soon be over, and morning will come."

She smiled again and settled back onto her pillows. "Goodnight," she whispered as she closed her eyes.

39

I took a steadying breath and turned to Liza, the moon still shining in her eyes.

"And so I left, sneaking out as if I was never there," I finished.

"And...and the little girl?" Liza asked. "Did the Ubyzniki send another assassin after her?"

I smirked. "I do not know. But they likely would not have found her if they did. Before I left, I wrote a note, warning the boyar and his wife that persons unknown wanted to do them and their daughter harm. I followed the newspapers for a while. It seems the boyar and his family disappeared. A relative took over his title and his place in the upper house of the Duma, but no bodies were ever found."

"But what happened after that? Is that when you left the Ubyzniki?"

I nodded. "Yes, but not before I returned home and confronted my father. Ugly words were exchanged. He accused me of insubordination, and I...I had much worse things to say to him. As a key member of the Ubyzniki, I knew he had known who I was sent to kill." I shook my head. "I will never forgive him for that."

Liza lowered her gaze but didn't say anything.

"All the way back from Minsk, I wondered who else had been killed. Were these killings just? Had any of these magical beings deserved to die? What could this little girl have possibly done to deserve to be assassinated? It made me question everything I had ever been told, everything I had been taught."

Liza was silent for a long while. She stared out into the trees around the chapel, her eyes unfocused and far away. "Some of them do deserve to die, Aleksandr. Perhaps not that little, half-Fae girl. Perhaps not her mother and father. But there are others that do deserve it. Like the strzyga that killed my family, that killed my entire village."

I didn't say anything, I just stood silently beside Liza, waiting to see if she wanted to share her story with me or not.

"I was fourteen, and I lived in Khomyne with my parents and grandparents. Our house was not big, but it was warm."

She paused for a minute and closed her eyes before continuing.

"My mother always went to Nizhyn on Saturdays to sell her needlework at the market. But my grandpa was sick, so I offered to take it. Papa did not like the idea of me going to Nizhyn alone, but I persuaded him. I told him I had been there many times with Mama. He eventually agreed as long as I asked Danya to go with me."

Her voice broke over the boy's name, and she took a steadying breath before she went on.

"Danya was an older boy, three years older than me, who lived near us. But I did not ask Danya to come with me because Danya and I had gotten into an argument the day before."

She laughed once, and it came out half like a sob.

"It was so stupid. He had promised to meet me by the big walnut tree, and he had been late. He was never very good at meeting anyone on time, and that day I was in a bad mood. We argued, and I threw a walnut at him. After he left, I found a magnolia flower on the ground. I do not know how he preserved it from the spring, but he always brought me little gifts when he did something wrong."

She smiled sadly at the memory.

"The day I went to the market, I was still angry with him. I knew we would make up in a few days, but I was not ready to forgive him just yet. So I went to the market by myself, despite what I had told Papa."

A single tear rolled down Liza's cheek, shining a thin trail over her freckles to her chin.

"It was very late when I returned home. I cannot remember what held me up in Nizhyn. But I knew my parents would not be angry because I sold all of the needlework I had taken with me. I remember it being very quiet."

Her voice dropped to a whisper.

"The lamps were not lit in the house, and I could not see anything until I struck a match... It was too late for my family. The strzyga had already visited. They were so pale...empty of blood; their insides—"

"I know how a strzyga feeds," I cut her off, trying to bring her back to the present moment.

She glanced up at me and nodded once.

"Mistress Yuliya found me as I wandered the path between my house and Danya's. She would not let me go there, telling me I was the only one left in the village. I sank to my knees, wailing and crying, and she stayed with me. She stroked my hair and promised me that the strzyga was dead."

"And then Yulya brought you here?" I asked.

Liza nodded. "I told her I had no family but the ones I had lost. She brought me back here, and the other servants took care of me until I was well enough to work."

"How did you go from being a servant to trying to get into the Ubyzniki?" I wondered.

"I was disturbing everyone with my nightmares. I would wake up screaming every night. To help me combat them, Mistress Yuliya trained me. And it worked. It was not unheard of. Many of the other servants have at least basic training. They need to, working for an Ubyzniki family."

"Yes, but none of them would be considered for induction," I pointed out.

Liza averted her gaze with a shrug. "Yes, well, I have always wanted to be able to save people the way Mistress Yuliya saved me."

So that was what the light of truth taught you. Those were the horrors that showed you what to fear and hate. "I am sorry you had to go through that, Kisa," I murmured, watching the moonlight dance on the leaves as the wind blew in their branches.

"As am I, Aleksandr. I understand why you left the way you did."

40

"Why?" Yulya demanded the following day after she'd summoned me to Father's study. "You have no idea what I had to deal with after your little display yesterday."

"They were outraged, yes?" I asked mildly.

"That is putting it lightly," she snapped.

"Good."

Her face flushed in fury, and I was a bit worried her eyes would pop out of her head.

"I do not want to marry Nika. I do not want to lead this family or the Ubyzniki as you well know. It is possible that Maksim will call off the wedding over what I said Sunday and yesterday."

"It is possible that he may take our entire family down for what you said too!" she roared. "Your actions do not only affect you. You are damaging our family legacy, my reputation, Masha's. Until I have undisputed control over this family, others will take what you say and do as a reflection of us all."

"But, surely, that can only help your claim. My

opinions are beyond unpopular. They are unacceptable to the Ubyzniki. That could mean that they turn to you as a better alternative," I reasoned.

"Or they could use this opportunity to rearrange the hierarchy and demote our entire family," she countered.

I frowned. The whole situation seemed entirely ridiculous to me.

Yulya fixed her glare on me. "Your time is up. I will not allow you to make a mockery of this family any longer. We tried it your way. It did not work. You are now fair game."

My heart squeezed as I stared into the icy eyes of my older sister. "I never wanted to hurt you, Yulya." My voice was soft but clear.

"Then that is yet another thing you have failed at," she spat.

I did not acknowledge Liza as I left my father's study. I knew she had likely heard everything from her place in the hall. I just walked past her and went down the stairs. She, of course, followed.

As I passed through the foyer, a booming knock —slow but demanding—emanated from the front door. I went to answer it.

Nika's black eyes raged at me from the doorstep. She didn't wait for me to invite her in but pushed past me. With long strides, she made her way to the parlour. I was left to shut the door and trail after her.

No sooner had I entered the room than Nika whirled around and fixed her predatory gaze on me. She was as angry as a snake who'd been stepped on. Her eyes flicked quickly to Liza who had followed me into the room, but she must have decided she didn't care about an audience because she immediately revealed the purpose of her visit.

"I have been nice thus far," she hissed. "I have been gracious and downright pleasant. You may have changed a great deal over the last ten years, Sasha. But I have not. And you know that I can be equally unpleasant."

I kept my expression smooth, distant, uninterested.

"I wanted to start this marriage off on good terms. I hoped we could grow to care for one another. At the very least, I thought we could be polite and cordial." Her tone darkened even further somehow. "But it does not have to be that way. I can be spiteful, Sasha. Vengeful. And while you may not care for your reputation or the reputation of your family, I do. I will not have you disrespect me the way you did yesterday. From now on, you will be amiable to me, or you will not even make it to the end of the glaz smerti."

I tilted my head and raised my eyebrows only slightly. "You seemed to have filled your head with many expectations about what this marriage would be without bothering to learn about the man you are marrying. Perhaps you should use the past few days as a preview to what your life will be like. If you want to follow such outdated traditions as an arranged marriage, then you will get all of the traditions that go with it. For instance, the tone you just used with me is inappropriate. That is not how an obedient wife speaks to her husband."

Her jaw clenched at my words.

"And you can threaten me all you like though it

will not help you. For one, if you kill me, you will not get what you want. And secondly." I smirked darkly at her. "You say you want to marry me because I am the best the Ubyzniki has ever seen. Is that who you want to challenge? I have told you I am not as good as I used to be. But if you want to marry me, you clearly do not believe that to be true. Would you risk your own head for that wager?"

"If you killed me, my father would never lift the glaz smerti," she said confidently.

I smiled. "Then I would be dead either way. I might as well take you down with me. Is that the sort of romance you are looking for?"

She didn't say anything. She just stood seething in impotent rage.

"But you are right about one thing. We do not have to be this way. You could easily tell your father that you do not want to marry me. Then you do not have to be affected by anything I might do to my family's reputation. I am sure most of the Ubyzniki would understand, even applaud, that decision."

She squinted at me. "So that is your play, is it? Act in such a way that would make me not want to marry you so I will call the wedding off." She laughed. "I knew you could not have changed so much. I have seen the thrill of the hunt in your eyes. That bloodlust is not so easily abandoned."

I frowned. "It is true that I do not want this marriage as both you and your father know. But the opinions I have expressed are honest."

She smirked. "Of course they are," she said in an overly sweet tone.

Then she approached me, swaying her hips in

smooth, seductive strides. Getting into my personal space, she rested her fingertips on my chest. Even that light brush of her touch rolled my stomach, but I didn't pull away.

She gazed up at me, her mouth quirked in a playful smile. "I think you have forgotten me, Sashen-ka," she cooed, drawing out each syllable as if tasting it. "I would make your everyday a living hell before I admit defeat. You may argue that I would be suffering in this marriage alongside you. But you would be wrong. Because causing you pain and mental anguish would be all the satisfaction I would ever need."

Then she smiled a sweet, innocent smile that was sinister and ruthless. My throat burned with threatening bile.

"I will be back, Sashen'ka," she promised. "But now I have to go and speak to Papa. He has the silliest idea of calling off our wedding. Can you imagine? But do not worry." She patted my chest. "I will talk to him, and everything will be fine."

I don't know how long I stood there after Nika left. I didn't have the mental wherewithal to decide what to even do next. But after some time, my legs moved me to a nearby couch.

I blinked as Liza sat down beside me. Looking over at her, I saw that she wore her usual composed expression.

"If I asked you to kill me, Kisa, would you make it quick and painless?"

Her grey eyes met mine. "I do not take orders from you, Aleksandr Sergeyevich," she said soft and simple.

I snorted and the motion broke something within me. I began to laugh, heaving hearty chuckles that brought tears to my eyes. By the time I was finished, my sides hurt, and every deep breath brought a new, sharp pain.

Glancing over at Liza again, I said, "I think my plan is working. Do you not think so?"

Her mouth twitched into a tiny smirk. "You have certainly gotten under her skin."

41

The rest of the day was uneventful compared to how my morning had started. I went to the training field, my muscles willing my mind into submission.

I knew my approach to dealing with Nika was a risk, that she was just as diabolical as she threatened. But what she didn't know was that I was willing to die rather than give in to her demands. Of course, that wasn't my first choice. But I knew she wouldn't get her way in the end. And that conviction allowed me to face the situation with a calm mind.

The following day, after I'd trained and showered, I sat in the parlour with Liza. L'vitsa purred contentedly, sunning herself while Liza stroked her silky grey and black fur. I was again twisting the tiny bands of my father's puzzle box, softly humming the tune of *My Cossack Girl*.

The moment was quiet and peaceful, which of course meant it wouldn't last long. Quick footsteps announced an interruption right before Petya entered the parlour.

I looked up at my friend. His hair was windswept, and his eyes were bright. His cheeks were flushed, and he grinned.

I smiled at whatever had brought him such excitement. "Do you bring good news, Petya?" I asked, noticing the large, cream envelope in his hand.

"I do," he agreed, slightly winded as though he'd run. He crossed the room and handed me the envelope. Then his attention had no more time for me; his eyes found Liza and fixed on her. "A royal messenger just delivered that," he explained.

I turned over the envelope and broke the golden wax seal, which indeed bore the imperial double-headed eagle. Then I unfolded the thick paper.

"What does it say?" Liza asked before I could even begin to read.

"It says: The Ober-Kammerherr is commanded by the Empress Alexandra Nikolaevna Romanova to invite Aleksandr Sergeyevich Volonov, Adrik Adrianovich Rostavich and his wife Yuliya Sergeyevna Volonova, and Maria Sergeyevna Volonova to a Grand Ball in commemoration of Her Imperial Majesty's 33rd Birthday at the Winter Palace on October 20, 2017, at 9:00 p.m. An answer is requested to the Ober-Kammerherr. Full evening dress or white tie."

I looked over the invitation at Petya. "But why were you so excited about a ball at the palace, Petya? You have seen the royal messengers before."

Somehow Petya's grin widened. "Because the messenger told me that there would be a commoner's dance for all the servants who work for the families invited. And it is also in the palace!"

"How very generous of the empress," Liza agreed.

Petya nodded. "Would you accompany me to the dance, Liza?"

I stilled. Her grey eyes met mine. The moment was heavy. It lasted forever; it lasted less than a second.

"It seems the empress wishes for the servants to have a night off," I told her. I didn't say that I would undoubtedly have to take Nika to the ball. I didn't say that unless I brought her as my guest, she wouldn't be invited. I just waited for her answer.

Looking back at Petya, she smiled politely. "Thank you, Petya. I will accompany you." Her voice was a warm, gentle breeze. Nothing like the hot and cold gales she blasted at me.

I smiled at my friend's success, patting him on the shoulder as I walked out of the parlour. By the time I started up the stairs to deliver the news to Yulya and Masha, my frown was heavy.

Masha was overjoyed at the prospect of a grand ball at the palace. She had been to balls, of course, but she had never attended one hosted by the empress. It brought me joy to see her so excited, and to see Yulya smile indulgently at her.

Masha would have a new gown. Yulya assured her that she would send for the seamstress that very day. With a sigh, she also added that she would call the tailor for me. Luckily, he already had my measurements, so we would only have to tell him the dress code. He would take care of the rest.

I, for one, thought this was a brilliant opportunity for my situation with Nika. A room full of boyars, Duma deputies, foreign dignitaries, not to mention the empress herself? Nothing could be a more perfect stage for embarrassing a woman into calling off an engagement.

The more I thought about it, the more I smiled. In a little over a week, I would be free of all this nonsense. I could go anywhere I wanted. I could go to Switzerland, Egypt, Mexico. I could go to Canada or France. The world would again be open to me. Or even better, I could find a quiet place to settle and rest, where I didn't have to be on the move anymore, where I didn't have to run from the Ubyzniki because they would have given up on me.

I promised myself all of those things and more while I descended the stairs with my coat.

I raised an eyebrow as Liza exited the parlour alone. "Did Petya leave already?" I asked.

She nodded. "Where are you going?"

I grinned happily at her. "To visit Bes, of course. I would not wish her to think that I have neglected my duties as her betrothed. The empress is having a ball, and I mean to bring my beautiful nevesta for all to see."

Liza tilted her head at my uncharacteristic declaration. "You are planning something," she stated.

"Now, Kisa," I said with a smirk. "Why would you think that?"

Her answering grin made my heart beat faster. I sobered at the sensation, my smile faltering as I stared at her.

"What is it?" she asked, noticing my change in demeanor.

I averted my gaze. "Nothing," I murmured.

"Aleksandr, what is it?" Her tone held the faintest hint of anxiety. "Did you think of something that ruins your plan?"

I looked down at her again, her grey eyes bright and insistent. My heart jumped.

"Ruins?" I muttered to myself more than to her. "No, not ruins. Just...complicates."

42

The Ivashkin family home had not the expansive grounds Volonov Manor had. While they were aristocratic—boyars in their own right—they were awarded their nobility purely because of the Ubyzniki, nearly one hundred years after the Volonovs.

The Ivashkins had always been master hunters though they primarily hunted fox, wolf, and bear for their fur trading enterprises. But when Catherine the Great conceived and conglomerated the Ubyzniki, she saw fit to not only include them but give them a title as well.

Liza silently trailed behind me as we twisted through the many hidden courtyards of Saint Petersburg. It was still before noon, and the sun's rays did not reach the chilled hollows of the courtyards, lit only by the dim streetlamps.

I glanced back at Liza as we walked. She was soundless and light-footed as she moved. The only indication she was there was the gravity of her presence, the way the air moved that said there was something there.

"So," I started conversationally, slowing my pace to walk beside her. "Are you excited about the dance next week?"

She didn't slow down as she likely would have done had I not spoken, but continued beside me. She shrugged. "It will be interesting to visit the palace."

"And Petya?" I probed. "Are you not looking forward to an evening with him?" I acknowledged how my stomach fluttered as I waited for her answer, but my smile did not slip.

"Sure," she agreed. "He is easy to be around, always so kind and courteous."

My stomach flopped as though I'd been personally insulted. "If that is what you are into," I said with a shrug.

She snorted a laugh. "Women do tend to like men who are nice to them."

"I am nice. I am extremely nice, very accommodating," I argued.

She smirked wryly. "Not to me."

"Well, you..." I started, then finished much quieter. "Are different."

Liza's smile seemed to sour. "That is right, Aleksandr Sergeyevich. Because I am not a woman to you."

A thrill shot through me, and the hair on my arms stood on end. *Did she hear me talking with Tanya? Or is she just coming to that conclusion on her own?* I stopped walking and turned toward her; she halted as well. Taking a slow, deep breath through my nose, I stared down at her, analyzed her.

Her long, dark hair was loosely braided and resting against her collarbone. Her nose and freckled cheeks were flushed from the cool wind, and her grey eyes were clear and bright in the dim light of the shaded courtyard.

My eyes traveled lower, following the curves of her body. She was slender and strong, well built for speed and stealth. Her breasts and hips were average in size, not overly large but substantial enough that she could not hide her sex. Her clothes accentuated her lines, close-fitting as if she were ever ready for a fight. Her legs were lean muscle, but her thighs were thick enough to compliment her hips, thick enough to grab ahold of and to relish the feeling of doing so.

I met her eyes again. "Do you want me to see you as a woman, Kisa?" I asked softly, my voice a little more heated than I'd intended.

The blush from her cheeks spread to her ears. "Of course not," she huffed. "I told you before, Aleksandr Sergeyevich. I am not like other women. And I would not become one of your conquests."

My chest squeezed at her words, and I knew my answering smile had a subdued quality to it. "Of course not," I echoed.

When we started walking again, any comfortability we'd found since she'd tried to murder me in my sleep was stifled by a new sense of awkwardness.

She is right. She is not like the others. At least she did not let me get my hopes up. She has been straightforward from the beginning. And it is not as if all the women of the world are interested in me. I will just treat her as one of them. I can be friendly and courteous without the potential for romantic involvement.

I nodded to myself. *This interest is likely fleeting anyway. I have gotten over women far more beautiful, far more enticing, than her in the past. Even when something happened between a woman and me, it never took long for me to get over her not wanting to stay.*

My stomach dropped at the thought. *No one ever wanted to stay.*

By the time we reached the Ivashkins', I'd talked myself out of the little intrigue Liza had aroused in me. In fact, I was starting to wonder if I should change my ways altogether. After all, this woman had tried to kill me. Perhaps searching for the hope of romance wherever I could find it for so long had affected me somehow.

In any case, I hadn't time for any of that at the moment. I had an eye of death over my head, and there was only one way to get out of it. I needed to concentrate on Nika.

I knocked loudly on the front door of the main building of Nika's home. My call was answered by a surprised Kostya a few minutes later.

"Aleksandr Sergeyevich," Kostya greeted with the dip of his head.

I noted his fidgeting hands before he clasped them behind him.

"What brings you here?" he asked.

I squinted at the boy, wondering what he was guilty of that would make him so nervous around me. "I am here to call on your sister. Is she at home?"

"Nika? Um, yes, she is. Please, come in."

Liza and I entered the small foyer. I glanced up at the wide marble staircase some two sazhens away.

"Is your father at home?" I asked Kostya.

"Papa is due back quite soon. He is paying Svetlana Pavlovna Rostavich a visit this morning. Would you like me to let you know when he arrives?"

I frowned. *Adrik's mother? What are you up to Maksim Igorevich?* "I do not think I will be here long enough to see him," I answered.

Kostya dipped his head in acknowledgment, then began leading us through the home.

The Ivashkins' house consisted of a main building with a series of smaller buildings connected by corridors to form a sort of unequally spaced hexagon with a courtyard in the middle. Taking us to the library, Kostya pulled back a large tapestry to reveal a door.

My blood ran cold as he opened the door, which I knew led down to their dungeons.

43

As I followed Kostya down the polished wooden stairs, I was again struck by how elegant the Ivashkins' dungeons were. The hallways were well-lit and painted in delicate creams. I often wondered how they dragged the wounded magical creatures down there without marring the pristine walls. I suspected they had a very diligent housemaid.

The rooms where their prisoners were held were an entirely different matter. Heavy iron doors could only look so welcoming. Kostya stopped before the first door on the left. He pounded his fist on the metal, and the deep thumps echoed in the room beyond.

Muttered curses answered the call. And after a few moments, the door began to open. It scraped and screeched on its hinges, a warning to the creatures within that pain and death were coming for them.

"What is it?" Nika demanded before she'd even opened the door enough to see who was there. It was clear she was in a bad mood. Her face had blood spray on it, and red-brown streams and drips were dried on her hands and forearms. Her hair was loosely tied up, and she wore a marred leather apron over her clothes.

Over her shoulder, I could see her latest victim: a brindle-colored wolf laid out on a sturdy, metal table. My stomach hardened as I took in the sight. Its legs were held down at unnatural angles, angles that would have been appropriate for a man's arms and legs. Its torso was opened up like a botched dissection. I was grateful to see it was no longer breathing.

Nika smiled upon seeing me. "Did you come to play with me, Sashen'ka? I am afraid you are too late, but you can cheer me up by staying for tea. I am very disappointed. I was trying to kill the volkolak while it switched between forms. Can you imagine the prize that would be? But the bastard finished his transformation with his dying breath." She glanced over her shoulder at the being she had just tortured and murdered. "Still, I suppose his coat is worth something. It will make a beautiful hat and muff if I did not put too many holes in it."

I swallowed my disgust and forced my voice to be steady and indifferent. "Since you have been... occupied this morning, I am certain you have not yet heard of the empress's ball. It can, of course, be assumed we would go together, being betrothed. But I thought it polite to ask you in person, especially in light of our last conversation. I assume you smoothed things over with your father?"

Nika smiled broadly. "I am glad you have thought about what I said, Sashen'ka. We will both be happier for it. Papa was very angry to be certain, but he has agreed to defer to my judgment on the matter. Of course I will go to the ball with you. It will be a good chance to reintroduce you to Saint Petersburg society. You have been away for so long after all. And though we cannot officially announce our engagement until after your father's mourning period, it will serve to show people we are courting."

I nodded stiffly. "I cannot stay for tea. There is still much to prepare," I lied. "But, rest assured, I will send word of the particulars soon."

Her answering smile was bright, and it made my stomach drop. Anything that made Nika that happy wasn't likely good for anyone else. *It is fine. Your plan will work.*

"I must go," I stated, not wanting to stay there for a moment longer than I had to.

"I will see you soon," she promised.

I didn't respond but walked back the way we'd come, closing my eyes against the images of the carnage she'd so recently wrought.

Bidding goodbye to Kostya, Liza and I re-entered the street. The autumn sun had struggled through the clouds but brought no warmth with it. I glanced over at Liza. Her face was pale even in the golden light.

"Are you all right, Kisa?" I asked her softly.

She turned her grey eyes toward me. They were wide and anxious, the fluff of dandelion seeds that could be blown away at any change of the wind. "She cannot be allowed to lead the Ubyzniki," she said, her voice soft but urgent.

"Have you ever taken part in an Ubyzniki hunt?" I asked gently.

She paused for a moment before nodding. "But that was...eliminating a threat. It was not—I never..."

"You never brought the targets home to play with their insides."

Her coloring went a bit green, but she shook her head.

"My father never approved of such tactics. Oh, he would kill a magical creature just as soon as look at it, but he never made it suffer."

"Then why...why would he want you to marry her?" Liza wondered. "Did he not know what she was like?"

"He knew," I said assuredly. Then I sighed. "I do not know what he was thinking, why he did what he did."

"You cannot let this happen, Aleksandr," Liza said firmly.

"What would you have me do, Kisa?"

She opened her mouth to respond but closed it without making a sound.

I sighed through my nose and rested my hand on her shoulder. Though I knew she was capable of deadly strikes, she felt very delicate, very vulnerable, beneath my hand. "Do not worry, Kisa," I said gently. "Yulya will never allow Bes to be in charge of the Ubyzniki, not if she has anything to say about it. And, as I have told you, I will not be claiming the title. Without me, she has no hope of leading."

Liza frowned. "But what will you do if we cannot get you released from the glaz smerti?"

I smiled softly at her. "You have lost your coloring, Kisa. I think something warm to drink and the strong wind off the gulf will be just the thing."

With every day that passed, every day that brought me closer to the empress's ball, I felt more and more confident in my plan. I had tried to make Nika forsake me by condemning everything she stood for. That hadn't worked exactly, but it had certainly made an impact. Had she believed my opinions were genuine, I was certain either she or Maksim would have called off the engagement. Though they very much were true, convincing her of that would be difficult.

So I adjusted my approach. It was clear she cared very much about her reputation and her family's reputation; that had been confirmed. Now was the time to undermine that reputation in more subtle ways. To do that, I needed her to believe she had convinced me, which is why I'd invited her to the ball myself. Promises and threats, that's how Nika had always gotten her way. And so, I let her feel that her old tricks had worked yet again, at least for the moment.

It had been three days since I'd invited Nika to the ball. It was Sunday, and Liza and I didn't attend Divine Liturgy. Again, I offered Liza to go with the servants, but she'd declined as before. She wanted to train.

As we approached the armory, I said, "Let us do something different today."

Liza stopped and looked over at me, tilting her head by way of a question.

"I have heard you praised, Kisa. They say you are the best they have seen in a while. And I admit I am curious. Let us try sparring."

Her expression gave nothing away. "All right," she agreed. "What would you like to use?"

I smirked at her. "Excuse me, but I am still a little shy of giving you something stabby and asking you to point it at me. I think hand-to-hand will be enough."

She nodded and didn't quite stifle her answering smile successfully.

A few minutes later, we faced each other in the sparring ring, loosening our limbs for our bout.

"Do not go easy on me, Kisa," I warned, soft and smooth.

"Why would I?" she challenged.

"You may not want to hurt my pretty face," I suggested with a grin.

She jabbed at my face with her right hand, but I knocked the punch aside. She retreated, quickly, jumping out of my counterattack range. The match had officially begun.

"Who tells you such things, Aleksandr Sergeyevich? I am afraid you overestimate your appearance," she shot back.

I chuckled. "Your words land better than your strikes, Kisa."

Her eyes analyzed me, looking for weaknesses. She came in low, sweeping her foot at my leg. As she made contact, I shifted my weight and lifted my front leg. With her back now to me, she spun her back foot around and lashed out with her heel.

I grabbed her ankle as her spinning hook kick approached my head. "I can see why you attacked me with stealth in the dark, Kisa. You are quite slow." I pushed her foot away, and she hopped to catch her balance.

"Do you always talk so much when you fight?" she asked. "Or are you trying to annoy me into forfeiting?"

I shrugged. "I thought I might as well make it entertaining for myself."

Liza rolled her eyes. "I could have practiced with the doll, you know. At least he does not make small talk."

I smirked at her again. Striking out with my foot, I swept her front leg, knocking her off-balance. When she began to fall, I caught her as if dipping her while we danced.

"I know how to fall," she told me, her hands clinging to my shirt.

I righted her. "I had no way of knowing," I answered offhandedly.

She cleared her throat with a soft grunt. "Well, now you do."

I nodded once.

As we continued our match, I was surprised to see that Liza was not even as skilled as Dima. *Why did Yulya send her instead of Dima?* But, even so, she wasn't terrible. She clearly had some training. And though I could predict all of her moves, I could also see how controlled and practiced they were.

Not much longer into our fight, a flash of color over Liza's shoulder announced a spectator. I spared a glance and saw Nika approaching the fence.

I frowned, turning my attention back to Liza. If she'd noticed Nika's arrival, she paid no mind as she plotted her next attack.

Before she could decide, I threw a right hook, slowing it down just enough for her to counter. She deflected my strike, then kicked out with her leg. I went down.

The air rushed out of me when I hit the ground with a huff.

Liza's eyes were wide with surprise as she stared down at me.

I chuckled. "I am more out of practice than I thought," I said, still on my back.

With crinkled eyebrows, Liza offered me a hand up.

"You win this time," I conceded as she hauled me to my feet. I looked around as if embarrassed by my defeat. "Oh, Veronika," I acknowledged, bobbing my head in a straight-faced nod.

Liza's head snapped in the direction I was looking.

Nika frowned severely, her black eyes glinting with displeasure. "You need to train more often, Sasha," she censured. "You are clearly out of practice. Even I could have countered that attack."

Though Nika had a very high opinion of her own

skills, the insult was clear. I was Aleksandr Sergeye-vich Volonov. No one had beaten me in a fight since I was a child. How could I possibly let a nobody, a servant who was only an Ubyzniki apprentice, beat me?

I shrugged. "I can only be the best I can, Veronika. I told you I am not the man I was. You knew me when I was in my prime. I am still a Volonov. Am I not?"

My heart soared at the disdainful expression on Nika's face. I was not the Aleksandr she remem-bered. I was no longer the best. Yes, I was still a Volonov. But would that be enough when the other Ubyzniki saw what I had become?

I approached the fence where Nika stood. "Was there a reason for your visit?" I asked in an all-busi-ness tone.

"I had hoped you would accompany me to my ballgown fitting," she explained. Her nose crinkled as if she would spit. "But you are clearly busy at the moment. And...and there is no time for you to clean up before my appointment." Her tone said she was grasping at any excuse within her reach. She needed to think about what she had just seen. She was avoiding me.

It was a miracle I managed to keep my expres-sion smooth—that I didn't burst into the broad smile that beamed in my heart. I nodded seriously. "All right. Did you get my message about Friday? The details about when and where I would meet you at the ball?"

"Yes, I will see you then. But now, I must go. I do not want to be late."

As soon as she was out of earshot, I burst into laughter.

45

Two days before the empress's birthday, I sat in the parlour as Liza read near the hearth. The night was quiet but for the wind and a few crickets, whose slow chirps bemoaned summer's end.

I was nearly finished with the second layer of my father's puzzle box. I could now see the features of the little doll. She had not the usual rosy-cheeked smile but frowned up at me with icy blue eyes. Her hair was dark beneath her red kerchief.

I still had a few rows to lock into place before she would reveal her secrets, but I suspected there would be another doll inside. I just didn't know how many layers I would need to get through before discovering what my father wanted to tell me.

A cold wind rushed into the room as someone opened the front door. I paid it no mind until I heard a sniffle and hitched breathing. Putting the doll into my pocket, I started to rise from my seat when Masha passed by the doorway.

"Masha," I called to her, taking a step toward the foyer.

She appeared in the doorframe. Her face was red and her eyes were swollen, but she had forced her expression into a small smile. "Yes, brother?" she asked, her voice steady but soft.

"Come sit with me, Mashen'ka," I said.

She opened her mouth, her eyes saying she would argue.

"Please," I urged before she could speak.

She lowered her face but nodded. As she sat beside me on the couch, she looked at Liza, who still read by the hearth as if we were of no concern to her.

"Elizaveta, would you mind asking the kitchen maid to brew us something warm? Masha just came in from outside."

Liza met my eyes, then glanced over at Masha. She dipped her head without argument and left the room. She even closed the door on her way out.

Once she'd gone, I turned my full attention to my younger sister. "Why were you crying, Mashen'ka?" I asked gently.

"I was not—" she started to contradict me but cut herself off when her gaze met mine.

In the silence she'd left, her big blue eyes shined in the firelight as they filled with tears. When they spilled over, I lifted my hand to her cheek and wiped them away.

"Was someone cruel to you?" I asked.

Masha shook her head. "No, not cruel."

I waited for her to explain, internalizing all my impatience so as not to rush her.

"I did not want to tell you this way," she admitted. "But I do not want to lie to you." She took a deep breath, then let it out in a long sigh. "I am in love, Sasha."

A shiver ran through me, and I must've worn my astonishment on my face because she snorted at me.

"You are so surprised? You have been gone a long time, brother. I am not a little girl anymore. Did you think it would never happen?"

"No—I am not..." I sighed, resetting my expectations. "Why should you being in love make you cry?" A thought occurred to me, and my whole body flushed. "He did not hurt you, did he?"

"No, of course not," she assured quickly. "In any case, I would be able to defend myself. I am a Volonova too, you know."

I took a deep breath and held it before letting it out slowly.

"We... I thought we felt the same. He had not told me he loved me in so many words. But I was certain he did," she explained. A line formed between her eyebrows. "But...lately, he has been distant. I do not know why. I do not think I have done anything to make him dislike me. I thought perhaps it was because...but no..." She hunched her shoulders and wrapped her arms around herself. "Maybe he just does not like me anymore, or maybe he never did."

"Why do you think he does not like you anymore?" I asked.

"He stopped coming to see me. And when I have seen him, he hardly speaks to me. He will not even look at me. And...and the ball is in two days. I thought he would ask me to go with him. But he did not." Her voice got quieter as she continued to speak. "So...so I asked him instead."

"And what did he say?"

"He did not say anything." Her eyes filled with tears again. "He just closed his eyes and shook his head. I—I could not take it, that coldness where there had only ever been warmth. So I left."

My heart ached for her. I knew the raw sorrow that was rejection. It wasn't something I would ever wish for my little sister. Wrapping my arm around her, I pulled her closer. She settled against me, resting her head on my shoulder.

"We cannot force others to love us, Mashen'ka," I murmured to her. "However much we want them, we can only ask that they be honest with us."

"Have you ever been in love, brother?" she asked.

I almost laughed at the question. It just seemed so absurd in that moment.

"Have I?" I mused. "Sometimes I wonder. I would say I have loved a great many in my own way. But they never seem to love me in return."

She was quiet for a while before she asked, "How did you know that they did not love you back?"

"They never stayed. I gave them whatever they needed. I gave them beauty. I appreciated them. But if they want to leave, they will leave."

Masha leaned away and glanced up at me, her brow crinkled. "You sound as if *you* were not honest, Sasha. Did you ever tell them you loved them? Did you ask them to stay?"

I smiled softly at her naivety. "There was no place for me. If I had asked them to stay, I would have been a burden. I would be holding them back with my desires. Can I even call it love if I tried to tie them down?"

"If they loved you, you would not be holding them back or tying them down. If she loved you, she would be glad to be bound to you. You would be bound to each other. A relationship is between two people, brother. She has no more right to have her needs met than you do. Both people should get what they need. It is a partnership."

Masha sighed softly, then shook her head. And when she looked up at me again, she smiled sadly. "My tender-hearted brother, I will tell you this because I think you need to hear it. You deserve love, Sasha. You deserve for someone to give *you* beauty, to appreciate *you*. You are right. Honesty is the best way. We can only ask them to be honest, and that is also what we should give them. I will tell him how I feel about him. And brother, I hope you will do the same."

A short while later, Liza must've decided it was safe to enter because she brought Masha and me some herbal tea. After our discussion and a delicately sweetened glass of ginger cinnamon tea, Masha already looked better. Her face was still red, her eyes still swollen, but she didn't have to force her smile.

I couldn't help but admire my little sister. She was so brave to tell this boy how she felt about him. The last time I had been so open with a woman... Well, I hoped it went better for her than it had for me. I'd been honest with Tanya, as honest as a person could be. I'd told her I loved her truly. It was only long after she'd left me that I realized she'd never said it back.

As I twisted the last few bands of the puzzle box into place, I thought about what Masha had said. I wondered if I was a coward. I wondered if I'd really loved those other women after all. Perhaps it hadn't been love. It certainly wasn't the all-in, soul-consuming love I'd felt for Tanya. But, then again, first love is always a bit different. Perhaps it had been the promise, the potential, of love. Maybe that was why my memories of Tanya were so different; they only ever brought sadness. But my memories of Ember, Monique, Nataliya were bittersweet at first but lost their sting over time, leaving a mellow, rose-colored glow.

Is Masha showing wisdom at the tender age of eighteen? Or is her youth and optimism coloring her reality? I didn't know which was the truth, but I hoped she had no cause to change her outlook.

I smiled to myself as the matryoshka clicked and opened, revealing—as suspected—yet another layer beneath. Putting the new puzzle into my pocket for another day, I kissed my sister goodnight and went to my room.

46

Though I had not been used to Grigori helping me dress for my father's funeral, I was grateful for his help the night of the empress's ball. I would never have gotten my tie as straight and perfect as he did. I felt awkward at first. It had been so long since I'd worn a tailcoat and trousers that tight. But I had adjusted by the time Grigori had slipped the white gardenia into my buttonhole.

I looked at my watch before tucking it into my pocket. I would be late meeting Nika. I smiled to myself as I left my room.

"Oh, Aleksandr," Liza said behind me in the hallway. "I thought you had already left."

I turned toward her, inhaling sharply when I saw her. She wore a bright blue sarafan with an embroidered belt emphasizing the curve of her waist. Her hair was loosely bound with a blue ribbon, and the color she'd painted on her mouth made her lips plump and entirely kissable.

"Kisa," I breathed.

She froze, color rising in her cheeks as she gazed back at me.

I took the gardenia from my buttonhole and reached toward her. She didn't pull away as I tucked it gently into her hair. I smiled, not hiding my admiration. "You look beautiful."

She frowned. "Are you ever serious, Aleksandr Sergeyevich?" she said, her tone tinted with bitterness. She started to reach for the flower, but I stilled her hand with mine.

"Leave it," I urged gently. "It suits you."

She held me in her gaze and didn't argue.

I released her wrist, so thin, so warm beneath my fingers. "We are already late. You would not want to keep Petya waiting."

She lowered her face by way of a nod, and we both descended to the foyer.

Yulya sighed. "Finally," she complained.

I gave my sisters compliments on their appearances and helped Masha with her stole. Then we went outside to the carriage, leaving Liza to wait for Petya. After Adrik had climbed in, I handed Yulya and Masha into the carriage before getting in after them. As we pulled away, I looked over at Liza, her shapely silhouette highlighted as she waited in the doorway. The echo of her wrist in my hand made my fingers tingle.

I faced forward, looking at Yulya who sat across from me in the carriage. Her expression was smooth and content.

I tilted my head at her unusual mood. "You are pleased to be going to the palace, sister?" I asked her.

She smiled. "I am happy to celebrate the empress's birthday."

I schooled my expression so as not to give away my thoughts. *You have plans. Well, so do I.*

The closer we got to the palace, the more congested the traffic became. By the time we arrived, we were well over an hour late to meet Nika.

As I entered the long hallway where they stored the cloaks, Masha's hand tucked into the crook of my arm, I had no trouble locating Nika. Her black eyes announced her foul mood.

"Good evening, Veronika," I greeted her with a polite bow of my head.

"You are late, Sasha," she huffed.

I didn't make an excuse for myself but looked around for Maksim and Kostya. "Where are your kinsmen?" I asked.

"I told them to go on ahead. Father was getting impatient, and I did not want to listen to him complain."

She stepped closer to me, expecting to take Masha's place. Masha loosened her hand to concede the spot, but I rested my hand over hers to keep her where she was.

I raised my eyebrows at Nika. "You do not mind if I escort Masha. It is her first imperial ball, and she does not have an escort."

Nika frowned but said, "Of course not. She will be my sister too after all."

I didn't reward her with a smile. Instead, I led Masha down the hall and trusted that Nika would follow behind.

"Brother," Masha whispered. "That was impolite. She is your betrothed. I could have followed behind."

I glanced over at her and smiled. "I would not hear of it, Mashen'ka. You are to be presented to the empress. I want to be there with you. Are you nervous?"

"A little," she admitted.

I patted her hand. "Do not be. You will do beautifully."

We walked up the stairs to the main vestibule and on through the columned hallway that led to the Jordan staircase. As I led my younger sister up the red carpeted, white marble stairs, she looked around, her mouth slightly open.

I chuckled quietly. When we reached the statue of Justice on the first landing, she looked up at the ceiling, where a painting of the Greek Olympians stared down at us. The gilded white walls, the statues, the paned windows, I remembered being awed by it all the first time I saw it.

I took the stairs on the right, leading her to the next landing, making sure to take it slow so she could admire the sight and not trip on her long gown.

The orchestra music playing on the second floor grew louder with every step. When we reached the summit, an officer in the Russian navy, his dress uniform polished to shine, directed us to the left.

We entered a large antechamber with golden chandeliers. At the far end, the master of ceremonies stood announcing people to the empress in the room beyond.

The antechamber was crowded with boyars,

politicians, and foreign dignitaries waiting to be received.

As we moved comfortably among the crowd, I saw more than a few people of whom I used to have the acquaintance. I wondered how many more I knew but just didn't recognize.

Maksim and Kostya were not in the room, having no doubt been received already. With Nika's eyes boring into my back as she followed after me, I went to work, smiling and greeting all the ladies I remembered. I, of course, made sure to introduce Masha to them.

"Sasha, is that you?" a woman's voice called from behind me.

I turned to see a dignified brunette smiling at me. She had the red ribbon that signified a member of the lower house of the Duma pinned to her dress, the red ribbon that remembered the blood spilled during the 1905 revolt, the blood that bought the average citizen a voice and sparked the reforms that would restructure Russia as a constitutional monarchy.

I recognized the woman's green eyes immediately. "Sonya." I smiled warmly, offering her my hand. "Or should I say, Deputy Sofiya Vladimirovna Lukina."

She placed her hand in mine, and I kissed it gently.

She chuckled at my ceremony. "I see you are the same as ever as if no time has passed."

"And do my old ways make your heart beat as they used to?" I asked playfully.

She blushed but waved her hand dismissively.

"Our youth is many years behind us." She eyed me again. "At least mine is."

"I do not believe that, Sonyechka," I murmured.

Nika scoffed behind me, but I paid her no mind.

"You." Sonya smiled, shaking her head with a nostalgic sigh. "You are incorrigible."

"Does that mean you will save me a dance?" I asked.

"Of course."

47

As time went on, Nika grew more and more furious. I was the accommodating and flirtatious Sasha she had hoped I would be—with everyone except her.

Finally, she pulled me aside, utterly ignoring that Masha was well within earshot.

"What are you doing, Sasha?" Nika demanded in a hushed voice.

I raised my eyebrows. "I do not know what you mean, Veronika."

She glared at me. "You have flirted with every woman here. Do not pretend you do not know it."

I shrugged. "You cannot expect love and attraction from an arranged marriage. That is not how business works. You want to be joined to me? Fine. I have agreed to give you my name. But you cannot force me to give you my heart."

She quivered with rage. "I can expect fidelity," she spat.

I raised an eyebrow. "Why would you think that?

Did I ever agree to such a thing? Have I ever given the impression that is who I am? You want to marry me? You may want to think more carefully about your assumptions."

Before she could respond, I turned to Masha, who was wide-eyed at our exchange. I smiled kindly at her. "Come, Mashen'ka, it is our turn. Are you ready?"

She took a deep breath to calm herself and nodded slightly. I tucked her hand into the crook of my arm, then led her toward the master of ceremonies.

After he'd given us the go-ahead, I escorted Masha into the small throne room, all decorated in reds and golds.

"Aleksandr Sergeyevich Volonov and his sister, Maria Sergeyevna Volonova," the man announced.

We walked into the small room where the empress sat on her understated throne of red velvet, the prime minister standing beside her. I bowed low at the waist, and Masha curtsied beside me.

"Aleksandr Sergeyevich," Empress Alexandra said warmly.

I looked up to see her bright blue eyes smiling at me.

"I am glad to see you home," she pronounced. "Will you be taking your father's seat in the upper house of the Duma?"

"I do not yet know, Your Imperial Majesty," I answered. "Much is still in flux after my father's death."

She inclined her head in acknowledgment. "I

was sorry to hear about Sergei Nikolayevich. You have my condolences."

"Thank you, Madam."

She turned her crowned head toward Masha, analyzing her dress and demeanor. Then she smiled graciously at her. "Beautiful," she declared. "Absolutely stunning. I expect to hear many great things about you, Maria Sergeyevna. You have quite a legacy to live up to."

Masha curtsied again. "Yes, Your Imperial Majesty. And may I wish you a joyous and prosperous birthday, Madam."

The empress smiled at Masha again, dipping her head. "Just charming," she said. "Enjoy the festivities."

We thanked the empress, and I led Masha out of the throne room and back the way we'd come.

After we'd returned to the antechamber, Masha sighed with relief.

"You did wonderfully," I praised, patting her hand.

Nika was presented after us, and I graciously waited for her to return, giving Masha time to recover her composure.

As we made our way from the antechamber back toward the staircase, we turned left into the forehall, where a bronze and malachite pavilion shaded a table with glasses of champagne.

I retrieved glasses for Masha and Nika but did not take any for myself. Nika stiffly accepted my offering, and I advised Masha to drink hers slowly.

Finally, we entered the ballroom in the great hall. White columns gleamed as the lights from the crystal chandelier sparkled off them. Musicians played in the gallery as couples twirled around the floor. There were too many people to see through to the other side. But I could see that the dark doors were thrown open and light shone in the concert hall beyond, no doubt providing more space for the attendees.

Masha's eyes twinkled at the spectacle, and my heart warmed to see it. *I am glad I was here for her first ball at the palace.*

Turning seriously to my sister, I bowed my head. "May I have this dance, Maria Sergeyevna?" I asked formally.

She lifted her chin and smiled. "Of course, Aleksandr Sergeyevich," she said, playing along.

After asking the unamused Nika to hold her glass, I led Masha out onto the dance floor for a waltz. As I'd expected, it was not long before we were noticed. I'd been away for quite some time after all, and Masha was young and pretty. I soon handed Masha over to a young man who'd asked to cut in.

As soon as I was off the dance floor, I looked for anyone I might know, anyone who was beautiful and not Nika. The sight of familiar red hair and pale shoulders drew my attention to an old friend. "What is your secret, Nataliya Igorevna? You have not aged a day."

The woman tilted her head at me. "That voice..." she murmured. "Sasha?"

I dipped my head in assent.

She graced me with a broad smile. "I heard you were back, but I did not think I would see you."

"You are as beautiful as last I saw you," I told her.

"And your words are as sweet as they ever were," she countered.

I offered her my hand, and she took it. As I bent to kiss her fingers, I noticed the large ring on her right hand. "Who is the lucky man?" I asked.

"It has been a long time, Sasha. I married Ivan Sidorov almost ten years ago. We have three children already."

I remembered Ivan. He was a boyar and had long been taken with Nataliya. "So soon after our little tryst?" I asked in an amused tone.

She smiled at the memories. "As if you would have stayed," she scolded lightly. Then she laughed. "Oh, but we had fun, did we not?"

I nodded. "We did indeed."

She sighed. "We were wild."

I smirked. "I still am," I assured her. "What do you say, Tasha? Would your husband begrudge me a dance, do you think?"

When I offered her my hand again, she smiled that old eager smile that used to light a fire in me.

"Of course not," she said, taking my hand and following me to the dance floor.

48

As the evening wore on, I managed to dance with Nika only once. Manners wouldn't allow me to snub her completely. But I made sure the interaction was polite and distant, nothing like the laughs and smiles I shared with the other women I danced with.

At some point, Empress Alexandra entered the hall, accompanied by a pale-haired man in foreign military dress. I didn't recognize him. And when the music started again, the empress danced with the man.

"Who is that?" I asked the matron beside me.

"That is the King of Denmark," she murmured back. "Rumor has it that he wants a match with the empress. Apparently, his country does not have a lot of saulht to make minte, and the economy is struggling. I do not know about such things, but that is what my husband tells me."

Another lady beside her joined the conversation. "But she would never marry him," she argued. "I heard the Sultan of the Ottoman Empire wants the empress for his youngest son."

The first woman scowled at her. "A youngest son is not good enough for our empress."

"Perhaps," the other woman said. "But even the youngest son of the Ottoman Empire is rich enough to bring quite a bit to the empress's table. It was their alchemists who discovered how to turn saulht into minte after all."

The first matron nodded. "But what about the Austro-Hungarians?" she asked. "Their prince is very handsome, I hear."

The second woman agreed. "Whoever she chooses, it is past time for the empress to marry. We need a tsarevich or a tsarevna."

Everyone within earshot of the two women nodded their heads. It seemed I'd been too long away from the happenings of the Russian boyars and legislators. Their concerns, their gossip, were almost foreign to my ears. *When had Russia stopped feeling like my home?*

With that melancholy thought swirling in my head, I left the great hall and wandered back into the forehall, turning right into a long hallway. I faced a portrait of Feodor Nikitich Romanov—father of Mikhail I, founder of the Romanov Dynasty. The hallway was dimly lit, not off-limits but not inviting. It was just the place I needed to take a rest.

I'd never tried to make a woman jealous before. I'd never tried to make a woman give up on me. And I found the effort exhausting.

Sighing, I started down the long hall, glancing at the Romanov portraits I passed on either side. Not even halfway to the end, I stopped before a portrait of Catherine the Great in her coronation robes. The first thing I noticed was her scepter and orb, but that was quickly overshadowed by her grey silk gown embroidered with golden, double-headed eagles. The artist had expertly captured how the light would shine off the fabric.

Finally, I looked at the empress's face. She was serious, confident. But her mouth held the slightest hint of a smile. *What was she thinking of when this portrait was painted?* I couldn't help but wonder what that hidden smile signified. *Did she know what the Ubyzniki would become when she established it?*

In the great hall, just on the other side of the wall I was facing, a song came to an end. In the few seconds of silence between the music quieting and the answering applause, I heard a soft click...tick...tick...tick...

My mind didn't have time to process the sound before my body started moving.

...tick...tick...fffpp

I ran farther down the hall and dove into a room. The space was fairly dark. Only the soft light spilling in from the hallway and the stars shining far above the curved glass ceiling illuminated the winter garden. A fountain gently tinkled a merry melody from the center of the space, surrounded on all sides by massive tropical plants.

I hid among the leaves, silently watching the entrance.

Less than a minute later, Dima appeared, his right arm held out before him. I couldn't see the small, mechanical dart gun in his hand, but I knew the sound it had made.

I rolled my eyes. *Never trust high-tech gadgets when your life is on the line. At least I know why Yulya was in such a good mood on the way here.*

As Dima squinted into the poorly lit indoor garden, he cautiously crept into the space. With every silent step, he drew closer and closer to my position.

My heart hammered in my ears. I held my breath. Closer, closer he got, not knowing how near he was.

When he was within my reach, I jumped out of my hiding place. Grabbing his outstretched arm, I used my free hand to punch him on the side of his jaw. He went down without a fight.

I stared down at his sprawling form, shaking my head at my unconscious opponent.

"The things people do for love," I murmured to myself.

With a sigh, I bent over and lifted Dima as best I could, dragging him to the far corner of the garden. There, I hid him behind a particularly thick fern of some kind. Then I unstrapped his little dart gun from his wrist and threw it in the fountain on my way out of the garden.

The marble column near the entrance had a small dent where the deadly dart had bounced off.

Back in the long hallway, I turned left, continuing the way I'd been going. I paid no mind to the portraits of the Romanovs on either side, getting more modern as I traveled farther down. Nearly at the end of the hall, I turned left and took a comparatively ordinary set of stairs down to the first floor. The light green banister the only feature worth remarking on.

As I made my way back to where I'd first entered the palace, I overheard two guards speaking farther down the hall.

"There is a problem upstairs," one guard said to the other.

I quickly ducked behind a nearby column just in case that problem had been caused by me.

"Seems something happened at the servants' dance. They are asking for assistance," he continued.

My heart thumped in my chest.

The second guard sighed as they started to walk. "I knew inviting them would only be trouble for us."

Continuing down the hall, I reached the main vestibule. I looked to my left, down the stairs that would lead me out of the palace. Then I watched the guards turn right farther down.

I clenched my teeth and followed after them.

49

It wasn't difficult to trail after the two guards on the first floor. They weren't looking behind them, and I could be very quiet when I wanted to be.

This part of the palace consisted mostly of long hallways lined with statues and suits of armor. At the very end, we turned left twice and headed up a flight of stairs. On the second floor, I cautiously followed the guards through a series of comparatively subdued rooms.

The distant sounds of music grew louder with every room we passed through. It wasn't the elegant melodies of a full orchestra playing a waltz. It was the earthy tones of the balalaika and the accordion, the tones that reverberated through every Russian's very soul.

In a room adjacent to the gathering, the guards met with one of their compatriots, who was holding a man steady by the arm.

"What is this?" one of the guards asked.

"Had a little too much to drink and caused a stir. Nothing huge, but he was troubling the women."

The first-floor guards nodded. "All right there? Let us take you downstairs and get you sobered up."

The man in question made no comment as the two guards led him away. I hid before they passed me. With his task complete, the guard who remained returned to the party.

The tightness in my chest eased. *Well, I am already here. I might as well take a look.*

Nearing the door to Alexander Hall, I looked in at the servants' dance. It was far livelier and more fun than the party I'd left. Men and women in traditional dress, stomped their feet and practically hopped around the dance floor. The room had been built to commemorate the reign of Alexander I and Russia's victory over Napoleon, a matter of extreme pride even in modern day. The walls and ceiling were a light blue with key scenes from 1812 and the ensuing European campaigns elaborately carved in white.

My eyes found Liza almost immediately, and I smiled to see her in such good spirits. Her cheeks were flushed with exertion as she grinned over at Petya while they danced.

Loud whistles punctuated the instrumental music as the tempo increased until it abruptly halted at its height. The dancers froze, striking their poses to mark the end of the dance.

Laughter and cheers erupted from the crowd, and Liza's grey eyes shined as Petya held her in his arms.

A second later, his lips were pressed to hers, and the room stood still.

The pounding of my own heart drowned out the sounds of the musicians, a hammering assault in a deafening silence.

I did not blink. I did not breathe. I just watched as they slowly pulled away and stared at each other.

Her eyes were clear and bright and said something. What, I did not know. Or rather, I did not want to know. My stomach hardened, and I had trouble swallowing with my jaw clenched as it was.

I turned on my heel and left, traveling back the way I'd come. I was down the stairs and straight out a door into the night before I'd even thought about where to go. The chilly air rushed over my face and neck but didn't cool my agitation. I hadn't retrieved my cloak. I just shoved my hands into my trouser pockets and bent my head against the wind.

The area around the palace was lively, too joyful for my bruised heart to take at the moment. Setting off in any direction that took me away from the sounds of merrymaking, I just started to walk. And eventually the only sound I heard was the gentle shuffle of my footsteps on the pavement.

I was miserable, and I knew it. Jealousy left a bitter taste in my mouth, and I spat onto the ground though it didn't help. I was a fool, but I wasn't an idiot. I knew what it meant. I knew how I felt toward Liza. There was no arguing at this point.

Who in his right mind cares for a woman who tried to kill him, a woman who is only around him so someone else can try again? Am I so starved for affection?

I frowned at the thought.

I helped Petya get close to her. It makes no sense to be jealous now.

But there was no reasoning with the knot in my gut. I was jealous. It wasn't a feeling I'd felt often, but I was self-aware enough to recognize it.

She has no interest in me. She does not want me to see her as a woman. She refuses to call me anything but my proper name. She has never felt anything but irritation and contempt for me.

The image of Liza laughing and smiling just before Petya had kissed her rose to the surface of my mind.

She has never smiled like that because of me. I sighed. *Will my heart ever want someone who will want me back?*

The quiet night was disturbed by the clamor of distant cheers. I looked around me. The electric streetlights of the more prosperous parts of the city had given way to flickering gas-lamps and lanterns.

Farther down the mostly dark street, warm light spilled into a hushed courtyard when someone exited a late-night establishment. The patron eyed me as he passed, no doubt finding my white tie attire out of place. As I nodded my greeting, he readjusted his scarf. His poorly maintained glamour flickered only slightly, revealing the untamed eyes of a Fae.

I let him pass to go on his way but continued toward the door he'd just left. I stopped outside the tavern, peering in through the front window. The inn had no name, just a number and a small seven-pointed star painted in one corner of the window.

A place for magical creatures to gather in the

middle of Saint Petersburg? How did they avoid detection by the Ubyzniki?

Curious, I went inside.

As soon as I entered the tavern, the patrons' sounds of merrymaking quieted, and their eyes fixed on me.

Lowering my gaze, I placed a clenched fist over my heart. "Do not mind me. I am but a traveler," I declared, speaking the phrase that told them I was a friend.

After a tense moment, they went back to what they'd been doing. Some of them even dropped their glamours.

I glanced around the space. It was a tavern, same as many others around the world. There was a sturdy wooden bar with stools lined up against it. There were full benches on both sides of marred tables. There was a roaring fire and plenty of dark corners. Making my way through the crowd, I sat on an empty stool at the bar.

The bartender, a Fae woman whose glamour didn't quite manage to mask her untamed eyes, asked me what I wanted to drink. I told her I would take whatever was on tap, and I drank deep of the dark ale she passed me.

"You must be a long way from home," the man beside me said in English.

I glanced over at him and saw that he eyed my attire. As I met his gaze, he dropped his glamour. He had chestnut hair and the untamed eyes and pointed ears of a Fae.

"Not as far as you are, I imagine," I countered in the same language.

He quirked a small smile. "That's true."

"What brings you here?" I asked conversationally.

He shrugged. "I needed some time alone. This was as good a place as any."

"This city is not safe for people like you," I said, careful to control my tone so it didn't sound like a threat.

"Why is that?" he asked.

"Some humans use their fear as an excuse to get violent."

The bartender, who hadn't hidden the fact she was listening to our conversation, jumped in to reassure her customer. "This is a safehouse," she said. "We have permission to be here. As long as we follow the rules, we will not have any trouble."

"Permission from whom?" I asked.

But before I could get an answer, a man stumbled into the bar, hitting his chest hard on the wood. "Another round, barkeep!" he slurred. "Tonight, we celebrate!"

I could smell the scent of stale alcohol coming off

him. It was clear he'd been celebrating for quite some time.

The bartender shook her head. "You have had enough, Christof."

Christof frowned seriously before grabbing what was left of my ale from the bar and lifting it into the air. "The Queen is dead. Long live the King! Long live King Pika!"

His declaration was met with enthusiastic cheers, and he downed the rest of my drink.

"Oi, that was not yours," the bartender scolded.

I waved my hand to tell her I didn't care. But she sighed and drew me another with a smile of apology.

I turned back to the Fae beside me, raising an eyebrow. "Someone die?" I asked.

His chestnut hair fluttered into his face as he nodded. "We just got word that King Pika killed his mother. With Queen Helena gone, many believe that the human sympathizer persecutions will end. Those who were exiled can finally go home."

I nodded. I'd heard rumors of human sympathizer persecutions from the Fae I'd met in Rome. And that thought led me right to Ember.

"You would not happen to know a half-Fae called Ember. Would you?" I asked.

His untamed eyes flicked to mine, and I caught a look of recognition before he masked his expression. "I have met someone who matches that description," he said noncommittally. "Can you be more specific?"

"Dark hair, pointed ears, human eyes. She is tough, not afraid to pull a knife on you if you step out of line. Lean build but strong. Last I saw her, she was with a blond man called Reilley."

He frowned, and his eyes took on a sort of lost quality as he stared into his drink. He nodded. "Yeah, that's her," he murmured.

My heart squeezed. "You have seen her? Recently?" My voice was a little too urgent. I lowered it. "The last I saw of her, she was in trouble."

The man sucked his teeth, then replied, "As far as I know, she's fine. She and Reilley traveled with us a bit before they left. From what I hear, they're safe in Faerie now. They're staying with her brother, the king, at the moment."

Her brother the king? I put that new information aside for later when I recognized the miserable, all too familiar, look on the man's face.

"You...knew her well?" I asked.

"Not as well as I would've liked." He paused for a moment, then sighed. "Our parents wanted us to marry."

I stifled a cringe at having known Ember far better than her betrothed had though it didn't stop my stomach from hardening.

"How did you know her?" he asked, glancing over at me.

"We..." I cleared my throat. "We worked together for a time."

He smirked bitterly at my hesitation. "She got to you too, didn't she?"

Memories of Ember flashed in my mind. Her smiles, her breathy giggles as we made love in the shower room of the airship. But the way she'd looked at me was nothing compared to the way she'd looked at Reilley.

I smiled, the memories no longer bittersweet. "It was a pleasure to know her," I told him.

I could tell by his answering smile that his memories of her had not yet lost their sting. "That it was," he agreed.

We both enjoyed our drinks for a quiet, companionable moment. Then I turned back toward him and introduced myself. "I am Sasha, by the way," I said, holding out my hand.

"Andrei," he answered, grasping my hand in the human way.

"You know Ember. I do not suppose you also know a Fae woman who goes by Charlie?"

Andrei shook his head. "I don't. Sorry. Was she also in trouble?"

I frowned and nodded, pausing before I asked, "Do you know anything about magic?"

He quirked an eyebrow. "Such as?"

"Do you know if there is any way to get out of an eye of death without the cancellation order?"

His expression darkened. "There is," he said softly. "But the life you'd have left isn't a life worth living."

My heart sank.

After another silent moment, while the rest of the patrons partied around us, Andrei lifted his glass toward mine. "To sorrow," he said. "Because nothing reminds you that you're still alive quite like the depths of despair."

I clinked my glass against his. "To sorrow."

51

I left the tavern not nearly as drunk as I wanted to be. And as I walked out into the early October morning, the dewy breeze blew away any intoxication that remained from the stale air of the establishment.

I'd left my new friend Andrei much worse for wear, tucking him into an inn bed above the tavern. It seemed he also had a wanderlust about him. But from the way he talked about duty and family, I had a feeling he too would return home sooner rather than later though I hoped not under the same dark circumstances that I had.

While I made my way to the nearest canal in search of a taxi, it occurred to me that I never did find out what the bartender had meant when she'd said they had permission to be there. And I didn't know how I could find out. I had a feeling this rare taste of solitary time wasn't likely to recur anytime soon.

I was grateful that the driver of my water taxi

was the quiet sort and didn't feel the need to fill the silence with chatter though my thoughts gave me little peace. I wondered what had happened at the ball after I'd left. *Did Masha enjoy herself? Did Yulya ever find where I stashed Dima? Was my behavior enough to make Nika not want to marry me? How soon will I find out? Did Liza have a good time? Will she and Petya court more officially now?*

The sun was peeking over the horizon just as my water taxi turned from the Neva into the Fontanka. By then, I was tired, and my thoughts had lulled into a dull hum. My eyelids scraped against my eyes, and the chilly morning air no longer kept me alert. I leaned against the steam stack, the hot metal warming my back beneath my coat, waistcoat, and shirt.

As I spotted the Volonov Manor dock—growing ever closer with every passing moment—I noticed a figure moving quickly up and down the planks, pacing in long strides. The nearer we got, the easier it was to make out the features of the dock's sole occupant. The golden dawn light seemed to dye the cornflower blue of her dress violet. Her gaze fixed on me as the taxi approached.

I paid the driver his fare and disembarked, my shoes thumping on the wood of the dock.

Liza's eyes were wide, seemingly analyzing every minute detail of my appearance. I likely didn't look as dapper as when she'd seen me last, and I didn't have the energy to present myself in a more appealing light.

"Where have you been, Aleksandr Sergeyevich?" she demanded though her tone was not quite as sharp as I'd expected. "They found Dmitri Stepanovich, but you were just...gone."

"Were you worried for me, Kisa?" I asked wearily, without my usual playfulness.

I took a step forward, trying to make my way past her, make my way to the soft, warm blankets of my bed. But I wasn't nearly as steady on my feet as I'd thought. I stumbled, knocking into Liza as she reached out to catch me. She looked up at me, resting her fingertips on my chest.

"Do not disappear like that again," she said softly.

As she lifted her hand from my pounding heart, I saw a flash of white in her palm. It was the gardenia I'd tucked into her hair the night before. It was wilted and slightly crushed as if it had been passed from hand to hand, as if warm fingers had caressed its petals for too long.

"Aleksandr, I have something I need to tell you," she murmured.

My heart leapt into my throat. "What?" I whispered, not taking my eyes from hers. I held my breath for her reply.

"You stink. You really should bathe after you spend all night drinking." Her eyes danced as she smirked up at me.

Laughter bubbled up inside my chest, and I couldn't help but chuckle. I shook my head at her. "I have never met anyone quite like you, Kisa."

And in that shared moment, as she smiled gently back at me in the dawn light on the river, it didn't matter that she didn't feel the same way about me as I felt about her. It didn't even matter that my oldest friend had held her in his arms and kissed her only hours before. Because it was a pleasure to know her. Because being around her made my heart warm and my soul light. Being around her was a blessing that I was glad I had lived to experience.

She may not like me. She may even try to kill me again in the very near future. But she does not hate me. As I stared into her dancing grey eyes, catching the light like the grey silk of Catherine the Great's coronation gown, I knew with every fiber of my being that she did not hate me. And that was enough.

52

As Liza and I started back toward the house, all I wanted to do was sleep. In retrospect, I decided it would probably have been better if I'd slept somewhere else instead of commiserating with Andrei all night. But there wasn't anything I could do about that situation at the moment.

"Kisa," I murmured as we made our way up the path through the trees.

She looked over at me to tell me she was listening.

"If you do me this one favor, I will be in your debt."

She tilted her head.

"Find me a safe place to sleep. I am tired. It has been a very long night, and I just want to rest. I think perhaps my bed is not so safe after all."

"You trust me with this task, Aleksandr Sergeyevich?" she asked incredulously.

I gazed into her eyes. "You may call me a fool. But if you tell me I can rest easy, I will believe you."

"You are a fool," she said with a smile. "Follow me."

As we approached the gate, I eyed the gatehouse. But neither Petya nor Tanya emerged.

"Everyone is out looking for you," Liza explained when she noticed the direction of my gaze.

Did I ruin her date with Petya? "Did you have a good time at the dance?" I didn't want the answer, but I couldn't stop myself from asking.

She used the act of unlatching the front gate and then closing it behind us after we'd gone through to delay her answer.

"It was...illuminating."

I frowned at her vague response, but her set expression told me she wasn't going to give me any more than that.

As soon as we were on the inside of the gate, Liza veered from the path. I followed her through the trees, the fallen leaves softly crunching beneath our feet. We passed the house and headed right for the outbuildings on the edge of the grounds. I hadn't spent nearly as much time there in my life compared to the training field. And when I did go to this part of the estate, I was likely going to the stables.

Back on the paved path, Liza led me to a plain, brick building with three large doors. I followed her around the side and through a regular-sized door.

Once inside, she flipped on an overhead light, illuminating two carriages and an empty space for a third.

"The coach house?" I asked, eying the carriage closest to me. It was in bad repair. Its paint was peeling, and one wheel-less axle rested on a large wooden block.

"No one will think to look for you in here," she said.

Glancing around the space, filled with tack and tools, I had to agree with her.

She crossed to the three-wheeled carriage and opened the door, which squeaked on its hinges. "You can sleep in here. It's comfortable enough if you keep your legs bent."

I stuck my head into the carriage. It did have a long leather bench seat I could lay on if I curled onto my side. "Well, I have certainly slept in worse places," I declared, testing my foot on the step to ensure it could handle my weight.

Nodding, I took off my coat and unbuttoned my waistcoat. Then I climbed in, balling my coat up to use as a pillow.

"Would you like me to fetch you a blanket from the stables?" Liza asked.

I smiled. "No, thank you, Kisa. It is stuffy enough in here to keep me warm."

As she began shutting the carriage door, I asked, "Are you not staying? You have also had a long night." I motioned toward the other bench across from me.

She quirked a smile. "Should I not rejoin the search for the missing heir?"

"For once, it was not you who tried to kill me, Kisa. Let the rest of them continue to look. Perhaps they will think of this sleepless night before they try again. You found me. I think you deserve some rest."

She thought for a moment and then climbed into

the enclosed space, taking the opposite seat. With a satisfied smile, I lay onto my side, my back to the bench. Liza did the same, resting her head on her bent arm.

I met her eyes across the small space, the only sound the quiet hush of our soft breathing. As she lay facing me in the dim light, I couldn't help but think her beautiful. The blue skirt of her sarafan bunched at her knees, revealing her pale skin between her boots and the hem of her skirt. The blue ribbon at the end of her dark braid nearly touched the floor as her hair streamed off the bench.

"I thought you were tired," she murmured, her voice a gentle caress in the soft light.

I was tired. My eyes burned with the effort it took to keep them open. But I didn't want to miss this moment. I wanted to remember her just like this.

"Go to sleep, Aleksandr. You are safe here." Her soothing tone lulled me. And eventually, even the artistic charm of the scene before me couldn't keep me awake.

When I awoke hours later, I was greeted by a pair of grey eyes staring at me. My heart jumped, and I blinked rapidly against my headache. Liza didn't move but watched me steadily. I didn't speak right away, taking a deep breath through my nose.

"Do you know what time it is?" I asked, my voice raspy from a dry throat.

"I do not."

Sitting up, I winced against the stiffness in my neck and shoulders. Then I dug into my waistcoat pocket and pulled out my watch.

"It is well past midday," I told her.

Liza sat up as well, the move much more elegant than mine had been.

"I suppose that is time enough," I said. "Back into the viper pit to tell my sister I am alive and well."

I'd expected Liza to defend Yulya. I at least expected her to make a sound of irritation. Instead, she just followed me as I climbed down from the carriage and headed toward the house.

53

I entered the foyer through the front door, and I was greeted with an immediate flurry of activity.

Masha had apparently been very worried; she rushed to embrace me. "I thought you had left without saying goodbye," she said into my chest.

I patted her head in an attempt to soothe her.

It was clear to me that Yulya hadn't bothered to tell our younger sister about her ongoing attempts to end my life. So when she met my eyes from across the foyer, I just said, "Were you worried, sister?"

She curled her lip at me.

"Well, you need not have been. Your faithful Elizaveta found me without err."

When Masha pulled away, she wrinkled her nose up at me. "Brother, I think you had better bathe and change your clothes."

I chuckled. "I agree with you. While I do that, will you ask the kitchen staff to make me something to eat?"

She nodded and flitted away to do as I'd asked.

As soon as Masha was out of earshot, I asked Yulya, "How is your Dima fairing today?"

Yulya trembled with barely contained rage.

"Are you not going to thank me, sister?"

"For what?" she spat.

I tilted my head at her. "Do you care so little for Dima now that you wish him to die? I could have killed him, you know. I hope you remember that the next time."

Yulya let loose a very colorful string of obscenities. A crash from the kitchen answered her.

"Tsk, tsk, sister. You know how that upsets Granddad."

"Zhri govno i zdohni," she snarled before storming from the room.

I turned to Liza. "I think Yulya is upset with me," I told her, my voice tinted with disbelief.

Liza sighed through her nose, rolling her eyes.

I smiled and headed up the stairs to my bathroom to bathe.

The hot water of the bath was heaven on my sore limbs, and the sweet scent of lavender and peppermint from the bath oil, cleared my last bit of headache.

After scrubbing away the previous night, I got out of the bath. Singing as I dried myself with a towel, my voice echoed off the tiles of the steam-filled bathroom.

"Oh, Cossack girl, fierce and brave,
You wield your sabre like a dance.
On the battlefield, none are your match.
Your grey eyes burn like fire coals.

Oh, Cossack girl, tender and true,
Put down your sabre and kiss me.
In my arms, no one is sweeter.
Your grey eyes are deep and pure.

My Cossack girl, fearless and faithful,
Pick up your sabre once more.
And though apart, you are with me,
Forever haunted by your grey eyes."

While I released the last note, I pulled open the door in a rush of cold air. As I strode purposefully into my bedroom, one hand holding the towel at my waist, I slammed into someone who'd been waiting on the other side.

Finding my footing, I steadied my visitor with my arm around her waist.

"What—?" I started, looking down at Liza.

"I am sorry," she said quickly. "I was just about to knock when you suddenly opened the door."

She glanced up at me, her eyes meeting mine. Her lean body was pressed against me—warm and firm—and her hands clung to my bare chest and arms where she'd tried to steady herself. The fabric of her clothes chafed against my naked skin, a thin layer between us. My heart pounded in my chest. And as a blush rose in her cheeks, desire stirred within me. Heat gathered in my loins, and my cock stiffened.

"Why are you here, Kisa?" I asked, my voice hushed and husky.

Her breasts heaved against me—heavy but soft—as she gathered the breath to speak. "I-I—"

Before she could order her words, my bedroom door opened without so much as a warning knock. "You will not keep me waiting..." Nika said, trailing off as she took in the scene.

Her expression hardened and grew cold. "I see you are not yet...finished. Very well. I will wait for you in the ground-floor library."

Without another word, Nika closed the door, leaving Liza and I in a very thick situation.

Looking back at Liza, I saw that her blush had traveled all the way to her ears. I wondered if they would be hot to the touch. *Are her ears ticklish? Or are they sensually sensitive?*

She cleared her throat and squirmed against me, her hands gently pushing on my chest. I immediately released her, being sure my hand still had a firm hold on my towel.

"I came to tell you that Bes was here and that she was getting impatient about waiting."

Her gaze traveled down my still damp body to the towel that covered me. I didn't look down but stared directly at her eyes. I knew what she was looking at. The towel would not have done a good job of hiding the erection I was flourishing, and my cock jumped at the attention she was paying it.

Her eyes flicked to my face for only a moment before she averted her gaze from me entirely. "Get dressed," she said, then cleared her throat when her voice came out broken and thick. "You do not want to keep her waiting."

I smiled as she turned her back to me and made for the door.

I didn't know what that blush had meant; blushes can mean a lot of things. But as I dressed to go see what Nika wanted, my heart was light. It wanted to find out.

54

When I entered the ground-floor library, I found Nika calmly browsing the book-shelves.

"Veronika," I greeted. "What brings you here?"

Nika looked over her shoulder at Liza and me. "Would you mind giving me a moment alone with my zhenikh?" she asked Liza.

Liza glanced at me, and I dipped my head in assent. She would be listening from the foyer anyway, so it didn't really matter. As requested, Liza left the library and closed the door behind her.

"We need to talk, Sasha," Nika started.

I raised an eyebrow at her but didn't answer.

"Based off your behavior at the ball yesterday, it is clear to me that we need to reevaluate the nature of this marriage."

I stilled.

"I am not angry. You can only be who you are after all."

"Get to the point, Veronika."

She faced me directly, her black eyes flat and cold. "I want to make a deal with you. As you said, this marriage is business. I will not ask for your affection. I will not ask for your fidelity though I would like you to try to keep your affairs quiet at least. I do have a reputation to uphold. I am sure you have figured out that all I want from you is your name and position. With you as my husband, I can easily rise to lead the Ubyzniki."

"And what exactly do I get out of this arrangement?" I asked blandly.

She quirked a smile, and it was a truly sinister expression. "Your sister, Yuliya. She is trying to have you killed, yes? I can help you with that. If you do not want her dispatched outright, I can protect you. I can give you a safe place to sleep at the least."

"I seem to be protecting myself just fine so far as I can tell."

"For now."

"And if I refuse?" I asked.

Her answering smile was amused. "I suggest you think hard on this decision, Sashen'ka."

"There is nothing to think about, Veronika."

"I will give you time to reconsider," she said graciously.

"Is this really what you want your life to be like?" I wondered. "A husband who does not love you? A husband who finds solace in another's arms? Have you no self-respect? Is your ambition worth losing face before the Ubyzniki, the boyars, the empire?"

"I have faith you will see the wisdom of this arrangement. So I will not have to worry about saving face."

"Nika," I murmured, my tone soft.

Her forehead crinkled as her eyebrows rose.

"This is not a good arrangement," I urged, trying to get her to see the truth. "We are mismatched. We will only make each other miserable."

She stared at me blankly as if not hearing a word I said.

I shook my head. "If this is the road you would choose, then I will not make it easy for you." I kept my voice low and soft, making my threat that much more menacing.

"The mourning period is over in three weeks, Sashen'ka. Think about what I have said."

Nika left without another word. She didn't even look back at me.

I sighed, despair painfully tightening my chest. *What can I do now? It is obvious my behavior has gotten to her but not enough for her to call off the wedding. Will continuing to chip away at her reputation even work? Is there a better way?*

I clenched my fists as frustration overtook the hopelessness. With an inhuman growl, I swiped my arm across the reading table beside me. The lamp shattered on the floor with a satisfying crash.

I froze as the gentle touch of a slender hand rested on my back. My heart pounded in my ears, but I didn't dare look over my shoulder.

"Do not give up," Liza said, her voice too soft compared to the breaking glass still ringing in my ears.

My anger melted in the warm tone of her words. I closed my eyes, taking strength from her quiet presence, from the faint pressure of her fingertips.

I didn't know what I would do next. And in that moment, it didn't matter. When had my life ever been safe and secure? When had I not been fighting some dangerous enemy or on the run from assassins? Did I ever have any assurance that I would live to be an old man? I'd never had such guarantees, especially compared to those who led ordinary lives.

And as Liza lent me her tender strength, I decided I wouldn't worry. Perhaps Nika would call off our wedding, perhaps she wouldn't. At the very least, I had nearly a year before the glaz smerti took me. I might die well before then from something entirely unrelated.

That didn't mean I wouldn't try to break the curse. I had three weeks before Nika expected me to marry her. And if ruining her reputation in that time didn't work, I could always threaten her straight-on. There really was no reason to go to the mage though he was far less able to defend himself in a real fight.

In the next three weeks, I would become as lethal as I had ever been before. I may have sworn off killing, but I wasn't a saint. I'd killed the pirates without flinching. And Maksim and Nika? They were just as bad. They would call off this wedding, or it would be the last thing they never did.

Turning to face Liza, I took her hand in mine. Then I brought her slender fingers to my lips and brushed a feather-light kiss to them.

She met my eyes.

"Thank you, Kisa," I murmured.

She nodded slightly and gently pulled her hand from mine. "Do you know what you are going to do?" she asked.

I smiled at her. "I am going to fight," I told her.

And as she gazed up at me, I could feel her analyzing my expression, my determination.

"There you are," she said with a smile. "There is the Aleksandr Sergeyevich Volonov I have heard so much about."

55

That evening, at dinner, Yulya told us that she and Adrik would be going away for a few days.

"Where are you going?" Masha asked.

"We heard from one of our scouts. The Mistress of the Mountain has been spotted. We, and a few others, will be taking the Ubyzniki's airship to the Urals to try to capture her."

Masha opened her mouth to respond, but Yulya cut her off.

"You will be sitting out this hunt, Masha," she ordered. "If it was not for Kostya, you could have been seriously injured in the last hunt. I want you to stay behind and train. I do not know where your mind has been lately."

Masha lowered her gaze to her plate.

"You are not even a full member of the Ubyzniki yet. We only allowed you to participate in such a dangerous hunt because it was in Father's honor," she continued to lecture. Then Yulya shook her head seriously. "But not this time, the Malachite Maid does not take kindly to women in her domain. She is a powerful enemy. And you are not ready to face her."

Masha didn't argue. She just nodded her acknowledgment.

"Good," Yulya said. "We leave this evening, and we are not likely to return for a few days. I trust you will keep up with your studies during that time."

Masha nodded again.

I had to admit, I would sleep soundly knowing that the Ubyzniki's best and brightest would be far away for at least a few days. I could be fairly confident that no attempts would be made on my life until they returned.

But as I stared up at the ceiling in my dim bedroom that night, sleep did not come easily to me. I wasn't worried that I wouldn't live to see the morning. My rest was chased by images and memories. I could still see Liza's blue dress, bunched at the knees as she lay across from me in the carriage. I could still feel her clutching my bare skin as she tried not to fall in my bedroom. And her eyes. Her serious, grey eyes that gave nothing away.

My room felt big and empty, my swirling thoughts my only company. I analyzed everything Liza had ever said or done. Was there something hidden in her reactions? I didn't think she hated me, but there was nothing to suggest she was fond of me either. Was she merely indifferent? It was true that she had shown me small kindnesses, but they weren't so great that she wouldn't have done the same for a complete stranger.

I squeezed my eyes closed, willing the thoughts

to let me rest. I sighed a long groan and threw the blankets off me. *Perhaps a glass of milk will help me sleep.* At the very least, going to the kitchen and getting a drink would provide my busy mind with something to do.

I shuffled through the dark house, not particularly careful to muffle the sounds of my movements. I descended the stairs and headed to the kitchen, squinting when I saw that a light was on ahead.

As I entered the kitchen, Liza was sifting flour into a bowl. There were small containers of ingredients spread out onto the counter before her. She concentrated on her task, a line between her eyebrows as she stared down at her work. The white apron she wore over her clothes accentuated her figure as she delicately shook the flour through the sieve.

"Do you do this every night, Kisa?" I asked.

She started, looking up at me with wide eyes. A bit of flour jumped out of the sieve, dusting her freckled cheek.

Aleksandr," she said with a sigh, pursing her lips ever so slightly. "What are you doing down here so late?"

"I could ask you the same."

She gave me an exasperated stare. "You can see for yourself that I am baking."

"But *why* are you baking, Kisa? And at this time of night."

"I like to bake when I cannot sleep. And Petya asked me to tea tomorrow. He mentioned that Mila liked chocolate spartak cake. So I thought I would make one for her even if I cannot come to tea."

My stomach dropped, and I averted my gaze, staring at all the ingredients she'd assembled for her task. "I did not know you could bake," I said, failing to sound as offhanded as I'd wanted.

"Did I not tell you my father was a baker?" she asked.

I nodded slowly. "Why would you not be able to go to tea?"

She raised an eyebrow at me.

"I do not have any plans tomorrow, so you do not need to accompany me anywhere."

"I will go then," she declared, and every word punched me in the gut. "Now, what is your excuse for being down here at this time of night?" she asked.

"I could not sleep. So I thought a glass of milk might help."

She gestured to a bottle of milk on the counter before her. "Take as much as you like. I can go down and get more if I need to."

I didn't reach for the bottle. "You said you are making spartak cake? That must take many steps. Would you like some help?"

She stared at me silently for a moment. "Have you ever baked anything, Aleksandr Sergeyevich?"

I shrugged. "I am not helpless in the kitchen."

Another silent moment passed with Liza's eyes on me. "All right," she said with a nod. "Would you mind putting some minte in the stove? Then you can help me make the cake batter."

I smiled and followed her orders. Unlike the traditional stove at the gatehouse, the stove in the manor's kitchen was the best, and most modern, that money could buy. I approached the fuel pot and opened the grate. Taking a hunk of minte from a nearby bucket, I tossed it into the fire and shut the door. The pipes that carried the heat from the fuel pot to the stove and oven made a quiet cracking sound as they began to reheat.

"What would you like me to do now?" I asked upon returning to Liza.

She glanced over at me. "Did you wash your hands?"

I gave her a guilty smile. "Right."

When I'd done that, she gave me a bowl and a whisk. "Beat the egg and sugar together," she instructed.

Liza hadn't understated her skills. Her hands were graceful and well-practiced. She made baking look effortless. And she didn't scold me for my clumsiness.

After she'd rolled out two layers of cake with the rolling pin and placed them in the oven, she went back to the counter to roll out two more.

"Before you do that," I said, raising my hand to stop her.

She crinkled her brow in confusion.

With a smile, I reached out and brushed my thumb against her cheek. "You have had flour on you face for a while now."

"Oh," she said, staring up at me as I rubbed her face. "Thank you."

"You are welcome," I murmured. After I'd gotten the flour off, I paused, my fingers still on her jaw. I gazed at the shape of her cheeks, her nose. Her lips were pink and parted, and I wondered what she tasted like.

"Is it gone?" she said.

I didn't answer.

"Aleksandr?"

"Yes," I whispered, dropping my hand. "It is gone."

She thanked me again and began to roll out more layers of cake batter.

I watched her skilled fingers go about their practiced movements. There was a bit of chocolate batter on one knuckle of her left hand. I wanted to lick it off. Would she show me that same easy indifference if I did, or would she flash anger at me? My heart thumped, and warmth again pooled in my gut.

"All right," she said after sticking the last of the layers into the oven. "Let's start making the cream."

Again, I followed her directions, and we were soon assembling the cake. As she decorated the cream frosting with leftover cake crumbs, which had been cut away so it was perfectly round, she smiled down at her accomplishment.

"You did good," I praised her. "I am sure Petya and Mila will like it."

"No, Aleksandr," she said. "*We* did good. It has to sit overnight, but I am sure they would not mind if you had a piece. We cannot eat a whole cake between us after all."

I found it difficult to answer her with a smile. "Save me whatever is left over. You made it for them." I paused for a moment, the silence awkward in its uncertainty. "Well, I had better try to go to sleep."

I turned to leave.

"Wait," she called.

I halted and glanced back at her. She went over to the cupboard and pulled down a glass. Then she poured milk into it and held it out to me.

"Thank you," I murmured.

As I took the glass from her, my fingers brushed hers. My heart jumped, and I glanced at her face.

She smiled politely. "You are welcome. Goodnight."

"Goodnight," I echoed softly. Then I left the kitchen.

56

Even after my glass of milk, I slept horribly. But considering I hadn't expected to sleep at all, I took that as an accomplishment. Despite my lack of rest, I trained hard the next morning. I went through the exact same regimen I was doing before I'd left home. And even though I'd been practicing over the last few weeks, my body was not prepared to take that level of abuse yet.

As far as I knew Liza was at Divine Liturgy with the other servants, taking advantage of Yulya's absence. She'd told me she would go to tea at Petya's right after.

But as I lay, stretched out on the cool grass, my limbs screaming at me, I was grateful for the pain. I knew I would have no trouble going to sleep that night.

"What are you doing?" Masha's voice said before her head blocked my view of the clouds.

I didn't answer her. I didn't really have an answer for her.

Before I could muster the strength to rise, Masha lay down in the grass beside me, not seeming to care that she was still wearing her clothes from Divine Liturgy.

We sat in comfortable, companionable silence for some time before I spoke. "Are you upset that Yulya made you stay behind?"

When she didn't answer, I turned my head toward her. She continued to look up at the sky.

"Can I be honest with you, brother?"

"I hope you will."

"I do not want to be a member of the Ubyzniki," she whispered.

My eyes widened, and I raised myself onto one elbow to better look at her face. "Masha...have you told this to anyone? Does Yulya know? Did Father?"

She shook her head. "Do you remember when I was very young? I was so clumsy, and Papa was worried I would hurt myself while training. Do you remember that he hired that ballet instructor to teach me dance?"

I nodded. "He hoped that it would be safer than weapons training, and he was right. You did beautifully, and you improved greatly."

She met my gaze, her blue eyes wide and pleading for me to understand. "I do not want to hunt. I hate killing magical creatures. Even if I know they are bad and they hurt people. I cannot stomach the sound of screams, the sight of blood. I want to dance. I want to be in the ballet. I have worked so hard at it, and my instructors say I could be professional if I continue to."

I reached across my body and took her hand.

"Oh, Masha. I am sorry I have left you for so long. I never thought you would want a life outside of the Ubyzniki."

"You showed me I did not have to follow the path they laid out for me, brother."

I smiled softly down at her. "Listen to me, Mashen'ka. There is always another path. Your destiny is your own. You know that I do not want to inherit the title. I have already tried to hand it over to Yulya. And as soon as I can get out of marrying Nika, I will leave again. If you want, you can come with me. I can take you to Paris. You could enroll in ballet school there."

"Ah, that is why you have been so cold to Nika. You do not want to marry her. Based off our conversation about love and the fact that it happened so quickly, I gathered it was an arranged match. But I did not know you were against it."

I shook my head. "No, I do not want to marry her. I am still trying to forge my own path, one that Father did not lay down for me."

She nodded solemnly, then gave me a sad smile. "Thank you, brother. I feel better for having told you. I do not know what I will do. But I will think carefully about leaving with you."

I squeezed her hand. "Yes, it is a big step. Think carefully." Laying back down beside her, I said, "The boy, have you told him how you feel yet?"

"No," she answered with a sigh. "But I saw him at the palace."

"Did you dance with him?" I asked, trying to remember the few young men I'd seen her dance with before I'd left the party.

"He left before I got the chance to ask him."

"He left?"

"Yes, and he seemed in a great hurry to do so. But I will try again. I will tell him how I feel when the time is right." She paused for a moment. "Are you really not going to marry Nika?"

I shook my head. "Nika and her entire family are the worst kind of people. Though I take no particular pride in being a Volonov, I would not let them sully the name with their depravity. Do not worry, Mashen'ka. You will never have one such as her for a sister-in-law."

Silence answered my declaration.

I smiled over at my sister. "Everything will be all right," I promised her. "Just think of the bright future you have ahead of you."

"I will."

I stretched my back, groaning at the soreness in my muscles. "Now, will you help your brother up? I fear I have overdone my training today."

Masha laughed, a bright, happy sound that I hoped to hear many times again. "You are getting old," she pronounced as she pulled me to my feet.

"Old? Old, you say? Well, I bet I could still beat you back to the house even as old and tired as I am."

Her eyes sparkled. "You dare challenge me? Maria Sergeyevna Volonova?"

"Whoever loses buys the pryaniki," I wagered.

She smirked. "You, my dear brother, will not win."

"We shall see," I countered, lowering myself into a running position.

Without warning, Masha took off toward the house, her laughter following behind her.

"Oi!" I called, waiting a few seconds before jogging after her. "I did not say go!"

57

Supper that evening was almost pleasant with only Liza, Masha, and me. There were no cutting remarks or murderous glares. There was only companionable silence punctuated by moments of polite conversation.

At the end, Liza offered us each a piece of spartak cake. "As I thought, we did not eat it all," she said.

"You had tea with Petya today?" Masha asked as she accepted the cake from Liza.

Liza nodded and offered me a plate as well, which I took.

"You also went to the empress's dance together. Did you not?"

"How did you know, Mistress Maria?"

Masha waved her hand dismissively. "Please, Yulya is not here. You can call me Masha." She smiled mischievously. "I know things," she answered vaguely.

"Y-yes, we also went to the party together."

Masha continued. "The dance a few days ago, tea today. Do you have any plans to spend time with Petya again soon?"

Liza cleared her throat. "He invited me to celebrate Unity Day with him week after next."

The sweet cake turned sour in my mouth.

"And will you go?" Masha pushed.

"I do not know," she answered, glancing at me.

I swallowed with difficulty.

"Well, I think you should," Masha said. "Petya is a nice man, he takes good care of his family, and he has long had eyes for you."

Liza didn't respond but took another bite of her cake.

The following day, I kept watch over my father's coffin so that everyone else could attend Divine Liturgy in honor of the Feast of Saint James the Just. Yulya and Adrik were still hunting in the Urals.

Liza decided to keep watch with me. The silence between us was heavy, or at least I thought so, as I glanced over at her while I twisted the bands of my father's puzzle box. But Liza didn't seem bothered by it.

It was clear to me my attraction to Liza was not just a moment's urge. Never had I felt so jealous over a woman, and especially not toward a friend.

With Liza, the entire situation was different. I only started to flirt with her as a way to tease her, and her reactions amused me. She'd tried to kill me and then was ordered to follow me around. Irritating her seemed like pale retribution in comparison.

But now that those feelings were real, it all felt like a farce, a buffoonish mockery of things too serious to joke about. Perhaps if she'd shown any real interest in those times, I would tell her what I was feeling now. Then again, if she had shown real interest, I would've felt guilty for teasing her to begin with.

As it was, it was clear to me that she was not interested. She had Petya, who was just as kind and honorable as everyone praised him for being. And I was just a licentious fool who had yet again messed up his chances. The truth was I no longer knew how to act around her. So I settled for silence.

The days that followed were quiet, and would have been peaceful with all the Ubyzniki gone had I not been so melancholy. I trained and kept watch and worked on solving my puzzle box. And Liza was ever present, ever watching, her beauty ever plucking the strings of my heart.

On the Feast of Saint Demetrius of Thessolaniki, five days after the Ubyzniki had left, they returned.

Judging by Yulya's expression as she entered the house, I was positive they had not been successful.

"Did the Mistress of the Mountain give you a hard time, sister?" I asked.

"Are you still alive and talking?" she snapped, ascending the stairs without another word.

"You should not provoke your sister like that," Adrik warned, his face weary from the failed hunt.

I stared at him blandly. "Perhaps you should provoke her a little now and then, Adrik. Maybe then she would not be in such a sour mood all the time."

Adrik's face flushed at the clear insult to his manhood. But, as expected, he said nothing and followed Yulya upstairs.

"I do not know why they went after the Malachite Maid anyway," Masha commented as we watched Adrik disappear. "She has never been caught, all these hundreds of years."

"Do you know why the Volonovs have such prestige even among the Ubyzniki?" I asked my younger sister.

"Well, we have the best record, and the most illustrious hunters are Volonovs, like you, brother."

I winced. "Right, and it was capturing the zharptitsa that gave us that place. If Yulya could have successfully led a hunt that captured the Mistress of the Mountain—"

"Then she would have no trouble claiming the title," Masha finished with a nod. Then she frowned. "Still, it was a great risk. By all accounts she can be quite malicious. Yulya could have been seriously injured, even killed."

"You know what they say about risk and reward," I countered.

And though I understood Yulya's bad mood, I couldn't stomach her when she was in a temper. The following day, already tired of the noise battle she was waging with the domovoi, I went out to buy the pryaniki I owed Masha for standing her up and winning our race.

The late October day was unseasonably warm though not so warm that I forgot my jacket. As always, Liza accompanied me on my errand. She was particularly interested in the variety of breads the bakery I stopped in offered. And I didn't rush her, my heart warming uncomfortably to see her eyes so keen with interest.

Once outside the bakery, she grabbed my arm to get my attention. "All right," she said as if she'd been holding the words in for a long time. "What has gotten into you lately?"

My mouth went dry. "I do not know what you mean," I managed to say.

She squinted at me. "There is something off about you, Aleksandr Sergeyevich. You have been too quiet. You have not been teasing me as you usually do; you have not called me Kisa in days. What is going on?"

I smirked, but I knew it was only half-hearted. "You have been telling me to stop doing those things since we met. Now, you complain because I finally listened to you?"

She frowned and sighed. "No, that is not it. I just do not understand this change in behavior. It is my job to watch you, and a change like this could mean something. Are you planning something, Aleksandr Sergeyevich? Are you giving up on resisting Bes? Are you planning to run away?"

I curled my lip and sighed through my nose, starting across the busy street. Anger pumped in my veins. Why? I didn't know, and I didn't care. I strode with purpose to the other side not looking back at Liza, needing to put some distance between us.

And therefore, I didn't see the carriage coming. I didn't hear the sounds of wheels and hooves, of shouts and screams. I just felt an impact as I was thrown to the ground.

58

My heart pounded in my head, and my hands stung, scraped where I'd caught myself on the cold pavement. I clenched my jaw against the pain in my knee as I looked around.

The pryaniki I'd bought for Masha littered the sidewalk. Crumbled and crushed, their white glaze smeared on the grey bricks.

The carriage that had nearly run me down was nowhere in sight. Bystanders approached, asking if I was all right. I nodded, holding up a slightly bloodied hand in reassurance.

And then I saw her.

A chill ran through me, and I couldn't breathe. Liza lay on the ground nearby, her back to me. I rushed toward her, my limbs awkward as my head spun.

"Elizaveta," I called with a shaking voice before I'd even reached her.

She didn't answer.

The woman who had bent to check on her prudently moved out of my way.

Another few heartbeats and I was kneeling beside her. My hands trembled as I reached out to touch her arm.

"Liza?" My tone was thick and broke in the middle.

She hissed and rolled onto her back, her grey eyes finding mine. "That is going to bruise," she complained, holding her shoulder.

I let out a shaking breath. My eyes started to burn, but I managed to hold back my tears. "You... Are you all right?"

She smirked up at me, still lying on the ground. "I told you I knew how to fall."

I chuckled unsteadily.

Sitting up, Liza analyzed me. "Are you hurt?" she asked.

I waved a hand at her. "I am fine."

"You are bleeding," she said, grabbing my hand and examining it. Her fingers were cool, but they sent warmth through me. "It does not look bad."

"The carriage is gone," I told her, frowning as she let go of my hand.

"It does not matter," she said. "I saw who was driving."

"It was not an accident then?"

She shook her head.

"Dima?"

She nodded.

"Then why..." I crinkled my eyebrows. "Why did you push me out of the way?"

We both knew that Yulya was trying to kill me.

Liza was only following me to keep Yulya informed of my movements. It was, therefore, presumable that she had told Yulya where I was going, and that is why such an attempt was made.

Liza froze, then cast her eyes about her as if looking for something. "I do not know. I did it without thinking."

I forced my gaze on her, staring at her eyes until she met mine. "Thank you, Kisa."

"Do not get used to it," she advised, but she quirked a small smile.

"Yulya will be angry with you," I told her. "Are you certain you would not like to run away now?"

She shook her head and rose to her feet. I followed suit, glad my knee was not nearly as sore as it had been immediately after impact.

"We had better get home," she suggested.

"I do not know how wise it is to return immediately to people who keep trying to kill me." I frowned down at the ruined pryaniki. I would have to buy more when I wouldn't smear blood around the bakery.

"Where else will you go, Aleksandr Sergeyevich?" she asked. "Will you take Bes up on her offer and stay with the Ivashkins?"

I scowled at her. "I thought you knew me better than that by now."

"Did you?"

I frowned. "I was thinking a hotel would be better," I clarified without answering her question.

"Do you really think so? You would not be as familiar with a hotel, and there are many ways to get in and out, not to mention what can be bought through bribery. And, if you went to a hotel, it would be more difficult for you to train and keep watch at the chapel. Also, how are you going to explain that to Mistress Maria?"

"Did you save me from that carriage only to deliver a more gruesome death to me at home?"

She smirked. "Are you no longer confident in your own abilities, Aleksandr Sergeyevich?"

I sighed, waving my hand in front of me to tell her to lead the way. But, as always, she followed behind.

All the way back to the manor, the absolute dread I'd felt when I'd thought Liza had been killed replayed in my mind. I'd told myself my feelings for her were merely persistent attraction. But I now knew that was not the case. *When had everything gotten so twisted? And what am I going to do about it?*

I didn't have an answer.

Yulya was livid when we returned to the manor, and she immediately demanded that Liza follow her into Father's study. I didn't attempt to listen in this time. I sat in the secondary library and worked on my puzzle box. Concentrating on the little bands gave my jumbled mind a rest.

This layer of the matryoshka was a rosy cheeked girl with big blue eyes and golden hair. It clicked open to reveal yet another layer as Liza walked into the secondary library.

She flopped into an armchair not far from mine.

"Yulya gave you an earful?"

She pursed her lips but didn't answer.

"Are you homeless now?"

She shook her head.

"You must be quite persuasive. She did not punish you?"

Liza glanced over at me. "She took me off surveillance. So you got exactly what you wanted, Aleksandr Sergeyevich."

Not exactly. "What will you do now?"

She huffed. "Mistress Yuliya was gracious enough to let me choose in what capacity I would serve the household though she strongly suggested the stables."

I raised an eyebrow at her. "That was nearly sarcasm. Are you certain you are the same stalwart Elizaveta you were before?"

She frowned, squinting her frustration at me. "My loyalty to the Volonovs will never be in question."

I held up my hands in defeat. "So what will you do?"

Liza heaved a deep sigh. "I do not know. I will likely ask around and help whoever needs it at any given moment."

"I suppose this means we will be seeing a lot less of each other," I said carefully.

"Yes, I suppose it does," she agreed seriously. "Well...I guess I should go and move my things back to the servants' quarters."

I nodded slowly. "Yes, I guess you should," I murmured.

59

The next few days were strange and lonely. I never thought I would miss Liza's constant spying. I felt as though I was more alert to potential danger, which was weird considering I didn't have an assassin at my back every moment of the day. But I wasn't overly worried about it. Yulya and Dima had failed thus far. And if I paid attention, they would continue to fail.

I spent most of my time training. It was only a couple of weeks before I would have to confront Nika and Maksim one way or the other, and I wanted to be ready for any potentiality. I was making fast progress, and it didn't take my body long to remember what it had been taught my entire youth.

But training did nothing for my heart. It kept my mind busy for a moment, but as soon as I put down my weapon, as soon as I stopped moving, my chest would tighten and begin to ache.

It wasn't as if I didn't see Liza in that time. I did.

I made sure I did. But she was always busy, and it was always in passing.

One evening, right before I went to keep watch in the chapel, Masha stopped me in the foyer. "Yulya wanted me to remind you that tomorrow is Unity Day. All of the servants will be off, so we will have to fend for ourselves. But the kitchen staff is making some things ahead of time so we will not go hungry."

I managed not to roll my eyes. Yulya hadn't been speaking directly to me since Dima had failed to kill me again. "All right."

"What are your plans for tomorrow, brother? Will you be going to a concert or street fair?"

"I do not know. Perhaps I will invite Nika to a concert."

"Will you invite her only to embarrass her again?"

I shrugged.

Masha shook her head. "I do not think she will accept your invitation then. Nika is smart. She knows what game you are playing. You need to try something else if you want her to give up on you."

I frowned. "Any suggestions?"

She pursed her lips. "I will think on it."

"And what about you? Do you have plans tomorrow?"

Masha gave me her best mischievous smile. "Perhaps."

I chuckled. "Well, good luck with whatever that is."

"Thank you."

When I awoke the next day, I didn't feel like training. Though the November sun was shining, dancing on the autumn leaves, the colors just reminded me that the leaves were dying.

I dressed and went down to the kitchen to get breakfast, grateful that everyone had already gone for the day. The kitchen staff had left bread and cheese, fruit and hard-boiled eggs for us to eat. I settled for a slice of buttered bread, a piece of cheese, and an apple, not even bothering to put any of it on a plate.

All across the empire, Russians would be celebrating—waving their flags, dancing, singing—to commemorate when all classes banded together to oust Polish-Lithuanian forces from Moscow in 1612. In modern times, it was a day to celebrate the mixed heritage of the Russian Empire, to concentrate on what unites us rather than what divides us. And I didn't feel up to participating in any of it.

That morning, as everyone else set out to enjoy the holiday, I wallowed in this low point of my life. My father was trying to force his expectations on me even from beyond the grave. I had a curse on my head, and the only way I could see to dispel it was to do something I'd sworn to myself I wouldn't do. My heart's deeper feelings had finally been reawakened, and the woman in question had been either averse to me or indifferent altogether, not to mention she was courting my oldest friend.

I didn't feel like I had anything to celebrate. And as I stood in the deserted kitchen, I made a decision. I would leave. There was no reason for me to stay. If I was going to die, then I would die with my honor intact. I wouldn't let Nika and Maksim turn me back into a murderer. I would leave a note for Masha to meet me in Paris. I could at least help her follow her dreams before the glaz smerti took me.

Determined, I strode through the house, coming to a halt when I saw Liza in the foyer. She wore a long skirt and a jacket with a kerchief covering her hair. She glanced over at me as I entered the hall.

"Good morning, Aleksandr."

"Are you going to meet Petya?" I asked, the words spilling out of me so fast that I nearly stumbled over them.

"Yes," she said.

My heart leapt into my throat. "No," I murmured.

She tilted her head.

"Do not go to him," I said more clearly. "I have no right to stop you. I know. But please, do not go."

Liza stared at me seriously for a long moment. "I know you think this is entertaining, but I do not find it funny."

I winced. "I am being serious."

"You are being foolish," she countered.

"Fine." I nodded, moving toward her as I continued. "I am being foolish. It is true."

I took her hand gently in mine.

"Elizaveta," I said. "Liza," I murmured. "Put me out of my misery." I stared into her grey eyes, pleading for her understanding. "I cannot tell you when it started. But, at some point, I found myself drawn to you. I know you will say that you will not be another conquest to me. I do not want that either. I am suffering. My heart aches when I do not see you. And I cannot stomach the thought that you would be in another man's arms." I paused, closing my eyes for a moment before meeting her steady gaze again. "Petya is a better man than I," I admitted.

"Petya and I are just friends."

I froze, taking a shaky breath. "But the dance..."

"At the dance, Petya kissed me. And I realized that I did not feel that way toward him. He *is* a good man and agreed to be just friends with me."

My heart hammered in my ears, and I had trouble swallowing my hope. "You are not just another woman to me," I whispered.

"I thought all women were unique to you," she argued.

I nodded. "I have been very foolish," I said again. "I have looked for love in the worst way, and I know why I have not found it."

"And why is that?"

"Because I was too scared to ask them to stay. I was too scared to make myself vulnerable in that way."

"And you are not scared now?"

"I am more afraid of not saying anything. Liza, please. What can I do to show you that I love you?"

She gave me a soft smile. "I sort of like it when you call me Kisa," she said.

60

I scarcely breathed as her bright eyes gazed up at me, my heartbeat loud in my ears. "Kisa," I whispered, turning her hand over and pressing my trembling lips to her palm.

Her answering smile was warm, the type of smile that I never dared believe she would show to me, she would direct at me.

"I have to be honest, Aleksandr Sergeyevich," she murmured. "I...I have kept so many things to myself for so long. I do not know how to act right now."

My heart swelled so much that I thought it would burst. "Do not worry about that, Kisa. I can lead."

She nodded slightly, blushing when I slipped my arm around her waist. And as I leaned down toward her, her breath caressing my face, her eyelashes fluttered closed.

Her lips were soft and supple when I kissed her, and I had never felt anything so warm, so real.

"Aleksandr," she breathed before I again covered her mouth with mine.

"Sasha," I murmured, meeting her eyes. My nerves stood on end, every fiber of my being needing to hear her say it.

She smiled softly. "Sasha," she repeated, and the sound sent a shiver through me as though every one of those threads had been plucked.

When I lowered my lips to hers again, I slipped my tongue ever so slightly into her mouth. Her answering hum traveled through me like ripples on a still lake.

I pulled back only a little, seizing control of the need rising within me. "Tell me to stop whenever you want," I told her.

She nodded, but I saw the hesitation on her face.

"Open yourself up to me, Kisa. You can show me how you feel."

"I...I do not want you to stop, Sasha."

"Then follow me," I urged, my whisper thick and graveled.

I crushed her to me, trailing my fingers up her back and into her hair as I declared my thus far restrained passions with a kiss. Her hands urged me closer, clutching at my shirt, encouraging me, imploring me. My cock stiffened.

I shifted our position, pressing her back into the door, pressing her harder against me. Her breath rushed out of her, and she breathed deep through her nose as she pulled me even closer.

My head swirled, intoxicated, and I felt dizzy as if the solid wood were moving.

I froze, holding my breath. But it happened again, a gentle nudge from outside.

"Someone is trying to get in," I told Liza, taking in her expression.

Her kerchief had slipped from her hair. Her cheeks were flushed and her eyes bright. Her breathing was heavy and uneven. She wouldn't be able to hide the fact that she had just been kissing me. And even if she could, I didn't want anyone to see her like that.

I released her and motioned for her to stand to one side. She nodded, and I opened the front door slightly.

Petya was just turning to head around the side of the house to another entrance. "Oh, Sasha." He paused, crinkling his brow as he looked at me. But if my appearance was disheveled, he didn't say anything about it. "Have you seen Liza? We were supposed to meet today."

I glanced over at Liza, who stood behind the door out of Petya's sight. She shook her head.

"I was told that Liza is not feeling up to going out today," I said.

"She is unwell? Perhaps I should stay and look after her. All the staff is off, so there will be no one to help her."

"That is not necessary, Petya. I have no plans today. I will make sure she is well taken care of."

Petya nodded, then smiled. "All right. Well, thank you for letting me know. I must go meet Tanya and Mila before Mila gets any more impatient."

I waved a hand at him. "Have a good time."

Closing the door, I turned back to Liza.

She moved toward me, her long skirt swishing with her hips. And when she reached me, she slipped her arms around the back of my neck.

I frowned when I saw how hesitant the action was. "Do you love me, Kisa?" I asked seriously, my heart squeezing in anticipation of her answer.

She stared up at me just as serious. "Come with me," she said. Then she slid her hand into mine and led me through the family rooms to the servants' quarters.

I had to remind myself to breath with every step she didn't respond.

Her room was small and clean with little decoration. She had a single bed, a dresser, and a tiny writing desk. At the threshold, she released my hand and crossed to her dresser.

After opening the top drawer, she pulled out a simple wooden picture frame. She held it out to me, and I entered her private space to take it from her.

As I stared down at the photograph, my breath hitched. It was a picture of me. And judging from my age, it had to be taken just before I'd left home. I couldn't remember the exact occasion, but I was dressed very nicely in white tie attire.

I glanced back at Liza, who was watching me.

"When we first met, you asked me if I had heard of you. I told you I had. But that is not the entire picture," she explained. "You can imagine that you left quite the reputation behind you. And when I came here, all I heard about was Aleksandr Sergeyevich. He was so talented. He was so handsome. He was a legend. I admired you... I idolized you. When I cried out in my sleep from nightmares, I would look at that photograph and take solace knowing that there were people like you out there in the world. People who would protect the innocent. And when I began to train, I would look at it and take strength."

She frowned, taking the photograph from me and putting it back as she continued. "I did not believe the things Mistress Yuliya said about you. Until...until I met you."

I scowled at myself. "Until you met me, and I was just as licentious as she had told you I would be," I provided bitterly.

Liza took my hand in hers, her eyes demanding that I look back at her.

"I also saw your heart, your conviction, your free spirit. And even though I knew you were not serious when you flirted with me, I was moved. I was tempted."

I reached up and brushed the pad of my thumb along Liza's cheek. "Why did you not tell me?"

"I thought you were only teasing me. And besides, it was too late. I was in a pattern of behavior. And then you kept pushing me toward Petya. And...I did not want to admit to it. If I admitted it, then I would have to face how much it hurt that you were not serious."

My chest ached. "Kisa, I am sorry," I murmured, pressing a kiss to her fingers. "Did I tell you how much of a fool I am?"

She gave me a soft smile. "Without those misunderstandings, we may never have gotten to this place."

Pulling her hand from mine, she placed her palm on my cheek. "I love you, Sasha," she whispered.

"For all your faults, for as much as you irritate me, for when you make me laugh, for when my heart has hurt because of you, for your honor, for your conviction, for your kindness. I could not help but love you."

I closed my eyes, swallowing the emotions that rose in my throat. "Kisa," I whispered. Then I met her earnest grey eyes again. "Will you be my wife?"

61

"Sasha," she said seriously. "You do not have to prove yourself to me in this way. If you say you love me, I believe you."

I took her hand from my cheek, gently squeezing it in mine. "I do not want to waste any more time. Even without the glaz smerti, I could die at any time. We both could. Nothing is guaranteed. I love you, and I want to spend the rest of whatever life I have left with you. We can leave this place. We can live freely."

My hands trembled as I held my breath, awaiting her answer.

She wore that same closed expression, and I could not see what she was thinking. She paused so long that my stomach clenched.

"But let us break the glaz smerti before we leave," she said finally. "I do not want my husband to die so soon after our wedding."

Adrenaline shot through me as my heart drummed in my chest. "You will?" I whispered.

Liza smiled. "Yes, Sasha. I will marry you. My loyalty is solely with you."

An incredulous laugh escaped my lips, and I wrapped my arms around her, crushing her to me.

"Today," I told her, grabbing her hands. "Right now."

She laughed, a joyous sound that warmed my very soul. "It is a holiday today. Who will marry us? We do not even have witnesses."

"Priests do not take holidays," I argued. "Surely there is one in this city who will marry us today."

"And the witnesses?"

I frowned.

"And today is Saturday," she pointed out. "Would it not be better tomorrow?"

I took a deep breath. "You are right, Kisa. Today we can find a priest and witnesses. We can marry tomorrow."

But as I started for the door, she stiffened her hands in mine. I raised my eyebrows and looked back at her.

The look in her eyes heated my blood in an instant.

"We have time enough for that later this afternoon," she murmured, a comely blush blooming behind her freckles. "We have the entire house to ourselves after all…"

My balls tightened, and my cock swelled.

She swallowed, then wet her lips. "Will you… make me yours, Sasha?"

I shuddered with fever. "Only if you make me yours, Kisa."

As I wrapped my arms around her waist, she

pulled me down into a kiss. Her fingers sliding through my hair sent tingles to my very bones.

I teased her tongue with mine, and she moaned against my lips. My head spun at the gentle vibration, at the erotic sounds Liza made, at the sounds I elicited from her. And when I pressed fervid kisses down her neck, she panted, "I have imagined this day."

I brought my lips to her ear. "It will be all that and more," I promised.

She shivered against me. And when I sucked gently on her earlobe, she squirmed, groaning through closed lips. I smiled to myself. *I will enjoy discovering her.*

And discover her I did. By the time her knees wobbled and she leaned heavily against me, I already knew how sensitive her ears were and that she enjoyed a bit of teeth.

When I slowly lay her down on her small bed, she pulled at my shirt with feeble tugs. Her eyes devoured me as I gratified her wishes and removed it, and my cock jumped at the knowledge that the sight of me pleased her.

She trailed her slender fingers down my chest and abdomen. And even that little enticement had me biting back a moan. Her gaze traveled down to my trousers.

"Are you hard for me, Sasha?" she asked.

I huffed a laugh at her ridiculous question. I lowered myself on top of her, pressing my fully erect cock into her thigh. Her eyes widened, and she smiled.

"Does that answer your question, Kisa?"

Lifting one hand to my face, she pulled my mouth down to hers while she slipped her other hand between us. I nearly choked on my moan as her fingers wrapped around my shaft. I broke our kiss and blew out a steadying breath.

"You are already wet," she whispered. "So am I."

"Are you trying to kill me?" I teased.

"Never."

I slid through her fingers as I pulled my erection from her grasp. Kissing her deeply, the buttons of her jacket and shirt popped easily through their button-holes while I undressed her. The laces of her short stays made the softest shuff against their eyelets as I untied them, hardly perceptible over the sounds of our heavy breathing.

I gazed down at her, her breasts and stomach laid bare before me. And I frowned at the dark bruise on her shoulder, just starting to yellow.

I reached out, my fingertips trembling over the wound, too nervous to touch it. "Does it hurt?" I asked, my hushed whisper cracked and uneven.

Liza sat up to meet me, guiding my eyes back to hers with a hand on my chin. Her grey eyes captured mine, compelling me to take her words as the utmost truth. "This pain is nothing compared to what I would have felt had I lost you."

My heart swelled, and she drowned whatever sorrow I felt with insistent kisses and provoking caresses. It didn't take long before I again wanted nothing more than to make this woman—this woman who would risk her life for me—mine.

Her skin was smooth and soft beneath my finger-tips as I stroked her. And my every touch, every brush of my skin against hers, told me just how much she enjoyed it, how much she wanted me.

When I closed my mouth around her pink nipple, she arched her back, hissing as her fingers in my hair urged me closer. She writhed against me, every movement, every vocalization made my cock throb in anticipation.

I trailed ever-so-slow kisses down her torso, her skin warm and trembling beneath my lips. And when I got to the waist of her skirt, I knelt on the floor before her. I gently removed her shoes and kissed her ankles. Every bit of skin I exposed by slowly pushing up her long skirt was greeted with kisses, hot breaths, and soft licks. And her gasps and stifled moans told me she enjoyed every moment of it.

By the time her skirt was bunched at her waist, I saw that she had not lied to me; the fabric of her underwear was slightly darker with slick heat.

As I slid the fabric down her legs, I met her eyes. They were glazed and feverish, urging me on as she watched me.

Trailing my hands along the supple thickness of her outer thighs, I dipped my head between her legs. She shuddered, she twitched, she cried out as I licked her thick and slow. And it wasn't more than a minute before she breathed, "Sasha, please. I want you inside me."

My heart raced, and I met her pleading grey eyes. "Do you have a condom, Kisa?" I asked, her nectar still on my lips.

"Tomorrow, I will be your wife," she answered.

I stared at her seriously. "Are you sure?"

Sitting up, she reached for my trousers, never taking her eyes off mine as she unbuttoned them. The cool air of the room did nothing to reduce my erection once it was released.

My heart pounded as she led me down to her, one hand on my hip and one wrapped around my manhood.

At the very brink of her core, her legs wide to accommodate my hips, she lifted her head and kissed me. But as I slid slowly into her slick warmth, she tensed beneath me.

I froze.

Then she relaxed, and I pushed in the rest of the way. And as I pulled back then slowly slid back in, her eyes showed no hesitation.

"I love you," she breathed.

My heart ached as if it would weep. "I love you, too."

And as we rocked together, and as she cried out my name and I cried out hers, the grey skies of her eyes seemed the sunniest, most beautiful sunrise I'd ever seen.

62

Later that afternoon, after Liza and I had bathed and dressed, we walked hand-in-hand back through the servants' quarters toward the kitchen. But once I opened the outside door, Liza let go of my hand. I looked over at her, my question clear in my face.

"Until the glaz smerti is lifted or until we leave, I think it is better if we are not too open about our relationship," she said, not looking at all happy about it.

I knew she was right. The chance of Maksim lifting the curse when he found out I was with Liza would be slim to none. But that didn't stop my heart from sinking as she spoke. Still, I nodded. It was just something we would have to endure for now. At least she walked beside me rather than following behind as we made our way to the stables.

The grooms were nowhere in sight. I assumed after they had cared for the horses, they went about their holiday.

I watched Liza approach one of the horse's stalls,

her backside beautifully accentuated by the tightness of her riding trousers. "Do you ride often?" I asked her as the horse stuck his head out to greet her.

She smiled at the beast. "Not as much as I would like to."

"Then you will be glad that our destination is nearly an hour away."

"So far?" she asked, looking over her shoulder at me.

"As you said, Kisa, we cannot risk those we cannot trust finding out about our marriage until the appropriate time. I know a little church where they may be able to help us."

She nodded, and we went about saddling the horses for our ride.

Once we were out of the crowded streets of Saint Petersburg, the ride was enjoyable. The wooded path was bright with fall color, and the horses were happy to be able to gallop and trot at a free pace.

It was late afternoon by the time we reached the little church and tethered our horses to a nearby tree. The church was nothing so grand as the cathedrals of Saint Petersburg. It was a simple, unpainted wood without even a bell though it did have a very small dome.

Tucked into the trees, far away from anyone we knew, I slipped my fingers through Liza's and lifted her hand to my lips. Then I led her into the church.

The warm wooden walls of the space were not entirely covered with icons as some of the more elaborate churches. There was but a small table before the iconostasis, covered with a white tablecloth.

However, there were golden candlestick holders stationed at intervals around the room.

"How do you know this place?" Liza asked as I led her over to a group of mostly unlit prayer candles.

I took one of the thin, beeswax candles and lit it. Then I placed it back in its holder.

"My mother," I told her. "She grew up around here. She once told me that she came here after every hunt."

"Valeriya Nazarevna Lyubeznova," a deep voice said from behind us.

I turned around and faced the aged priest in his black cassock, who'd spoken my mother's name. His beard was grey but full, and his dark eyes held the light of joyful sorrow.

"You have grown well, Aleksandr Sergeyevich," the priest said. "Your mother would be glad to see how strong you are."

I had only vague memories of the priest. I dipped my head in greeting. "Father," I said respectfully.

"But what brings you all the way out here?" he asked. "Not that I mind the company. So few come to our little church these days."

"Father, I am to be married," I explained. "And I was hoping you would marry us here."

The priest turned his attention toward Liza, whose head was bent beneath her kerchief.

"This is your nevesta?" he asked.

"Yes, Father."

After gazing at her for a short while, he nodded his approval.

"Certainly. I would be loath to refuse to marry

the son of our Valeriya. When will the ceremony be?"

"Tomorrow. We want only a small wedding."

His eyes widened and flicked to my face. Then he chuckled. "With such a beautiful nevesta, I understand that you are in quite the hurry. Very well. Tomorrow after Divine Liturgy. Bring your witnesses, and I will marry you."

I bowed my head to the man. "Thank you, Father."

"Now go," he said, making a shooing gesture with his hand. "You no doubt have much to prepare before the ceremony."

We thanked him again and said we would see him the following day.

The ride home was invigorating. Even the rush of the cold wind on my face could not deter my smile. My heart was light with hope in a way it hadn't been for a very long time. And as I looked over at Liza while we rode back toward the city, her smiles made me thank whatever God existed that I'd lived to see this day.

"Who will we bring as witnesses?" Liza asked after we finished wiping down our horses back in the manor stables.

"Do you have anyone you want to be there?"

"Not particularly."

"All right. Then I have just the two. Leave it to me."

She smirked up at me. "When did you become so reliable?"

I scowled at her. "That hurts me, Kisa."

"You will get over it." Her grin widened.

I wrapped my arm around her waist and pulled her to me, the length of her body yielding and warm against mine. "How did you ever manage to keep any of your smart remarks to yourself?"

She looked around, making sure no one could see us, and snaked her arms behind my neck. "With much effort, and I still was not terribly good at it," she said before she stood on her toes and kissed me.

My body responded to her, and I let out a long sigh as she pulled away. "You will be the death of me," I told her.

"Do you remember what I told you? I said you would beg me for mercy."

"You are a woman of your word." I chuckled.

She frowned, breaking our little moment. "When I think it is the right thing to do."

63

Just as I tilted my head at her change of mood, a stable lad entered.

"Oh, Master Aleksandr. I mean, Master Volonov. Can I help you, sir?" the boy, who was around Masha's age, asked.

"What is your name?" I asked him, marking that Liza was putting more distance between us.

"Kirill, sir, but everyone just calls me Kirya."

I nodded. "Thank you, Kirya. We took these two for a ride." I gestured at the stalls where the horses we'd ridden were now resting. "We have already wiped them down."

Kirya dipped his head. "Yes, sir. I will take care of the rest."

Just as I moved to leave, I paused. "Did you enjoy your day off, Kirya?"

The boy's eyes flicked to my face, and a slight blush rose to his cheeks. "Yes, sir. Thank you, sir."

I smiled at him. "Good."

The small distance Liza kept between us as we

walked to the house was the same as it had always been. She was not two steps away from me. If we both reached out our arms, our fingers would touch. But it didn't feel that way. It felt like an uncrossable chasm.

"Tomorrow, are you going to Divine Liturgy?" I asked as we walked.

She nodded.

"When you return, take a walk to the Summer Gardens, where your friend was selling walnuts before. I will pick you up there."

Her eyes clung to me, and I knew she didn't want to leave my side just as much as I didn't want to leave hers. It made my heart ache all the more.

"Until tomorrow," she promised.

"Tomorrow," I vowed.

We went our separate ways, her to the kitchen door and I around to the front. The house was a flurry of activity as servants returned from their holiday, laughing and telling stories of what they'd done with their day off.

I found Grigori in his office, and I knocked on the opened door to announce my presence.

"Master Aleksandr," he greeted with a nod. "How was your holiday?"

"Perfect. And yours?"

"Very nice," he answered.

"Grigori, tomorrow after Diving Liturgy, I need you to drive me somewhere."

He dipped his head in acknowledgment.

"Expect to be gone for a few hours," I advised.

"Yes, sir," he said, not asking for any more details.

I left him to enjoy the rest of his day and went in search of my sister.

I found Masha in her bedroom. I could hear her singing cheerfully even from the hallway.

I knocked, and she called for me to enter.

"I see you had a good day," I said, marking her bright smile as she danced around the room with L'vitsa in her arms.

She stopped dancing and faced me. "I did." She beamed.

"I am glad to hear it. Masha, would you mind accompanying me tomorrow?"

"I have Divine Liturgy in the morning."

I nodded. "I know. After that."

"All right. Where are we going?"

I smiled. "It is a surprise."

"But what should I wear?"

"Whatever you wear to service will be fine."

She stared at me hard, and I could see the curiosity simmering in her blue eyes. "Shall I try to guess?"

I chuckled. "You can try, but you will never get it right."

She pursed her lips. "Fine, but it better be good."

"It will be," I promised.

As I left my sister, I thought of the last thing I needed to get before the wedding. I just hoped that I could find some without being observed.

Heading back outside, I took the same path I used to use to sneak out unnoticed, the same route Liza and I had taken to escape Nika a few weeks before.

On the other side of the wall, I slipped into the

busy streets. Celebrations were still in full swing and would be for a few hours yet. It didn't take me long to locate a street fair, the road packed with vendors and stalls.

As I moved through the crowd, I scanned the booths, a magpie looking for treasure.

The first few places I stopped didn't have what I was looking for, despite the vendors insisting that they did. Finally, at the very end of the street, I stopped before a small table. It had not the professional setup the other booths had. It was a square table with a green kerchief laid out like a tablecloth.

The young woman behind it couldn't have been more than fifteen.

I bent closer to the bits and bobs. They were simple yet elegant, metal expertly twisted and polished to shine.

"Do you make these?" I asked the girl.

"No, sir," she answered. "My brother does."

I smiled at the little treasures. "You brother is very talented," I told her.

She dipped her head in thanks. "I will tell him you said so."

"I will take these two," I said, pointing at two rings made of braided silver.

She quoted me the price, and I frowned, shaking my head. Her expression tightened with anxiety.

"These are far too good to go for such a low price," I told her, handing her twice what she'd asked for. "Tell your brother to have more confidence in his work."

She bowed at the waist. "Thank you, sir."

I smiled. "No, thank you." Then I slipped the

two rings into my pocket and made my way back to the manor.

The rest of the evening was torturous. My mind whirled with excitement, and I couldn't manage to stay in one place for too long. Though I moved about the room—alternating sitting and standing—I occupied myself by twisting the bands of my father's puzzle box.

Eventually, I forced myself to lie in bed to try to sleep. I told myself it wouldn't do for me to be sleep-deprived on my wedding day, but my heart didn't want to settle. Finally, after some hours, I willed my eyes to shut and my breaths to even.

64

The next morning, I couldn't eat from anticipation. I dressed in a simple three-piece suit and retied my tie some ten times before I was happy with it. I actively avoided Yulya when the family returned from Divine Liturgy, not trusting myself to keep an even expression.

Grigori didn't bother to get down from the carriage as he waited for me.

I hid behind a column near the front door and called out to Masha after Yulya and Adrik entered. Her head snapped in my direction, and I stepped into view.

"I was just coming to look for you, brother. Will you tell me where we are going now?"

I smirked at her. "No. Get into the carriage."

"All right..." she said with a sigh.

Before climbing in behind her, I told Grigori to head toward the Summer Gardens and that I would signal to him when to stop. Reliable as ever, he nodded and didn't ask any questions.

As we made our way to the gardens, Masha said, "I hope we are going somewhere with food. I am hungry."

I smiled at my sister and handed her one of the sandwiches I'd made just in case this should occur. She raised an eyebrow but took my offering.

When we approached the Summer Gardens, I watched carefully out the window. I had no trouble spotting Liza. She waited beside her friend in a white sarafan embroidered with pink magnolias. Her hair was unbound, and she wore a simple pink kerchief over the dark tresses. My heart skipped a beat at the sight of her.

I knocked on the side of the carriage, telling Grigori to pull over.

"Are we stopping already?" Masha asked, mustard in the corner of her mouth.

"Just for a moment."

The carriage stopped, and I opened the door and got out. I gave Grigori directions of where to head, then handed Liza into the carriage.

Masha's eyes widened as Liza settled beside me. She shoved the last bite of sandwich into her mouth and wiped her lips with the napkin it had been wrapped in.

"Liza," Masha said finally once she'd swallowed her food. "I did not know you were coming with us. How pretty you look today, almost like a bride."

Liza's cheeks pinked. I slipped my fingers between hers and brought her hand to my lips.

"She is right," I told Liza. "You look gorgeous."

Masha gasped, covering her mouth with her

hand. Her eyes were so wide that they bulged from her head. "You..." she whispered.

I looked at her seriously. "Will you bear witness for us this day, Mashen'ka? We are to be married."

Another second passed, and Masha's face lit with joy. She squealed with delight, clapping her hands together before pressing them to her cheeks. "Oh my goodness! Of course! Oh, I am so happy for you." Her expression grew serious. "But surely this is not your plan to get rid of Nika?"

I shook my head. "No. I am marrying Liza because I love her. Nika is another matter entirely."

Masha smiled. "A secret wedding... How romantic! At least, I assume it is secret since we are sneaking off without anyone else and you made my sister-in-law wait in a garden when she lives in the same house." She raised an eyebrow at me.

"Yes, it is a secret. For now."

Masha squealed again, shaking her closed fists in excitement. Then she sighed. "I am so glad you took my advice, brother."

Liza turned to me. "Her advice?"

I pursed my lips. "Masha told me that I needed to be honest with the person I love. That if I wanted her to stay, I needed to tell her that."

Liza smiled at my sister. "Then it is partly thanks to you we are seeing such a happy day."

Leaning forward, Masha took Liza's free hand in hers. "You have always been kind to me, Liza. You are brave and true, and I would not want anything less for my brother. I know both of you have had less than happy pasts. I hope you will be each other's strength and solace. Thank you for letting me be part of your special day."

Liza dipped her head, smiling gently at my little sister.

All the rest of the ride there, Masha bombarded us with questions. When did we first know we loved each other? What did I say when I confessed? She wanted to know about Liza's relationship with Petya and how that had changed.

But when she got around to asking more personal questions like if we'd consummated our relationship, I changed the subject. I told her about the church we were going to and about our mother's devotion to it. And before she could turn the conversation back, we'd arrived.

Getting down from the carriage, I helped Masha and then Liza to the ground. Masha's eyes took in the little church, but I stared down at Liza, who smiled back up at me.

"You are sure about this, Kisa?" I asked. "You are not upset that we are not doing all the wedding traditions?"

She smirked. "Do not try to get out of it now, Aleksandr Sergeyevich. You promised to be my husband this day, and I will hold you to it."

A pleasant tingle traveled through me, and I kissed both of her hands. "Wait for me while I get our other witness."

She nodded and went to stand by Masha.

Approaching the carriage seat, I looked up at Grigori, who looked down at me.

"Could you come down here for a moment, Grigori?"

"Yes, sir."

Once he was standing before me, I said, "Grigori, you were my father's confidant and friend."

"It was my honor, sir."

I nodded. "I have known you my entire life, and I have always thought of you as a cherished member of our family."

"Master Aleksandr..." His expression was smooth, but his eyes seemed to tremble as if he would tear up.

"As such, I ask this of you, trusting in your discretion, trusting that you will keep what you hear and see today to yourself until I indicate otherwise."

"Sir?"

"Grigori, will you witness my wedding?"

Grigori took a deep breath through his nose, straightening his back. "It will be my honor."

I reached out and rested my hand on his shoulder. "Thank you."

He bowed his head.

65

When we entered the church, the priest was setting everything he needed onto the small table. Tingles of bliss and awe hummed through my body. Masha pulled Liza to one side and braided her hair into a single plait, tying the end with a pink ribbon from her own hair.

When he was ready, the priest turned to us, motioning us all forward. We approached, and I handed him the two rings I'd bought the day before.

After putting the rings on the table, the priest faced us and started the ceremony saying, "Blessed is our God, always, now and ever, and forever."

Without the assistance of a choir, we all answered, "Amen."

"Let us pray to the Lord," the priest instructed.

I followed the motions, chorusing where it was expected of me, my heart full of light as the woman I loved stood beside me.

After blessing us and reciting Bible passages, the

priest took up the rings for the ceremony of betrothal.

Turning to me, he held up a ring and made the sign of the cross over my head.

"The servant of God, Aleksandr Sergeyevich Volonov, is betrothed to the servant of God, Elizaveta Yurivna Zaporozhnaya, in the name of the Father and of the Son and of the Holy Spirit. Amen."

As I held out my hand, he placed the smaller ring on my finger. Then he turned to Liza, held up the other ring and made the sign of the cross over her head.

"The servant of God, Elizaveta Yurivna Zaporozhnaya, is betrothed to the servant of God, Aleksandr Sergeyevich Volonov, in the name of the Father and of the Son and of the Holy Spirit. Amen."

Then he placed my ring on her finger.

Turning toward each other, Liza and I exchanged rings three times before we each wore our own ring on the third finger of our right hands. Her hand was small and chilled, but she smiled up at me warmly. My heart swelled, and I vowed not to weep.

After more blessings and prayers, the priest asked me, "Do you, Aleksandr, have a good, free, and unconstrained will and a firm intention to take as your wife this woman, Elizaveta, whom you see here before you?"

I stared deep into Liza's grey eyes, her cheeks a comely pink behind her freckles. "I have, Father."

"Have you promised yourself to any other bride?" he asked.

I froze, startled by the question. *Not with a free*

and unconstrained will. "I have not promised myself, Father," I answered.

The priest continued, "Do you, Elizaveta, have a good, free, and unconstrained will and a firm intention to take as your husband this man, Aleksandr, whom you see here before you?"

"I have, Father," Liza said, her eyes sparkling with joy.

"Have you promised yourself to any other man?"

"I have not promised myself, Father," she answered without hesitation.

"Blessed is the kingdom of the Father and of the Son and of the Holy Spirit, now and ever, and forever."

Everyone answered, "Amen."

With still more prayers and more blessings, the priest handed us each a lit candle into our left hands and told us to join our right hands. Then he took his stole from about his neck and placed it atop our clasped hands. "Join these, thy servants. Unite them in one mind and one flesh."

As the priest spoke, I marveled at how small Liza's hand was in mine.

Then, as instructed, I repeated after him.

"I, Aleksandr, take you, Elizaveta, to be my wife. And I promise to love you, to respect you, to be always faithful to you, and never to forsake you. So help me God, one in the Holy Trinity, and all the saints."

And in her turn, Liza repeated, gazing into my eyes and speaking clearly. "I, Elizaveta, take you, Aleksandr, to be my husband. And I promise to love you, to respect you, to be always faithful to you, and never to forsake you. So help me God, one in the Holy Trinity, and all the saints."

"What God has joined together, let no man put asunder," the priest declared.

Turning around, he retrieved a crown of myrtle and autumn flowers. He placed it on my head, saying, "The servant of God, Aleksandr, is crowned in marriage for the servant of God, Elizaveta, in the name of the Father and of the Son and of the Holy Spirit. Amen."

"Amen," we answered.

He then placed a crown on Liza's head, saying, "The servant of God, Elizaveta, is crowned in marriage for the servant of God, Aleksandr, in the name of the Father and of the Son and of the Holy Spirit. Amen."

"Amen."

Blessing us again, he repeated three times: "Oh Lord, our God, crown them with glory and honor."

With readings and prayers, we all answered as was expected. Then the priest lifted a goblet from his table. He presented the cup to me, and I took a sip of wine. The sweet sting sung on my tongue. He did the same to Liza. Three times each we drank of the common cup, which symbolized the sharing of our lives' joys and sorrows.

Grabbing the ends of the stole, still laying upon our joined hands, the priest began to lead us around the table. Three times we circled it before coming back to our original positions.

Taking the crown from my head, the priest said, "Be exalted like Abraham, oh bridegroom, and be blessed like Isaac, and multiply like Jacob, walking in peace and keeping God's commandments in right-eousness."

Then taking the crown from Liza's head, he said, "And you, oh bride, be exalted like Sarah, and exult like Rebecca, and multiply like Rachel, and rejoice in your husband, fulfilling the conditions of the law, for this is well-pleasing to God."

With parting prayers, he proclaimed, "Grant, oh Lord, to your newly wed servants, Aleksandr and Elizaveta, peace, health, and happiness for many and blessed years."

"May you live," Masha and Grigori answered.

And as their blessings rang through the small, wooden church my mother cherished so well, I gazed down at my bride, my lovely and fierce Kisa, and I wished to live a long life with her.

66

On the steps of the church, I gazed down at my new wife. And with flushed cheeks and sparkling eyes she smiled up at me. Pulling her into my arms, I kissed her sweetly, savoring the moment I would remember the rest of my life, however long that would be.

"I love you, Sashulya," Liza told me.

Unexpected heat rose in my cheeks, which was only made worse when Liza giggled at me.

Leaning down, I kissed her again, silencing her laughter and covering my blush. "And I love you, Lizochka."

Liza chuckled at the name she told me she would never want me to call her. "To tell you the truth, I always wanted to hear you call me that."

"I knew it," I said, kissing her a third time.

"Not that I want to interrupt your happy moment, but you cannot stand on the church steps kissing all day," Masha said when we finally broke apart. "We still have a long ride ahead of us."

Lacing my fingers with Liza's, I led her back to the carriage and helped her inside. Then I handed Masha in behind her, following and closing the door as I climbed in.

At Masha's insistence, Liza sat beside her and turned her back to her as best she could.

"I know you will not be able to wear it like this once we get out of the carriage, but still," Masha explained as she unbraided Liza's single plait and rebraided it into two plaits.

As my sister's deft fingers slid through my wife's hair, I watched, unwilling and unable to stifle my smile.

Masha glanced over at me before turning back to her task. "You will not fool anyone if you walk around with that look on your face," she warned.

"What would you have me do?"

"Tonight is your wedding night, brother. And though you two want to keep it a secret, I do not want to think you would be robbed of it. So, as a wedding present from me, I will cover for you. If Yulya should ask after you, I will tell her you are not feeling well and are upstairs in your room. Then I will send Liza to you under the guise of bringing you food and checking on you."

And once we arrived home, Masha delivered her gift flawlessly. In the evening, as I restlessly paced my bedroom floor, a quiet knock sounded on my door. I rushed to open it, but Liza had already slipped in before I even reached it.

In her hands, she carried a plate covered with a towel, which she set on the small table beside the armchair.

Lowering her head, she said, "Yesterday, after we parted ways for the evening, I baked this."

She removed the towel to reveal a golden brown loaf of round bread—delicately decorated with birds and flowers.

"I know I should not have baked it myself, but I wanted us to have one."

I reached out and took Liza's hands in mine, giving them each a kiss. "It is fine, Lizochka. You made it with love, and that is what matters."

"Will you try it?" she asked, pulling her hands from mine and breaking off a piece.

"Of course." I opened my mouth and accepted the soft bread from her fingers.

Then I broke off a piece from the loaf and offered it to her. She smiled. And as I gently fed her the karavay, she closed her lips around the tip of my finger.

A shiver ran through me and heat pooled in my gut.

Smirking at me, she said, "It has been a long day. Are you tired, Muzh?"

My cock stiffened at her suggestive tone, at the glint in her eyes, at her calling me husband. "I have energy enough to make you my zhena," I told her, pulling her to me with a controlled jerk of her waist.

She brushed her fingertips against the side of my neck, a sultry smile playing on her lips. "That is good. You are going to need it."

Pulling me down to her, she kissed me forcefully, and my heart raced to catch up to the pace she was setting. Pushing and tugging, Liza soon had me right where she wanted me: half naked on my bed with her straddling my hips, her wedding dress gathered at her full thighs.

"You have known many women," she said, gazing down at me in cold judgment. Then she grinned a smile that sent a shiver down my spine. "But you have never known the unrestrained love of your wife who loves you. You will remember this day, Aleksandr Sergeyevich," she vowed.

And as I had said the day prior, Liza was a woman of her word.

Late into the night, when Liza had effectively shown me what the love of a wife could do, we lay wrapped warmly in each other's arms, the only light the dim flickering of the fireplace.

"It will be forty days since my father died on Friday," I murmured, staring up at the ceiling as I stroked the silky waves of Liza's hair.

She didn't answer right away, but her voice was serious and assertive when she did. "Do not worry, Sasha. I will make sure everything works out just the way you want it to. If you want to leave and live freely, that is what we will do. I will take care of Bes and Maksim or anyone else who threatens you. By the time the mourning period is over, you will not be chained by the glaz smerti."

I pulled away from her slightly so I could look her in the eyes. Brushing her hair from her face, I said, "Kisa, you do not know what these people are capable of. And I could never put you in that kind of danger. I will go to Maksim and Nika tomorrow and try one last time to convince them. But if that does not work..." I frowned, steeling my gut for what I may have to do to protect my future with Liza. "I will take care of it."

Liza's eyebrows puckered with worry. "You will take me with you?"

I nodded.

67

The morning after my wedding night was tense and strained. Liza had left my arms early and breakfasted with the servants while I went down to sit in the dining room with my family.

Masha had slept in that morning, according to Yulya, who was apparently talking directly to me again.

I didn't respond to her but looked down at the kasha the maid had placed before me. I raised an eyebrow at Yulya, knowing that she didn't like the buckwheat porridge, or at least she used to not like it.

She caught my expression and shrugged. "It is cold outside today; I thought kasha would be welcome this morning."

I pulled the milk to me and poured it over my porridge. But just as I was lifting a spoonful toward my mouth, a flash of red caught the corner of my eye. I turned my head to see the domovoi sprint through the room, his long, grey hair and beard covering most of his face and his red tunic.

Jumping from my seat, I dropped my spoon as my heart hammered in my chest. Yulya and Adrik started at my outburst, following me as I rushed to chase the creature.

But when I reached the foyer, having raced down the hall after him, he'd disappeared.

"What has gotten into you?" my sister demanded as I looked around for him.

"Granddad..." I murmured, dread clenching my gut. "Did you not see him?"

Yulya stared at me hard. "Have you lost your mind now? You are hallucinating."

I sighed and tried to shake off the bad omen as I made my way back to the dining room. Upon returning, we saw that L'vitsa had jumped onto the table and was drinking the milk from my bowl.

"Oi!" Yulya yelled at the cat. "Get away from there."

L'vitsa froze, staring at Yulya with her big, grey eyes. Then she jumped down as if no one had scolded her and she was leaving on her own terms.

I waved my hand at Yulya's expression. "I hope she did not get too much. Masha will be angry if she knows we let her drink any milk."

Yulya frowned and sighed. "I will ask them to bring you another bowl."

"It is fine. I will just get some bread from the kitchen." Leaving my sister and her husband to their breakfast, I went to the kitchen and asked the staff for a few slices of buttered bread, happy for a reason to see Liza again so soon.

After we'd finished eating, we left by the kitchen door to pay a visit to Maksim and Nika.

Kostya answered the front door of the Ivashkins' home, his face paling when he saw it was me. "A-Aleksandr Sergeyevich... Are you here to see my sister again?"

I glared at the boy, not attempting to rein in my disdain for him and his family. "Yes, your sister and your father."

Kostya's head bobbled as he nodded. "Of course, Papa is in his study, and Nika is... I will get her and tell her to meet you in there."

We followed him into the house. After closing the door, Kostya pointed to the stairs. "Second floor, first door on your right," he instructed, then scurried away to find his sister.

I met Liza's sharp, grey eyes—her eyes that said she would fight her way out with me if things should turn ugly. Sticking my hand in my pocket, I closed my fist around the wedding ring she'd put on my finger only the day before and started up the stairs.

I knocked firmly on the door Kostya had indicated once on the second floor.

"What?" the deep voice of Maksim Igorevich demanded from the other side.

"It is Aleksandr Sergeyevich. May I come in?"

After a quiet moment, the door opened and Maksim stood before us, his expression stern. He didn't ask us to come in, but he opened the door wider for us to do so.

Maksim crossed the room and sat behind his large, polished desk, lacing his fingers together as we came to stand before it. "Why are you here, Aleksandr?" he asked, his expression cold.

"I have come to talk to you and Veronika. Konstantin is bringing her now."

Maksim nodded, and we didn't have to wait long before Nika presented herself. I was grateful to see that she was not covered in blood this time at least.

She smiled that satisfied smile that soured my stomach. "Have you thought about what I said, Sashen'ka?" she asked, crossing the room and leaning her hip on her father's desk.

"I will not marry you, Veronika," I proclaimed.

She pursed her lips, squinting her black eyes at me. "Then you do not have a long life ahead of you," she said.

Maksim frowned. "Nika, perhaps...given that he is not who he used to be—"

"It does not matter if he is or not," she snapped, cutting her father off. "His name is legendary. That is all I need."

I shook my head at her. "You are such a spoiled child. If you wanted to lead the Ubyzniki, you should have done so on your own merit. Do not try to use me for your own ends. I have my own life to live, and I want nothing to do with you or the Ubyzniki."

Nika laughed, a cruel and maniacal sound. "You think you have your own life? The moment the glaz smerti was cast, your life belonged to me. You have two choices: you marry me, or you die."

My control snapped and fury bubbled up inside me. "I am already married," I declared.

The pressure in the room grew heavy as if all of the air had been sucked out of it.

"You are already married?" Nika said, emphasizing each word like the ticking of a bomb set to explode.

"You married someone else despite having promised yourself to my daughter?" Maksim asked, his tone incredulous and offended.

"To whom?" Nika murmured, soft as the whisper of a blade before it strikes.

"To me," Liza said, stepping up beside me, her chin held high as she stared directly back at Nika.

Nika's lips curled back from her teeth.

"You married a *servant*? An orphan? She has no background! She is not even a full member of the Ubyzniki!" Maksim raged.

"Stealing another woman's zhenikh... I should kill you where you stand," Nika growled, stepping toward Liza.

I thrust my arm out in front of Liza in a protective gesture. "That is my wife you are speaking to, Veronika. Watch your tone, and show some respect."

Nika smiled, and a chill ran down my spine, her eyes still on Liza. "Congratulations on your wedding, Elizaveta Volonova. I will give you some advice: enjoy being married while you can. You will be a widow before long."

I made a move toward Nika. I would have strangled her with my bare hands had Liza not grabbed my wrist, gently reminding me to be smart about this.

"Maksim Igorevich," I said, turning my eyes toward him and effectively ignoring Nika. "Will you lift the glaz smerti?"

Maksim stared seriously at me for a moment. "You have broken the terms of our agreement, Aleksandr. The consequences are on your own head."

"Then you have chosen your path," I stated. I turned on my heel and left the room, Liza close behind me.

68

B ack on the street in front of the Ivashkins' house, I trembled, my fists and teeth clenched. Small hands enclosed around my fist, smoothing it out. I sighed as Liza laced her fingers with mine, stroking the back of my hand with her fingertips.

"Well that was not a secret for very long," she said lightly.

"I am sorry, Kisa—" I started, turning my head toward her.

She held up her hand to cut me off. "It is done now. Sometimes the direct approach is the best one though I think we often forget that as assassins."

I raised her hand to my lips. "There is something I need to tell you," I said reluctantly.

She tilted her head to show she was listening.

"I saw the domovoi this morning."

She stiffened beside me, her hand freezing in mine.

"Did anyone else see him?" she asked.

I shook my head.

"If the domovoi is showing himself to you, you are clearly not safe, Sasha," she said, frowning, her brow crinkling in thought.

"Perhaps we should just leave, Kisa. Nika and Maksim are not going to change their minds. And if some unknown danger is going to befall me... I want to have as much time with you as I can."

Liza met my eyes. "I will not let you die so easily, Muzh. Give me a few more days, and I will take care of everything."

"You are so confident?"

She smirked. "I have a lot to fight for."

"Very well, Kisa," I sighed. "I will give you until the end of the week to come up with something. But if you cannot get the cancellation order, then we will leave and appreciate the time we have left."

She stood on her toes and brushed a soft kiss to my cheek. "Do not worry, Sashulya," she murmured.

But as she started the pull away, I wrapped my arms around her, crushing her to me. "Promise me that if you go after them, you will not do it alone."

She trailed her hand soothingly up and down my spine. "I promise." She paused before continuing. "Now that Bes and Maksim know of our marriage, there is no reason to keep it secret. So there should be no problem in keeping me near you. I would...feel better if you stay close."

I smiled down at her. "I suppose I should go home and tell my sister the happy news then." I took my wedding ring from my pocket and slipped it back onto the third finger of my right hand.

Taking my wife's hand into mine as we walked, I was grateful that I didn't have to hide my love for her, not that the secret had lasted very long. But as we approached the front gate of Volonov Manor, Liza pulled her hand away.

I frowned and snatched it up again. "He is going to find out eventually," I told her when her brow puckered.

She sighed and nodded in response.

Just as we were approaching the little gatehouse, the door to the cottage opened. Boris bounded out with Mila close behind. Then Tanya exited, glancing back over her shoulder at Petya.

"We will be back soon," she told him.

Upon noticing Liza and I, Tanya and Petya stopped, their eyes flicking to our joined hands. Tanya's expression was smooth, dignified, resigned. But Petya struggled to force a smile onto his face.

"Good morning," Petya greeted.

"Good morning, Petya, Tanya. We were just out for a walk and stopped to share our happy news," I said, my voice serious.

The siblings waited, their expressions fixed.

"Liza and I were married yesterday," I declared.

It was clear from their wide eyes they'd expected an announcement of less magnitude.

"We apologize for not inviting you," Liza murmured beside me. "It was a very private ceremony, only ourselves and the witnesses."

I nodded in agreement with her sentiment.

"Congratulations," Tanya said. And though her tone was not as cheerful as matrimonial good wishes ought to be, I could hear her sincerity. "I wish you all the happiness, Sasha."

"Thank you," I answered.

"Congratulations," Petya seconded, his tone far less convincing than his sister's. "For two people I love so dearly to find each other... It is a blessing."

And as my oldest friend met my eyes, I knew that he was hurting, that he would be hurting for a while. But I also knew he meant us well. Eventually, he would be glad for us.

Petya truly is a better man than I.

We thanked Petya for his kind words and took our leave.

"That was painful," Liza said as we walked toward the house. "Should love between two people cause such pain for others?"

I squeezed her hand, but I had no words of comfort for her.

As we opened the front door, we were assaulted by a woman's wailing cries. Liza and I glanced only momentarily at each other before following the sound to its source.

In the parlour, Masha knelt on the floor, her face buried in the seat of the couch. Yulya sat on the couch beside her, stroking her hair as the girl sobbed.

"What happened?" I asked.

Masha looked up at me, her face red and swollen as tears ran from her blue eyes. "Brother!" she cried, running to me and burying her face in my chest.

I patted her head, attempting to soothe her. "What is the matter, Mashen'ka?"

She answered, each word broken with hiccuped breaths, "L'vitsa..." she sobbed. "She is dead."

My blood turned cold. "How did she die?" I asked.

"I do not know," Masha wailed. "I was sleeping

late, and then I heard her crying at my door. I let her into my room. She crawled into bed with me, and then she just died. There was no blood. She was not injured. I do not know what happened!"

I stared at Yulya over Masha's head. Her expression was smooth and serious, and I knew she was hiding something.

I shushed Masha gently, stroking her hair. *She can never know how L'vitsa died. As upset as she is about her cat, knowing that her fate was meant for me would only make things worse.* "I know, Mashen'ka. But L'vitsa was not a kitten anymore. She was no longer young. Perhaps she just died of old age."

Masha sniffled. "But she seemed very healthy. She ate well. She played. She did not seem lethargic."

"Still..."

Masha nodded her understanding though tears still leaked from her eyes. "You are right," she murmured.

My heart ached at the pain she was feeling and for the memory of sweet L'vitsa.

"Would you like to have a funeral for her?" I asked my baby sister.

Her lips quivered, but she dipped her head. "There is a tree she loved to climb," Masha said. "Can we bury her beneath it?"

"Of course. I will ask Grigori to find a wooden box to put her in, and we can bury her after lunch. All right?"

Masha nodded.

69

L'vitsa's funeral was small but heartfelt. One of the gardeners dug the hole for her coffin, which was made from a fruit crate. I shed my tears for the feline who had died in my place. She had been an adorable and loving kitten, and she'd given Masha much needed solace when I'd left home. It was hard losing a pet, but I knew Masha would one day be able to remember her with fondness and fewer tears.

Later that evening, when Masha had cried herself into an exhausted sleep, Liza and I went in search of Yulya. We found her in my father's study, her face drained of blood as she stared down at a piece of paper. She looked up, her eyes wide and startled when we entered.

I lifted an eyebrow at her. "What is that?" I asked, nodding toward the paper. I approached the desk, but Liza stayed near the door as Yulya would expect her to do.

"Nothing," she murmured, balling up the paper

between her hands and tossing it into the trash bin beside the desk.

Given that her face had yet to regain its color, I was not convinced. But I didn't challenge her assertion.

"I bring good news, sister," I said, making my voice light.

She gave me a hard stare. "Anything that is good for you is likely not good for me."

"Oh, no. I think you will be very happy overall."

Yulya pursed her lips.

"I have been married."

Her eyes bulged. "You married Nika? How is that good for anyone?" she demanded, her cheeks flushing as her voice rose into a shout of fury.

"I did not marry Nika," I said calmly. "I married Liza."

"*That* was your big plan?" she sneered.

"You misunderstand me, Yulya. I married for love. Does that not please you?"

Yulya laughed a dark, cruel chuckle. "In fact, it does, brother. Because now you will never be the head of the family. Maksim will never lift the glaz smerti since you broke your word. And even if he does, you cannot lead with *her* at your side. She may be skilled, but the Ubyzniki would not even have considered her for an apprenticeship without Father's recommendation."

I looked back at Liza, her grey eyes cold and sharp like an icicle with a lethal point. Pride filled my chest to see her standing up to Yulya. But she didn't say anything, she just stared at my sister, whose flushed cheeks began to lose color again as they exchanged glares.

"You are as callous as ever, sister," I said. "I suggest you learn to be a little more gracious to your sister-in-law for the rest of the time we are here. I have been lenient on you until now. Four times you have tried to kill me, and I did not retaliate. I have always loved you, and I felt for the position Father put you in. But I will not tolerate this nonsense anymore. My wife and I will stay until the end of the week, and I expect you to treat her as an equal."

Yulya curled her lips at my threat. I knew she wouldn't outright insult Liza in my presence again, but she would never treat her as an equal.

"Are you done?" Yulya asked coldly. "I have work to do."

I dipped my head at my sister, and Liza and I left her to stew.

As we walked hand-in-hand down the hallway, with the eyes of my Volonov ancestors staring down at us from their portraits, Liza murmured, "You would have been a much better choice to lead the family."

I shook my head. "Yulya can uphold the long-standing traditions, the purpose for why the Ubyzniki was founded in the first place. I have not the heart to get behind that mission."

"Perhaps that is one of the reasons you would be better, Sasha. Your words at the memorial hunt were not wrong. You were not wrong to spare that half-Fae child. Perhaps your vision of what the Ubyzniki could be, would be better for everyone, human and supernatural alike."

I smiled sadly at her words. "The Ubyzniki would not accept such a change."

"You might be surprised. Sometimes people just need a leader to show them the way."

I stopped, turning to her and brushing my thumb along her soft cheek. "I did not know you had such thoughts, Kisa."

"But I would not impose such expectations on you. I have seen how much you struggle against such bonds."

"You have been watching me quite closely." I grinned. "Have you not, Kisa? And you wondered where my confidence came from."

Her scowl was quickly followed by a smirk. "I still wonder. You are not as pretty as you think you are."

I raised an eyebrow at her. "Am I not?" I asked, stepping in closer to her.

She shook her head resolutely.

Firmly grabbing her hips, I leaned my face down to her. "Truly?" I whispered, my lips hovering just above hers.

"All right," she murmured. "You are a little pretty."

I smiled. "Only a little?" My voice was low and hushed, thick and seductive as I looked at her through lowered eyelids.

She moved to kiss me, but I kept just out of reach. Her lips pouted, and I steeled my resolve in the face of such an appealing expression.

"Fine," she grumbled. "You are pretty."

"Not as pretty as you, my kisa," I whispered before I pressed my lips to hers. The kiss was indulgent and laced with need. My heated blood raced through my veins.

"Let us go. Now," Liza insisted, pressing her body harder against mine.

"You do not want to let the rest of the household know about our marriage?" I murmured, only a few words escaping at a time between kisses.

"Tomorrow," she said.

"If that is what you want, Zhena. Then that is what you will have." Then I scooped her into my arms and carried her upstairs to our bedroom.

70

L ate that evening, as Liza slept warmly in our bed, I slipped into the dark hallway. My training kicked back in effortlessly while I crept through the hushed house. The door of my father's study opened silently when I turned the knob.

I didn't flick on the overhead light. The drapes were open, the waning gibbous providing enough visibility for me to cross the room to the desk. After pulling a lamp from the table, I set it on the floor and turned it on, the desk hiding most of the light. Then I grabbed the small trash bin and retrieved the crumbled ball Yulya had earlier thrown away.

Smoothing it out, careful to make as little sound as possible, I gazed down at the handwritten note as I crouched on the floor behind the desk.

The clever cat who wants to live out her nine lives knows when to leave the mouse alone.

I crinkled my eyebrows at the note that had had

such an effect on Yulya. It was clear it was a threat. And based on her pallor, she had taken it seriously, despite saying it was nothing. *But who is it from? And what is it referring to? Is it a reference to L'vitsa?*

I frowned and replaced the paper the way I'd found it. Then I flicked off the light and returned the lamp to its place on the desk.

After creeping back to my bed, my thoughts on the note drifted away as I snuggled closer to my sleeping wife.

My whirlwind wedding was all the talk among the staff the following day though the celebrations were muted due to the household still in the mourning period after my father's death. Liza had breakfast with the family, and Yulya behaved herself though she didn't say a word. Masha was all achatter throughout the meal, and she insisted on taking Liza shopping that afternoon.

Liza's protests that the clothes she possessed didn't need replacing were feeble and ineffective. And she soon agreed to Masha's pleas.

Just before they left, Liza turned anxious eyes on me. "Are you certain you do not want to come with us?" she asked.

"I wonder if you are worried for me or yourself, Kisa," I said with a smirk.

She pursed her lips, and I leaned down, pressing a kiss to her forehead.

"I will lock myself in my room if that will make you feel better," I offered.

A slow smile spread across her face. "That would be good. Then you will already be just where I want you when I return."

"Oh, you are wicked to say such things just before leaving."

She stood on her toes and pressed a declarative kiss to my lips. "Wait for me, Sashulya," she murmured.

I tightened my arms as she moved to pull away, kissing her gently. "Be careful," I pleaded.

"I will," she promised.

Bursting through the front door, Masha sighed when she saw us. "Brother, let her go. It is my turn to spend time with Liza. You can have her back when we are finished."

Liza managed to stifle her laughter, but I couldn't hold in my chuckle. Releasing Liza into Masha's care, I told them to have fun as they walked out the door.

I was restless while Liza was away. Would Nika and Maksim target her? Would Yulya? Twisting the little bands of my father's puzzle box did little to occupy my mind.

I told myself Nika and Maksim wouldn't likely act so quickly. Perhaps they would just be happy with the glaz smerti killing me later. I told myself that Yulya would be better served just to let us leave at the end of the week though I was counting on her rational mind to overshadow any spite she might have toward us.

I thought about what we would do once we left, where we would go. I played out in my mind how I would ask Masha to come with us. She would love Paris, and I hoped I would see her dance on stage before my time was up.

My chest ached at the thought that I wouldn't be

alive this time next year. I might never see Masha dance in a ballet. I would never see Liza as an old woman. And if Liza were to get pregnant, I would likely never get to hold our child. Certainly, our baby would never know me.

Was keeping my morals, my vow to myself, worth giving up that future? Could I stomach becoming what I hated most to preserve it? It was clear Maksim wouldn't give up the cancellation order without persuasion of the threatening variety. And for all I knew, he wouldn't give it up even then. The mage certainly wouldn't tell me without it turning ugly.

I sighed and shook my head, sitting in my room all alone with only the hissing of the fireplace and the clicking of my father's puzzle box to accompany my thoughts. *No, I will not do it.* I loved my wife. I loved my sister. I wanted to live a long and happy life. But I wouldn't be able to look myself in the mirror if I resorted to those old practices. I'd done enough harm in my life already even if I hadn't known better at the time. I knew better now. Perhaps it was my punishment for all the damage I'd caused, that I would only know true happiness for a short amount of time.

"What are you doing there, alone in the dark?" Liza asked as she flicked on the overhead light when she entered the room.

I hadn't noticed how the fire had dimmed, that the sunlight through the windows was now soft with dusk.

I didn't answer her question but held out my arms to her. She crossed the room and sat on my lap, wrapping her arm around my shoulders as I grasped her hip and waist.

"Are you all right?" she murmured, kissing the side of my head.

"I am fine," I told her, my voice soft but resolute.

Then I rested my head on her shoulder as she stroked my hair.

71

The following morning Yulya informed us that there would be another hunt. Masha didn't complain when she was told to stay behind again. Because the Ubyzniki were hunting upyr', they would leave before noon to catch the creatures during their noon to midnight active time. Apparently, a small group of upyr' had been spotted within the city, a direct insult to the Ubyzniki's effectiveness.

As Yulya and Adrik prepared to meet the other assassins, Liza and I went to the chapel to keep watch for the day.

It was past dark when Kostya came rushing into the chapel, sweating and out of breath.

I raised an eyebrow at the boy. "Is the hunt over already? I thought Petya was to relieve me."

Kostya shook his head, his Adam's apple jumping as he tried to swallow. "Masha," he gasped.

The hair on my neck and arms stood on end at

the tone in his voice, at the fear in his eyes. I rushed to the boy, grabbing him by the shoulders.

"What about Masha?" I demanded.

His gasps turned to sobs as tears spilled down his cheeks. "She is gone."

"What do you mean 'gone'? Where is she?" I shook him by the shoulders.

"She...she was supposed to meet me," he explained, his words broken. "W—w-we were going to run away. But she never came. I thought she had changed her mind. But I found her bag on the ground nearby. Th-there is blood on it."

He held out the bag to me, and I took it with shaking hands.

"Who took her?" I asked, unable to pry my eyes from the dark red stain speckling the cloth.

"I do not know."

"Are you sure she was taken?" I asked, meeting the boy's wide, blue eyes. "Kostya," I snapped, demanding his focus. "Did you check the house?"

He nodded. "I went there first. She is not there."

My stomach curdled, and I swallowed the bile that rose in my throat. I watched the boy, who was pale and shaking.

"We are going back to the house to call Vladimir. And you are going to tell me everything you know."

Kostya bobbed his head and followed Liza and me to the house.

As soon as we arrived, I told Grigori to call Vladimir. But when he informed me that there was no answer, I asked him to tell Petya to take over my watch.

"Kisa," I said, turning to my wife. "Do you think you can go to Peter and Paul Fortress and bring back the mage?"

Liza nodded seriously and slipped into the night.

Then I ushered Kostya into the kitchen and made him some tea. Sitting across from him at the kitchen table, I placed the tea before him.

"Speak," I ordered as he wrapped his fingers around the podstakannik.

His eyes flicked to mine, then he gazed down into his cup. "Masha and I... We love each other. We have loved each other for a long time, but we never said anything. When you told me to stay away from her, I tried. But when she confessed, I could not do it anymore. She does not want to be an assassin, and I just wanted to be happy with her. So we decided to run away. When we found out about the hunt today, we thought it would be a good night to do it. I told my father I was not feeling well to get out of it. We were supposed to meet at Admiralty Fountain. Then we were going to go to the airfield and take an airship to wherever the next boat was going."

I closed my eyes against his words. This boy, whose face was still wet with tears, was not like his sister, not like his father. I could hear in his voice how much he loved Masha. He also didn't seem to have Nika's or Maksim's cool intelligence.

I sighed heavily. "I will deal with you, the both of you, once Masha is found. But finding her and bringing her back safe is what is important right now. Where exactly did you find her bag?"

"I found it near the monument to Vasily Zhukovsky."

"Was there blood around it?"

Kostya shook his head. "There were a few drops, but most of the blood was on her bag."

I frowned. "That could mean that most of the blood just stayed on her clothes, or they could have snatched her only to kill her later."

Kostya's face paled, and he looked as though he would faint.

"Did you see anything? Hear anything?"

"No. But Masha was a good assassin even if she did not have the stomach for it. She would know how to fend off an attacker."

I nodded. "There could have been more than one. Or they could have taken her by surprise."

Kostya's glass rattled in the podstakannik as his hands shook. "You do not think she is d-dead, do you?" he whispered.

I pushed down my own sense of dread. "I do not know. Let us concentrate on finding her for now."

Just as Kostya nodded, sounds from the foyer filtered into the kitchen. We both jumped to our feet and rushed to see who it was.

Yulya, accompanied by Adrik, wore a satisfied smile. "You are here, Kostya?" she asked as she glanced over at us. "You must be feeling better. You missed a successful hunt. We did not kill as many as we had hoped, but we did capture one. She is at your house now, in fact. Your sister assures us she will get the location of the rest out of her."

"Yulya," I called her attention toward me. "Masha has been kidnapped."

The smile slid from Yulya's face as did all of the blood. "By whom?" she murmured.

"We do not know yet. Kostya just finished telling me what he knows. I have sent Liza for the mage. I hope he can dowse for her."

Even from across the foyer, I could see Yulya trembling. "Tell me everything," she said.

72

"How much time have we lost?" Yulya asked, pacing the parlour from end to end.

"It has been nearly three hours since Masha was to meet me," Kostya answered quietly.

"Liza will be back soon," I assured.

"That is—" Yulya started to yell when the sound of the front door cut her off.

Hurrying to the foyer, we were greeted by Liza and a harassed looking Vladimir. His hair was mussed, and he wore an overcoat over his pajamas.

Liza returned to my side, and I nodded my thanks at her.

"Thank you for coming, Vladimir," I said. "We need your help."

He turned serious eyes on me. "Yes, Elizaveta told me of young Masha. Have you heard anything else?"

I shook my head. "We know her last likely location, but that is all. Can you dowse for her?"

"If she is on the earth, and if she is alive, I can find where she is," he assured.

"I have set some maps of the city out for you in the ground-floor library," I said, gesturing across the foyer.

As we stood over the map of Saint Petersburg, I pointed to the location of the monument of Vasily Zhukovsky near Admiralty Fountain. "This is where her bag was found," I told him.

Vladimir reached into his coat pocket and pulled out a chain with a small silver obelisk on one end.

"Can I have her bag, please?" he asked.

Kostya, who had been hugging the sack close to his chest, handed it over to the mage.

We held our breaths as Vladimir closed his eyes, his lips moving as he spoke silent spells and prayers. When he opened his eyes, he leaned over the map of the city, holding his pendulum over the point where Masha had last been.

The obelisk swung in wide circles as the mage slowly moved it over the map, trying to narrow in on a location.

Systematically, he moved it from district to district, but the circles didn't change.

"It is not working," Yulya raged, her angry voice breaking the silence of the room.

"Be quiet," I snapped.

She glared at me but didn't speak again.

As he hovered the pendulum over Moskovsky Avenue, the circles started to tighten. And over a little green splotch on the east side of the street, the obelisk stopped.

Vladimir's face paled as he leaned closer to the map. "Novodevichy Cemetery," he whispered.

My heart hammered in my chest. "Are you certain?" I asked him as Yulya shouted something I tried to block out.

The mage dipped his head. "She is there or quite nearby."

"Can you find out who has her?" I asked.

At that, Yulya's rage turned on me. "Why does it matter who has her? She is still alive. If we go now, she may still be alive when we get there."

I turned to my sister. "We need to know who we are up against. It may not be humans who took her. We need to be properly equipped to handle whatever we encounter."

"Waiting is a mistake," she spat.

Fury bubbled up inside me. "Do you think I am not just as upset as you are?" I demanded. "I want Masha back safe, but we cannot go in blind, or we risk not just Masha but everyone else."

"I am the head of this family, and I say we go *now*."

My stomach hardened. "No, Yulya. We do not go. You will send word to as many Ubyzniki as are available and tell them to come here. Vladimir will find out who we are up against. And once he does, we will arm ourselves properly and *then* go get Masha."

My sister shook with anger as she met my eyes. I stared back at her, unwilling to budge. And after a tense few seconds, she averted her gaze. Then she stormed from the room, Adrik close behind.

I turned my attention back to the mage. "Do it," I ordered.

He nodded and went about whatever spell he needed to cast to comply.

Closing my eyes for only a moment, I took a deep breath. Then I felt Liza's small hand in mine and looked down at her.

"What do you need me to do?" she asked softly.

I tried to give her a tired smile, but I couldn't seem to twist my mouth in that way. "Help Vladimir with whatever he needs."

She squeezed my hand before going to him.

In the corner of the room, his brow puckered and his eyes sad, Kostya stood with his gaze on the floor. Crossing to the boy, I rested my hand on his shoulder. He jumped at the contact.

"Kostya," I murmured. "Are you going to be all right enough to come with us? I cannot guarantee what you will see when we get there."

His head bobbled in response, and I lifted an eyebrow at him. He took a deep breath and sighed, straightening his shoulders. Then he met my eyes. "I want to be there."

I patted him on the back, nodding once. "Try to get yourself straight then. It will not be long."

Leaving the boy to his internal struggle, I exited the ground-floor library in search of my elder sister. I climbed the stairs to the second floor but stopped just outside our father's study, listening as Yulya talked.

"It is a long story," Yulya said. "Just come here. Hopefully we will know more by the time everyone arrives."

She paused.

"Yes, all right. See you then."

Satisfied that Yulya would carry out my orders, I went to my room. I changed into a pair of black trousers and a black shirt. After pulling on my boots, I stared at the leather vest I used to wear for Ubyzniki missions. There was no way it was going to fit my broader build now.

Without another thought, I went back down to the second floor, to my father's bedroom.

The room was chilled as the grave, no fire warming the space. The moonlight spilling in through the open curtains illuminated the dust particles as they swirled and danced. I crossed to the dressing room and opened the door.

My father's suits, shoes, ties, and shirts hung limply on their hangers and rested in their drawers. At the very back of the dressing room, hanging on the left side, was my father's supple leather vest. I took it down from its hook, running my fingertips over the scratched and scuffed surface. It had seen more hunts than I would ever know. And it had served my father well.

I slipped on the garment, adjusting the straps to fit my leaner gut. It was as if it had been made for me.

After buckling the final strap, I left the dressing room to lead the Ubyzniki.

73

When I reached Vladimir and Liza back in the ground-floor library, I was greeted by the mage's haunted gaze.

"Upyr'," he whispered, sinking into a chair.

My blood ran cold. "Liza," I murmured.

She turned to me, met my eyes, then shook her head. "I already know what you are going to say, Sasha. And I will not have it. I will not sit here at home while Masha is in such danger. I am coming with you."

"I cannot protect you both if you go."

Liza sighed, lifting her hand to my cheek. "Then I will protect you, Muzh."

I stared into her eyes, and I knew she wouldn't take no for an answer. I pressed her hand to my cheek, putting all my love for her into the small gesture. "Go get ready," I told her.

As Liza went to change, Yulya and Adrik returned to the first floor.

"Are they coming?" I asked Yulya.

She nodded.

"Good. We are going to need all the help we can get. Masha has been taken by upyr'."

Yulya paled. "No," she murmured, touching her fingers to her mouth.

"Yulya, I need you to tell me everything you know about the upyr' you went to hunt earlier today. We do not have much time before midnight, and they are not likely to keep her alive while they sleep."

"Like I said, we only got a few of them. At least four got away. They have been hunting in the Gorodskoy District. That is where we found them," she told me.

"Have they been killing their victims or just feeding on them?"

Yulya squinted. "Does it matter?"

"It matters, Yulya," I insisted.

"They have been killing, draining their blood and eating their hearts as upyr' do."

"They are not trying to be peaceful, Sasha," Liza said, rejoining us. "They are killing people."

I closed my eyes. "Then we need not spare them."

Looking at those assembled, I made a motion for us to head toward the armory.

"I assume you do not know where they sleep?" I asked my sister.

"No, being dead, we could not find them by dowsing. But Nika said she would get the location out of the one we caught, so we had planned to just find them once she had."

When we arrived at the armory, some of the

Ubyzniki were already there. Dima, Nika, our cousin Vasili—seasoned assassins.

"Is this everyone?" I asked Yulya.

"Everyone who could come quickly," she answered.

"Veronika, tell me that upyr' you captured is still in one piece," I said.

Nika curled her lips at me but answered. "She is more dead than when I first got my hands on her."

I growled my frustration. "We could have used her as a bargaining chip. At the very least, we could have followed her to their exact location."

"You wanted to let her go?" Nika asked, her voice rising in disbelief.

I held up my hand to silence her. "We will just have to go off of Vladimir's directions and hope we find her in time. Everyone," I stared at the group before me. "Arm yourselves for an upyr' hunt. This time, they have one of our own."

In the armory, the ranks of the Ubyzniki grabbed what weapons were useful against our revenant opponents. Vasili, who had exceptional aim, grabbed a bow and arrows. Dima took mechanical gadgets that would slice off heads or shoot stakes. Adrik filled his belt with vials of chemicals that would ignite when mixed. I grabbed a shashka, quite effective in decapitating an undead enemy. Along with the stiletto already in its sheath, Liza took a sovnya from the wall, its curved blade above her head as she held the staff in her grasp.

Armed with the weapons they felt most proficient in, the lethal assemblage turned their eyes on me.

"Novodevichy Cemetery is too far to walk in a short amount of time, and the airship will take too long to get ready. So we will be taking an open carriage. We will stop just shy of the cemetery and walk the rest of the way so we do not raise suspicion," I said.

Their steady gazes told me they were listening with rapt attention.

"It is not long before midnight. We need to find Masha before then. Normally, I would suggest we surround the cemetery and come at it from all sides. But since we do not have much time, and our priority is to find Masha rather than kill as many upyr' as possible, I think a clean sweep would be best. There are many gravestones and crypts at the site, many places where they can hide. So be alert. If they are holding her somewhere in a group, there are only so many places to keep her."

Glancing at each one in turn, I nodded. "All right. Let us go."

Returning to the front of Volonov Manor, I climbed into the driver's seat of the open carriage. Liza sat beside me. After everyone was in, I urged the horses on.

Once we were through the gate, I compelled them to go faster, and we sped through the dimly lit streets of Saint Petersburg as if the devil were chasing us. The cold night wind burned my bare face and hands. My throat was raw from breathing in the freezing air. The horses' hooves clattered, and the carriage wheels rumbled on the road. But none of these sounds overshadowed the pounding of my own heart.

As we approached the cemetery, I reined the horses in, coming to a stop a block away.

Out of the carriage, I tethered the horses to a lamppost. And after we'd all checked the status of our weapons, I unsheathed my shashka and signaled for us to move out.

As silent as shadows, we slipped through the night into the graveyard, where not everyone was sleeping as soundly as they should be.

The leaves on the ground were damp and smelled of decay. I followed the bricked paths past crumbling statues and moss-covered headstones. Sweeping my gaze through the darkness, my heart was steady and my breath even as I analyzed every shiver of a tree branch, every wisp of wind. We crept past crypts with peaked windows and weathered inscriptions that could no longer be read. But when we had reached the other side, we had not found Masha.

74

I blinked into the night, scrunching my brow in thought as I stared back toward the cemetery. But before I could think of what to do next, Yulya rushed toward me and punched me right in the jaw. The strike was more anger than precision, but it certainly stung.

"This is all your fault," she growled as I looked down at her. "We got here too late."

"It is not too late," I told her. "It is still fifteen minutes to midnight, and we have not found her body."

Yulya grabbed the front of my vest in her fists. "Where is she?" she demanded, pain and grief shadowing her icy eyes.

As I stared down at her, the wind blew through the trees, shifting the speckled moonlight that filtered onto the ground of the cemetery. A sliver of pink caught the light over Yulya's shoulder. I squinted at it.

Extricating myself from Yulya's grasp, I seized

the out-of-place bit of color. It was a satin pink ribbon with a dark stain.

"Is that...?" Liza asked, gazing at the ribbon in my hand. "Masha had a ribbon just like that. She used it to tie my hair."

I nodded. "It could be."

Analyzing the ground around me, I saw the leaves were disturbed, not the gentle blanket that falls from the trees or the windswept piles. Following the path with my eyes, I stared across the street at a crumbling building of brown brick. There were no windows, and the brick wall of the entrance had barbed wire on top.

"There." I pointed. "What is that building?"

I looked around at the assassins, who just shook their heads as if they had no idea.

"It does not matter. I bet Masha is in there."

"How do you know that?" Yulya demanded. She gestured down the road. "She could be in any one of these buildings. If that is her ribbon, it could have been dropped before they took her through the cemetery. She could be somewhere on the other side entirely."

I nodded at my sister. "She could be. But we do not have much time, and we need to make a decision."

"Will you take responsibility if she is not in there?" Yulya spat.

"Yes." I looked around at the others. "Are you coming or not?"

They glanced to Yulya then back at me, and it was clear their decisions had been made.

"All right," I said, motioning for them to follow me across the street.

The iron gate in the wall was unlocked, a good sign that someone who shouldn't be there was inside. We slipped in and approached the splintered, wooden door.

I gritted my teeth when it creaked on its hinges as I pulled it open. Holding my sword at the ready, I entered what appeared to be an abandoned warehouse. As trained, the rest of the group found cover behind pillars and old crates, stacked and broken.

We moved quickly but carefully through the shadows. My ears strained for any sound that said I had chosen correctly.

A shriek split the air, chilling my bones and setting my nerves on end.

Kostya rushed toward the sound, but I grabbed him by the collar, holding him in place.

The cry had come from above. I motioned them to gather in a cove between boxes. Then I whispered, "She is still alive, but we do not know how many there are. Kostya, we will make a path for you. You are to grab Masha and get her out as quickly as possible."

I met each of their eyes, and their focus was as sharp as their weapons. I nodded, and we moved on in search of stairs.

The staircase was through a doorway; its door leaned, unhinged, against the wall beside it.

As I crept up the stairs, I carefully controlled my footfalls so that no scuffling could be heard from my shoes. And I was relieved not to hear those behind me.

When I reached the second-floor landing, I saw a light flickering off the walls of a room ahead.

"Why did you wake her?" a female voice demanded as we moved closer to the light.

"I like the way fear tastes in the blood," a male answered.

"But someone could have heard," she said.

"All of our neighbors are dead," he scoffed.

"How much longer do we have to wait to open her up?" a graveled male voice asked.

"Until Roza returns," a third male answered.

"If she has not returned by now, she is not coming back, at least not tonight," the female said.

A sigh answered her assertion. "All right. But do not wake her up again, Ilya. Zhanna is right. We cannot risk someone hearing her."

At the threshold of the room, I peeked around the doorframe. Masha was lying on a table, five upyr' around her. Four of the five each had a limb. The sickening sounds of teeth sinking into flesh, muffled moans, slurping lips, echoed off the walls. But just as the fifth leaned down to Masha's jugular, Vasili let loose an arrow, which found purchase right in his unbeating heart.

The feeding stopped as the upyr' turned toward the assassins, who piled into the room.

To the untrained eye, the upyr' would have looked human, though some would find the blood leaking from their mouths unusual. But other than their fangs, they just appeared pale. Still, the average human would know to avoid them. If not for the fact that they were unwashed, they had a sort of dangerous, wild aura about them.

And as the one who had been called Zhanna lunged toward me, her dead eyes shined with a feral light.

The battle ensued. And outnumbered as they were, the upyr' were ferocious, frantically clawing and snapping their teeth.

As Zhanna and I stared each other down, Liza appeared at my side, facing the enemy with a determined stare.

"Help Kostya get Masha out," Liza said.

I started to protest, but she cut me off. "Go," she urged. "She has lost a lot of blood."

Striking out at Zhanna, Liza effectively put an end to the discussion.

I redirected my gaze toward where Masha lay, limp and pale on the table. One of the males slashed out at Kostya as he approached.

I charged forward, dodging weapons, claws, and teeth as assassins and upyr' fought for their lives.

Launching myself at the male, I knocked him to one side. We both scrambled to our feet as we squared off.

"Get her out of here, Kostya," I ordered without looking back at him.

"That is my dinner," the male growled, baring his teeth.

"That is my sister," I snapped.

He flicked out his tongue, still stained red with Masha's blood. "Does the spice of fear in the blood run in your family?" He smiled—flashing his fangs— and lunged at me.

I stepped out of the way, dodging his attack, but kept my eyes on him.

"You are a quick one." He grinned. "Are you afraid? I can hear your heart beating," he sang in a sing-song voice.

But when he came toward me again, I lashed out with a powerful strike, cleanly separating his head at the neck.

Glancing around, I saw Liza fighting fiercely with her sovnya. Her motions were clean and practiced. She had not the sloppy movements she'd had while sparring with me. She seemed to move like a polyanitsa of old: graceful, fierce, deadly. And with a mighty cry, she swiped with her sovnya and decapitated Zhanna.

The smashing of glass sounded beside me. I looked over as Adrik lit my opponent's corpse aflame with his mixed chemicals. Masha and Kostya were no longer in the room, and the remaining upyr' was not long for this world, surrounded by three Ubyzniki. With a gurgling cry, the last of the upyr' was dispatched. I trusted Adrik would ensure they would not rise again.

Meeting Yulya's eyes, I tilted my head, motioning for us to go find Kostya.

75

Not attempting to stifle the sounds of our movements, Yulya and I sped down the stairs. We found Kostya, Masha in his arms, outside. He was well into the cemetery already. He looked over his shoulder at us with wide, frightened eyes when he heard the sounds of our approach.

He sighed upon recognizing us.

"Put her down," Yulya ordered.

But Kostya clutched her closer to him.

"It is all right, Kostya," I assured. "She just wants to check her injuries."

Kostya bit his lips but lowered Masha to the leaf-covered ground.

"I need more light," she said as she knelt beside her.

I pulled a flashlight from my vest pocket and started to crank the handle. Then I knelt on Masha's other side while the little light flickered on.

"How is she?" I murmured as Yulya examined the bites on Masha's limbs and a gash on her head.

"She is unconscious. She has lost a lot of blood, but she is breathing, though shallowly. Her pulse is weak. We need to get her home. We need to call the Ubyzniki's doctor." Yulya pulled a roll of bandages from her pouch and began wrapping Masha's wounds tightly.

As Yulya attempted to stop the bleeding, Liza and Dima joined us.

"Is anyone else hurt?" Yulya asked Dima. And by the look she gave him, it was clear who she was asking after.

"Just a few bumps and shallow cuts," he answered. "I am fine. Everyone is fine."

Her eyes lingered on him for a moment, checking the veracity of his assurances. Then she turned her full attention back to Masha. "Dima, will you fetch the doctor to meet us at the manor?"

He dipped his head then left, running to accomplish his task.

As Yulya tied the last bandage, she said, "All right. That is the best I can do out here."

I nodded to Kostya, telling the boy he could lift her back up. Then I looked over at Liza, who stood quietly at my side. I don't know what expression I wore, but she smiled softly and reached out to touch my arm.

"Go ahead," she murmured. "I will stay behind with the others and let them know you are taking Masha home."

Leaning down, I kissed Liza on the cheek. Then I turned back to Kostya and my sisters. "Let us go. I will drive."

I was much more careful on the drive home than

I had been on the way there, not wanting to disturb Masha too much. Kostya held Masha in his lap, stroking her hair and whispering gentle words to her.

By the time the doctor had arrived, Yulya had already unwrapped and cleaned Masha's wounds. She was snugly tucked into her bed under a pile of blankets, with Yulya, Kostya, and I watching her labored breathing.

A thorough examination and a few pints of blood later, the doctor assured us that Masha would recover. She needed rest. And when she woke she needed food.

As the first rays of sun filtered in through the window of Masha's bedroom, the only sounds were the soft breathing of the two young lovers—Kostya's front half slumped on the side of Masha's bed—and the clicking of the puzzle box in my hands. Yulya had gone to see to it that Masha would have the proper food when she awoke. Liza and Adrik had yet to return, no doubt clearing any trace of the upyr' from the warehouse.

The matryoshka smirked up at me, his blue eyes sparkling beneath a mess of dark hair as I slid the last band into place. With an unobtrusive click, the doll opened, revealing a small slip of paper.

My heart pounded in my chest as I unrolled the note, which had three words written in my father's handwriting: *on your desk.*

I scrunched my eyebrows and quietly left Masha and Kostya as they slept. Down the hall, I entered my bedroom and crossed to the table I'd once used for writing letters. I hadn't even looked at it since I'd returned home, other than to notice that the books

I'd been reading ten years ago were still on it, undisturbed.

I stared down at the table. It held a few books and a box where I kept my writing supplies: paper, pens, wax, and seal. I opened the box, riffling through the blank stationery. Quirking my mouth, I reached for the top of the two books.

It was a collection of poems by Aleksandr Pushkin. Flipping through the book, I stopped when I found an envelope slipped among the pages. The poem on the page was "To the baby."

Taking the envelope from the book, I broke the wax seal, the family crest with the zhar-ptitsa, and opened the letter written in my father's handwriting.

My son,

> *You are angry with me, I am sure. And I do not blame you. From where you are sitting, you cannot understand the reasons for what I have done. Please, let me explain.*
>
> *Ten years ago, you tried to tell me something I could not hear. For that, I am sorry. Perhaps if I had listened then, I would have gotten to see your face before I die.*
>
> *I have always known you are a leader. I saw the signs early on. But my own pride would not let me follow, and I realized my mistake too late.*
>
> *That is why I have done what I did though you may never forgive me. I cast the spell tying you to Nika because I knew you would stay long enough to have it removed. She is not someone I would have you marry, and I knew*

you were never fond of her. I hoped that you would also not want to see the Ubyzniki in her hands. I pray that I was correct in my calculations.

I am sending Liza to you. I do not know how she will convince Yulya to let her find you, but she is clever. And I trust she will find a way.

It is in Liza that I found hope once you were gone. Have you seen what she can do yet? She is far better than I ever would have expected, the best I have ever seen. But it is her loyalty, her heart, that sets her apart from the others. I hope that people like you and Liza will lead the next generation of Ubyzniki.

For too long, we have been blinded by our own fear of those different from us. But I have met with members of the magical community now. I have seen that many are not very different. I even helped set up a safehouse for them here in Saint Petersburg though that does little to redeem me for the many I have killed.

I have thought many things since I found out I was not long for this world, and I have many regrets. I am sorry I did not get to see the man you have become. But I am certain, I know in my very soul, that you are a man I can be proud to call my son.

It is my hope that you will choose to lead the Ubyzniki into a new era. But I understand if you do not. Either way, I wish you a long life of joy and propriety.

In case you have not found and solved my riddle, read this aloud:

Black-and-white in equal measure.
Acrobats, Justice, golden treasure.
The knife's edge cuts more than your foe.
The wisest mind this truth does know.
Balance.

That is the cancellation order for the glaz smerti. You are now free to live the life you choose for yourself.
I know you will make it worthwhile.

Your father,
Sergei Nikolayevich Volonov

76

A tear dropped onto the paper, blurring the ink of my father's letter. My chest ached, and I wished I'd come home sooner. Why had I been so stubborn, so prideful? How many years had I sacrificed with my father? How many supernatural beings could we have saved together?

I squeezed my eyes shut, swallowing a sob as it tried to climb up my throat. With a deep breath, I steadied myself. Questions had been answered, problems solved. But his letter left more questions in its wake. And as my bedroom door opened, and my wife entered, I was determined to get the rest of the answers.

Liza met my gaze, and her eyes widened. "What is the matter, Sasha? Is Masha all right?"

I waved my hand at the question. "Masha will be fine. But *I* need some answers."

She crossed the room to stand before me. "Answers to what?"

Holding up the evidence, I said, "I found a letter from my father."

Her expression grew more serious, but she didn't speak.

"He told me he sent you to me."

"Yes," she murmured, hanging her head. "Yes, he sent me to bring you home. He wanted you to be the head of the family, and he charged me with the mission to make that happen."

My brows crinkled, and I shook my head against my confusion. "How does trying to kill me in the dead of night accomplish that?"

She frowned. "I was not really trying to kill you. When I found out your sister was sending someone to kill you, I volunteered. I just needed to find you and bring you back."

"And what if I had killed you?"

"I trusted you would not from what your father had told me, but it is not as if being an assassin is free of risk."

My gut hardened. "You are a good actress, I must say. Was everything all an act then?"

Her head snapped up, and her grey eyes pleaded with me to understand. "No, Sasha. No, not everything. I did not know he had gone to such lengths. I did not know about the glaz smerti. I did not know about why you even left. And my love—"

She reached out to touch my face, but I jerked my head away from her.

"My love is real," she vowed, tears welling in her eyes. "When you said you felt the same, when you asked me to marry you, I gave up on my mission. And even before that, I faltered. I saw what the expectations were doing to you. It was not right to force you to lead when you did not want to. I told you when I accepted your proposal that my loyalty was solely with you."

The sound of her voice, the desperation in her eyes, my heart twinged. "Why did you not tell me before now?" I whispered.

"Because it no longer mattered. We were going to leave. We were going to start a new life. And... and..."

"And what?" I pushed.

"And I did not want to see that look in your eyes, the way you are looking at me now. I was...afraid. I did not want to hurt you, and I did not want you to doubt me... I am a coward."

I closed my eyes and took a deep breath. "You should have told me, Kisa," I said seriously. "But I know why you did not." I sighed, snorting in a humorless laugh. "How long have we been taught to hide and scheme in the shadows? How can we expect honesty when all we ever do is lie and plot?"

"I swear," she vowed. "I will never hide anything from you again."

"That is good, Zhena. Because I am going to need your help if I am going to make the Ubyzniki into something better."

Her eyes widened, and I smiled gently at her.

"Getting them to understand that all supernatural beings are not bad, that we only need to kill the ones who are harmful, is going to take a lot of work. Tomorrow, the family, the Ubyzniki, will gather to mark forty days after my father's death. I will announce that I accept my place as heir." I reached out and touched her cheek. "Will you help me, Kisa? Will you be by my side?"

Pressing my hand to her face, she turned and kissed my palm. "I will," she promised.

I nodded. "But there is one more thing that needs addressing, Kisa."

She tilted her head in a question.

"My father tells me that you are the best assassin he has ever seen. I assume that would include myself. How much of your skills have you been hiding from me?"

Liza lowered her face, glancing up at me guiltily. "I may not have been completely honest on that front. I needed you to think that my attempt to kill you was genuine."

"You know how to shoot a bow?"

She nodded.

"And you are good at hand-to-hand?"

She dipped her head again.

I sighed. "Well, then I think there is only one thing that needs to be done." I quirked my mouth. "We need to have a rematch. I cannot very well lead the Ubyzniki if I do not know the skill level of its members, can I?"

She smirked at my light tone. "You will not be embarrassed to lose to your wife?"

"Oh, Kisa," I said, moving in close to her. "If you beat me, I will reward you most generously."

She shivered as I trailed my fingertips along her collarbone; her face flushed, and her gaze heated. "It is late," she murmured. "Perhaps we can have our match later?"

"You are wrong, Kisa," I whispered, leaning

down and hovering my lips just above hers. "It is early."

And as I kissed her, she wrapped her legs around my waist. Grabbing her rear firmly, I carried her to our bed.

77

Later that evening, as the sun dipped lower on the western horizon, Liza and I circled each other at the sparring field. Despite Yulya's protests, Masha had come out to watch. She sat to one side, wrapped in blankets, snuggled warmly in Kostya's arms.

"Do not go easy on me, Kisa," I told her, echoing my earlier words.

"You will wish you had not asked that of me," she said with a smile.

When I saw an opening, I lunged at her. A heartbeat later, I found myself flat on my back, the breath rushing out of me as I hit the ground.

Liza stood over me, her silhouette golden around the edges with the setting sun.

"Would you like to try again?" she asked, grinning a deliciously wicked grin.

I blinked at her. "I think I got the picture."

Taking her offered hand, I ignored Masha's cheers at Liza having beaten me so easily.

"You are swift indeed, my kisa," I said, staring down at her.

She smiled up at me. "You are not so bad yourself, my myshka."

My eyes widened as she called me little mouse. "You. You sent that note threatening Yulya."

"Well, I could not very well have her killing my husband, now could I?"

"Is there anything else you need to tell me? Anything else I should know?"

"Yes," she said, standing on her toes and wrapping her arms around the back of my neck. "I love you."

And as she kissed me in the golden light of dusk, on that cool autumn evening in Saint Petersburg, I felt that I was truly home.

EPILOGUE

The crowd cheered as the second act came to an end, and the curtain closed. Katya clapped her little hands together as she sat in my lap, the puffy blue fabric of her dress spilling over my legs.

"What do you think, Katya?" I asked. "Was not Aunt Masha beautiful out there on stage?"

"Pretty," the child agreed with a smile, her grey eyes sparkling.

As the applause died down for the between-act break, I turned around in my seat, looking anxiously at Yulya.

My sister smiled, her blue eyes bright and happy, as Dima brought her hand to his lips. My worry eased. This was Yulya's first public appearance since her divorce had become official, and I was relieved to see all the stares and whispers directed her way hadn't bothered her in the least.

"I told you," Liza whispered from beside me, following my gaze.

"You were right, as always, Kisa." Leaning over, I kissed my wife on the cheek.

"Papa," Katya complained, placing her hand on my face.

"Yes, my love," I acknowledged, smiling down at my daughter and giving her a kiss on the cheek as well.

The curtain to our box opened, and a grumpy looking Kostya entered. He stomped over to his seat and took the bouquet of roses he'd left there back into his lap.

"They would not let you backstage?" I guessed.

"I did not even get the chance to try," Kostya grumbled. "Oleg stopped me before I could get there."

I glanced back at the curtain just as our newest apprentice slipped into the box. He dipped his head in apology, his glamour firmly covering his untamed eyes and pointed ears. If I hadn't known better, I never would have suspected he was Fae.

"I am sorry—"

I waved my hand at his apology. "Do not worry about it, Oleg," I told him. "Kostya is just disappointed, and you were told to find me if you heard anything. So what have you heard?"

Everyone in the box, besides Katya, listened attentively as Oleg related his news.

"The vodyanoy... We have been keeping an eye on his lake as you ordered. He...he has taken a child."

I sighed, shaking my head. When I met Liza's eyes, she nodded.

"All right," I said. "Gather the others. We will meet at the airship."

Oleg hesitated. "Should I...call Maksim Igorevich?"

I frowned, glancing over at Kostya. Nika and Maksim had not been pleased at Liza and me taking over the Ubyzniki. They'd gone so far as to try to break off and start a separate organization. But the empress put a swift stop to that. She agreed with our new approach and had told those who'd left the Ubyzniki to accept the new direction or suffer the consequences. Maksim had reluctantly agreed, but it didn't take him very long to fall into line after the empress's threat. But Nika had refused and gone rogue. I strongly suspected that Maksim was still in contact with his daughter, despite his assurances that he was fully on our side.

I glanced at Liza, then shook my head. "Not this time, Oleg."

Oleg nodded and left as silently as he'd come.

I lifted Katya as I got to my feet, and everyone else rose as well.

Kostya frowned down at the roses. "Masha will be disappointed."

I rested a hand on his shoulder. "Go to her dressing room and leave a note. She will understand. There is a child in danger, and we have work to do."

AFTERWORD

Thank you for reading! I do so hope you enjoyed it. If you have a moment, I would very much appreciate a review on the store where you bought it. Tell other readers what you thought, and help them make a decision on this book.

If you'd like to stay updated on news about my books and events, you can subscribe to my newsletter on my website: www.dlieber.com

On my site, you will also find my blog, where I post all my fun little tidbits.

Thanks again! I hope you will travel through my worlds with me again in the future.

D. Lieber

ABOUT THE AUTHOR

D. Lieber has a wanderlust that would make a butterfly envious. When she isn't planning her next physical adventure, she's recklessly jumping from one fictional world to another. Her love of reading led her to earn a Bachelor's in English from Wright State University.

Beyond her skeptic and slightly pessimistic mind, Lieber wants to believe. She has been many places—from Canada to England, France to Italy, Germany to Russia—believing that a better world comes from putting a face on "other." She is a romantic idealist at heart, always fighting to keep her feet on the ground and her head in the clouds.

Lieber lives in Wisconsin with her husband (John) and cats (Yin and Nox).

LINKS

Website: www.dlieber.com
Goodreads: www.goodreads.com/dlieber
writing
Bookbub: www.bookbub.com/profile/d-lieber